No Mercy

Maisie Techs

Copyright © 2023 by Maisie Techs

All rights reserved.

No portion of this book may be reproduced in any form without written permission from the publisher or author, except as permitted by U.S. copyright law.

contents

01 | intrigant — 1
02 | accepted offense — 19
03 | the incriminated — 38
04 | the lion's den — 58
05 | villain of the story — 78
06 | off with her head — 98
07 | adora's teachings — 117
08 | the smell of death — 137
09 | reuben kang — 159
10 | son of a killer — 177
11 | justice or vengeance — 196
12 | fragility — 218
13 | sanctimony — 239

14 | welcome to angora	260
15 | tibbles	280
16 | renegade	299
17 | poppy winters	323
18 | ayako	338

01 | Intrigant

CHAPTER ONE — INTRIGANT

THE smell that day was a nostalgic blend of a sickeningly dry, sweet metallic scent and vomit.

Cradling her twisted arm, breathing shallow and agony glinting in her reddened eyes, she stooped and bowed. The pain, sharp and burning, had incapacitated her ability to think rationally, her body weak, disoriented, and perspiring. Her flesh bore the scars of the beating, not to mention her heart. They derived pleasure from agonizing a Powerless and that alone shattered something deep within her—something that would endure even after her skin and bones healed.

There was sadness in her eyes, a heaviness, an unyielding sorrow that stripped her of her once easy smile. She couldn't bear to meet their gaze, not when their conceited smiles and malicious grins awaited her. With mocking eyes, they counted her breaths, eagerly anticipating for the last to come.

She'd beg but the sea of unbearable pain that had washed over her was far too great and exhausting. Her stomach rumbled with uneasiness, maddening her to frustration and bitterness. Was it bad she was praying for respite from the suffering, yearning for her body to completely stop feeling, for her brain to permanently shut, for death, after too long of a wait, to enter?

When a chair clashed with force against her frail back and blood spluttered out of her dry mouth, staining Athena Takao's new shoes, she silently cackled. Her friends would tell her to fight harder, to make a run for the door or seize the nearest item and use it as a weapon but her body said to stay put, lying on the floor, wheezing from the throbbing ache, and wait for the end to come.

"The kingdom has treated you and your people like mere ants. . ."

"Ugh! You ruined them!" Athena bent and reached for her jaw, forcing their eyes to meet.

Breathing was slow and painful. Every single one of them, from the Yuscuessau girl whose heart was bursting with iniquitous delight to the Gochueze boy at the back of the classroom leaning against the cream white wall, could hear the loud inhales and exhales, each progressively decelerating. Even then, that did not stop Athena from digging her nails into her flesh, a swift formation of a bruise seamlessly merging with the rest, tainting her warm beige complexion.

Athena's hands squeezed her reddened cheeks. "These were my favorites too, Eun. Are you planning on washing them for me?"

In that moment, all she could manage was a slight nod.

"They have forced them into slavery and executed them mercilessly."

"I'm surprised you even made it this far," Athena spat. "I'm surprised you tricked us all long enough to turn fifteen. You really had us fooled, I'll give you that. But. . ." She leaned forward, her small, round lips curling into a sinister smile and her black narrow eyes sparkling with nefarious glee. "What are you waiting for, Eun? What's stopping you from picking up that rope I know you hide under your bed?"

Her forehead puckered, fresh tears running down her cheeks, newfound panic flaring in her eyes, seizing her brain. Who would have thought that someone she had so much faith in could be this wicked?

"Are you waiting for me to do the honors, Eun?" Athena's eyebrows raised with excitement, a jolly laugh fleeing from her mouth. "Or is it that you're. . . hopeful?" Next came a gasp dipped in contempt. "Oh no, you couldn't possibly be hopeful. I refuse to believe you're that foolish."

There had been hope before in the past, a sense of possibility in a brighter future, the future society claimed she was unable to achieve. With the open eyes of a child, she'd reached out, fingers extended. During that moment, people were given the choice between kindness and cruelty. It was no surprise the Powerless chose the former. One of them, she was. They suffered and wept together. And neither was it a surprise when Holders chose to cast her away. They were aware of her people's great affliction, witnessed their miseries but either did nothing or made it worse. Holders were all one and the same—the arrogance, the hate, the corruption.

She'd been misled by the woman from her dreams, the woman that promised her she was only born for great things, born with a different fate. That woman had uttered nothing but lies and empty assurances. No, she was merely a plaything to be toyed with whenever their hearts desired. Perhaps, it was her own fault for heeding these fabrications despite everything else the world told her.

"Eun, please," Athena snorted, "you'd be doing the world and yourself a favor. Finish it."

"Karma is like a rubber band. You can only stretch it so far before it comes back and smacks you in the face—and now, it's their turn to be confronted by their long-awaited fate."

That little innocent child she fortunately outgrew had been too hopeful for this kingdom.

The Holders were never going to change.

"Never let them see you in a moment of weakness. Never let them see you falter."

——..∘ ☽ ▫ ☾ ∘..——

Never let them see you falter.

These words stand out loudest among the hundreds of suffocating thoughts that are swimming through her mind, not just because they come from someone dear to her but because they're her drive, something that has sustained her through the shattering memories that refuse to leave her alone. She wakes up and the words are the first things she thinks about. Just as they're the last before she falls asleep.

As the girl saunters through the busy streets of Findara with her tamed midnight-black hair tied into pigtails and a small sword fastened to either side of her thin waist, she recites the words again and again to herself while her snow-white horse trots alongside her.

Never let them see you falter.

The greatest error she believes she ever made was trusting that there would ever be a day of peace between her people and those high in power, that they would come to understand the way they were born was never her people's fault. That day will never arrive, not until Holders drop to their knees and learn what it's like to beg for mercy, to beg for their lives to be spared. She understands that now and after centuries of the torture, the abuse, the damage, it's only fair she returns the favor.

Findara's tremendous crowd seems to have a life of its own, each individual moving just as though unseen hands are dragging them this way and that, pulling their eyes to one thing and then another. The vibrant clothes shimmer in the late-afternoon light and people move about like beguiling schools of fish. They respond in foreseeable ways, each with a daily objective in mind. There is chatter between sellers and buyers, young children running about, old friends catching up and new friends making.

Despite the cheery atmosphere, she knows better than to put her faith in the elated grins on their faces. Sure, it's a beautiful day but not for the Powerless on their knees, begging with tears for something—anything—to fill their empty bellies or for medicine to mend their loved ones. Not for the Powerless working without rest or preparing themselves for the gruesome tournament due in days.

How dare these Holders laugh and dance and look the other way when her people are suffering right in front of them, their bodies so thin that their bones are prominent and they can hardly move?

Even in the bitter September cold, she can feel the warmth of bodies pressing against hers as she maneuvers through an abundance of individuals. Worst of all, she can smell them too—a mighty accumulation of over-applied cologne, perfumes, and body odor.

A registration table she's been searching for eventually comes into sight and she begins her way toward it. For most people, today is a day like any other. But for her, today is the day a scheme she's put her blood, sweat, and tears into for three years officially commences. She can't recall just how many people have warned her that vengeance is never the answer—they were all wrong. Simply thinking about this scheme brightens her spirits.

Though half of her face is covered with a black handkerchief with a plan made not to reveal herself just yet, she can't help but notice that people are mumbling, pointing. Perhaps, not at her yet she wonders if there is a possibility she's already been recognized.

Being habituated to noxious attention has done a great deal of harm to her. Even after those three years spent far from this death-dealing kingdom, memories of past maltreatment never left her mind—and they never will. She's accepted that, accepted that no matter what she does, the scars she's acquired over the years will never fade, nor will her hatred for Holders. One day, they will all finally feel her people's wrath. Definitely not today. Maybe not next month or next year. But one day.

Even if she has to die trying.

She nears the registration table and pounds an arm against it to retrieve the attention of the man in charge, unconcerned about how ill-mannered the behavior may have appeared. The large Aryan man's dark brown round eyes stare at her for a moment before they dive down to her bare neck. He raises his eyebrows and opens his mouth to speak, revealing the small gap between his two front teeth.

"You aren't here for the academy, are you?"

"No, I'm here for bread," the conniver scorns after a light scoff, cocking her head to the side, her soft-arched eyebrows sculpting into a glare contemptuous enough to make the man grasp onto the fact he just asked an obvious question.

"Well, can you blame me for wondering?" He points at her neck with a scowl. The man is wary, she can tell. Holders normally come to register with an Amulet adorning their neck. "If you're a Powerless," he warns, "do understand that you'll be greatly punished for even stepping foot inside the academy. Watch yourself."

"I'm well aware of the rules."

Right then and there, she wonders just how many of her people have pretended to have an Amulet in their possession simply to gain access to a place they are not permitted to enter. She knows the Powerless only do this to steal food and any other necessities they manage to come across and she can't exactly blame them either, not when she's done the same exact thing when she was younger.

Her almond-shaped eyes concentrate on the dark brown pendant around the man's fat neck and scoffs again to herself when he caresses it as though it's his own child. The love these Holders have for their precious necklaces is far too great that it makes it impossible for them to love anything else just the same. She'll never comprehend that.

"Every student ought to be in possession of a real Amulet if they wish to apply for the academy," the man reiterates as though it isn't already obvious enough. He waits a few more seconds, and when she doesn't turn to leave, he eventually shifts a paper and an antique red-feathered quill pen her way. "Just write your full name here," he instructs, the puzzlement still clear in his voice.

She picks up the pen, at first scanning the paper, quietly reading the names of many others that have already registered while stroking the red feather.

The man's perplexed and judgmental eyes continue to examine her neck. "You know. . ." he says, "We wear our Amulets everywhere we go so we don't get mistaken for the Powerless. You would do the same if you were even half as intelligent. Where's yours?"

Avoiding the question, she pushes the writing materials back toward the man after printing her name. Her lips curve into a minor smirk. "I'd watch my tongue if I were you."

The man presses his thin lips together, slightly glowering at the girl. "You youngsters really don't know how to respect your elders anymore, huh?" he utters with a low scoff. He wants to believe she's lying, that she doesn't actually have an Amulet and this is all just a foolish plot to get inside the academy, but would a Powerless really be this brave? He'd deny her registration if it was up to him.

"At least, I'm not an elder who doesn't know when to stick to his own knitting."

Shrugging with a sneer, the younger steps away from the table. The aggravated man is still scowling even as she continues her walk, her sharp, wily eyes studying each direction of the immeasurable kingdom. How easy it is to tick these Holders off, she thinks mockingly. If only their self-control is as high as their ego, or even better, their injustice.

Nothing appears to have changed since the last time she was here—the Holders are more shrewd than ever and the Powerless have descended to such a demoralizing level that defending themselves is no longer possible.

In her eyes, Arya's new inclusion is merely another institution that'll only impart to younger Holders the belief that her people merit suffering, as the rest of them have done annually for centuries. The fact so many Holders are genuinely convinced that this academy is precisely what the kingdom needs to achieve supreme greatness intrigues and amuses her. None of them need any more power. Not now. Not ever. And it's time someone stripped them of the dominion they currently hold.

Seems like she hasn't come back for nothing.

Stopping a couple of feet away from two women sitting around a rounded wooden folding table, she glances around again. A particular family comes to mind straight away and once more, her lips extend into an ill-disposed grin as her heart pumps with great ecstasy from envisioning her scheme in motion.

One might wonder how the mere thought of vengeance—a simple image of her adversaries unable to form words from the agonizing anguish that's filled every aspect of their frail bodies tearing them apart, slashing through their perspirant skin, and searing their worn-out muscles—can bring her such joy. The planning process was not simple. In fact, she can still remember the exact number of times her mentor, Adora, pleaded with her to reconsider. But how can she when Holders never hesitated?

"This academy should have been opened a long time ago." The voice of one of the women around the folding table seizes the schemer's attention instantaneously. "But at least now, they'll be taught to use their abilities more efficiently, especially since the Outsiders have become more of a menace to this kingdom these days, wouldn't you agree? We weren't this fortunate back in the day. It's nice to have some protection."

The Outsiders? She's heard that term before. Her mentor brought it up a number of times during her training after she fled Arya three years ago. Although she's aware of their opposition to Arya, she's unsure whether she'll regard these Outsiders as allies or foes. Aside from her own people, nobody can be trusted these days.

"The Powerless, on the other hand, are just complete wastes of space. Their lack of contribution is absolutely frustrating," the second woman chips in with a derisive scoff. "If the Outsiders were to invade right now, their presence would be nothing more than a hindrance. Why do we bother to keep them around? They're just taking up valuable resources that could be used for those of us who actually matter. Honestly, I say we throw them to the Outsiders and let them deal with those cowards. Good riddance to them all."

Her opinion is clear and concise, leaving no room for ambiguity. Ah, so she's one of those. The young girl chuckles bitterly at the thought. She finds it quite comical that certain Holders hold the belief her people serve no purpose when in reality, they've been the ones handling every arduous task the Holders refuse to undertake. How disheartening that such a belief exists, given the clear evidence to the contrary. Or perhaps, the dissatisfaction stems from the Powerless doing their jobs with reluctance. What do these Holders want? For her people to smile while taking a whip to the back?

"Who would clean our houses or run errands for us, then?" the first woman insists, shaking her head. "As irritating as those Powerless are, we can't give them away. They can be good at what they do."

The young girl's eyes fly over to a Powerless visibly struggling to carry three hefty bags while a Holder is loudly urging her to move quicker. In the eyes of these savages, her people have been reduced to mere canines.

There is something that has always puzzled her even until this day. Her people are detested for not possessing their very own Amulet, pendants that have been deemed the most significant things in existence, items so powerful that they dictate the very fabric of life. Even the mere presence of the Powerless always seems to incite anger and frustration among Holders. Why not send them away, then? Why not simply expel them from the kingdom and relieve them of their apparent misery?

Holders often boast about their immense power and capabilities, yet they struggle with basic household tasks. Their free time is primarily spent indulging in partying, gossiping, and tormenting others. Worst of all, it's not that they're incapable of doing these things—they just choose not to. What's the point of washing my clothes when I could just force a Powerless to do it for me? Their only concern is deriving pleasure from watching Powerless individuals beg for mercy. Nothing else matters.

Her stream of thinking is interrupted by an abrupt altercation that can be heard nearby. It's not the bickering itself that catches her attention per se, but rather one of the voices, which she's certain is that of the same person she hasn't been able to shake from her thoughts for the previous three years. Pitiful she hasn't moved on, she's aware, yet on the other hand, picturing this person's battered body has done well in motivating her numerous times.

Well, well, well. We meet again.

She nears the quarrel in a matter of seconds and at the sight of Arya's Golden Girl screaming at a guard with both hands clenched, her lips draw back in a snarl. Although she has little interest in learning how the disagreement began, it doesn't take her long to notice the dark brown splotches all over Athena Takao's gown, which could have been caused by the guard mistakenly spilling something on her.

In the midst of what appears to be a little tea party, she dismounts her horse and walks over to the chaos. Of course, with Athena, tea parties always involve more chit-chatting than actual tea consumption. She would know, after all, they'd been previously friends back when she was still posing as a Holder.

At least, there's no need to pretend now.

Gathered around Athena and the guard are several other girls, each one of them cheering Arya's Golden Girl on as the screeching, hot-headed child hurls insult after insult at the soldier. Three of these girls stand out to her right away—mind-controlling Jade Lavender, rumor-mongering Akira Ito, and defamatory Sa-rang Lee. Three years later and they're still clinging to Athena like moths to a flame.

The guard, on the other hand, simply stands there, rolling his eyes and scoffing to himself, acting as though the taunts are not getting to him. It's easily understood that a tremendous part of him is too afraid of maligning the daughter of the king's closest friend.

Coward, she can't help but think. Yet at the same time, she has to concede that the previous registrant's man was correct. Younger Holders have grown to think that respect for the elders, or for anyone, in fact, is never required if they have power or are associated with someone who does. She finds the way this perverse doctrine has been disseminated from generation to generation to be the most unsettling. No one has ever made an effort to halt it.

Until now.

She walks up to the guard and takes his arm, yanking him away from the girls while sending him a warning death stare to flee while he still has the chance. At first, the guard appears offended at the idea of someone else stomping all over him. He's meant to be one of Arya's revered individuals, after all. However, the moment he believes he's pieced two and two together and surmises she is simply another one of Athena's close friends, he turns and speedily strides away. Again, coward.

Nothing about what she just did makes Athena any less irate. In an instant, Athena turns her rage from the guard on her. She shrieks even louder now, "Who do you think you are?" and takes a step forward. "I was still talking to that man when you inconsiderately interrupted."

The young schemer studies the girl for a moment. Athena, a Yuscuessau girl who's lived in Arya practically all her life, still has that smooth olive complexion, snub nose, round lips, and ridiculing black narrow eyes that her adoptive brother, Alvin, once remarked were beguiling. Even the girl's gait hasn't changed. She still obnoxiously swings her hips from side to side.

"Well, speak, you pig!" Athena hisses again. "Do you have the slightest idea who I am?"

"Do you have the slightest idea who I am?"

In the twinkling of an eye, Athena's glare deforms at the sound of her voice, an expression of bewilderment replacing it instead. She points an unsteady finger in an attempt to hold her undaunted demeanor but the discomposure can already be seen. "You better walk away this instant if you know what's good for you," the headstrong girl urges again through gritted teeth. "You don't want to mess with someone who's got the Royals on her side. I assure you that would be a grave mistake."

"Still using your status as an excuse for every little thing?" the younger shakes her head, although she can't say it's out of disbelief. "I'm not sure whether I should be disappointed or glad at the fact your character hasn't changed even now. What I am sure of is that you're going to make this incredibly easy for me, Athena."

"W-who are you?"

But even with the question, she knows she's already got it figured out. She knows Athena has matched her voice to that of the helpless youngster she used to torture day in and day out three years ago. Why else would her voice sound so unstable?

"I asked for your name, you fool! Don't you know it's rude to keep me waiting?"

Still sporting the same sly grin, she takes a poised step toward her stunned foe as her fingers reach for her mask. Once near enough to whisper in Athena's ear, she, with great pleasure, gradually lowers the piece of cloth down, revealing the entirety of her face.

"I'm the person who's going to bring this entire kingdom to its knees."

word count • 3844

02 | accepted offense

CHAPTER TWO — ACCEPTED OFFENSE

TOO many high expectations. Far too many classes.

This has always been Arya's issue—or any kingdom's, for that matter. Too much judgment.

They are beyond sympathy, beyond help. For years, Holders have espoused the nonsensical notion of perfection and nowadays, they've become solely concentrated on fixing themselves to fit in and conform to society's condemnation. Arya loves to divide, they love to compare, creating strife in an already unforgiving world.

To her, it is disheartening to see how Yeblil has prioritized beauty, wealth, and power above all else, and not just because she's been told countless times that she could never accomplish such things. It's become a common phenomenon that when asked about their life goals, individuals immediately mention these superficial desires as if they hold the key to happiness and fulfillment. The obsession with Amulets only serves to perpetuate this toxic mindset.

She can very clearly recall being questioned about the number of times she had been let down in life and a direct response was never given. That number was far too high. Before, she blamed the individuals that disheartened her and often even cursed them in moments of bitterness and self-pity. Now, she understands she was always to blame for expecting too much from people that gave too little.

Even now, this is one aspect of her younger self that she despises. Her people always warned her that hope was futile in a wicked game of survival where only the Holders, wealthy, attractive, and men could win. They made it clear that everyone else was doomed to suffer and perish. Why then did she choose to trust the words of a woman she'd never met before, a woman that was most likely formed from her imagination? Why had she ever entertained the idea that some Holders might come to love those unlike them, accept their differences, and make an effort to comprehend their struggles?

But that was who she was then—Eun Calinao, diffident, fragile, hopeful. Much to her dismay, she still sees a fraction of that little girl inside who she is now—Ivy Pearls, scrupulous and single-minded.

The day Ivy Pearls learned just how much appearances matter was the day she witnessed a Holder getting ridiculed for the way she looked and the way she dressed. A Holder! The girl couldn't believe her eyes at the time. She was only ten then, sitting at the very back of the classroom where every other Powerless sat when Clover Hermione walked in, repeatedly glancing over her shoulders, her steps slow, dragged. Several students, driven by disdain and hostility, were already waiting for her by the door and grabbed her long hair to yank her down the first opportunity they got.

At the mere age of ten, Clover was told that her facial appearance was unattractive, that she would be unable to form friendships, and that no man would dare marry her in the future. The incident was a clear indication of how shallow and cruel Holders could be towards those who did not fit into their narrow definition of beauty, even if it were their own people.

When they repeated this behavior the following day at the playing field, Ivy refused to stay quiet. She could have walked away—her tormentors hadn't noticed her yet. But watching someone, whether Holder or Powerless, get beaten especially for something beyond their control always had a way of causing sadness to thrum through her veins and rage to quicken her blood. The first thing she observed as she marched up to the students that would not leave Clover alone was that Clover's once-waist-length hair could now barely reach her ears, revealing more of her slightly rectangular face and a small scar almost the shape of a half-moon on her neck. Could she have possibly cut it due to how easy it was to take hold of it? It was no wonder some of the pupils were screaming that she now had such a boyish appearance.

Unfortunately, bravery was insufficient to overcome the harassers. Ivy became the new target. Needless to say, she foresaw this. To these Holders, being a Powerless was a lot more intolerable than being repulsive in appearance. Clover was given the time to finally catch her breath and wipe the blood off her lower lip while all the beatings and insults shifted to her instead. But she didn't worry.

At first, delight engulfed her. On the inside, she was smiling. It wouldn't be long before Clover came to her rescue just as she'd done for her. Yet when she lifted her head after more excruciating seconds had gone by, a fresh swell of despondency swept over her at the sight of Clover scurrying away. She did not look back. Not once. She did not care.

Attempting to push the abrupt memory to the back of her mind, Ivy concentrates on the tiny knife in her palm for a moment. However, her efforts prove futile as the memory of two individuals she dreads thinking about begins to consume her. Ivy sees nothing improper in recalling her past. They often remind her never to repeat her mistakes. Yet whenever two aching names begin to reverberate in her thoughts, she finds it quite impossible to focus on anything else.

Clover Hermione and her unfortunate choice to flee rather than help is not the only thing Ivy remembers from that day. She remembers the intense pain that grew the more breaths she took and the sensation of her body weakening with every hit she endured. She remembers feeling as though that day would be her last and how perhaps, that was for the best. And she remembers hoping when she glanced up from the ground that Clover would change her mind and return only to be met by the sight of two completely different girls running in her direction.

Benecia Patel and Delyth Nguyen—two Powerless girls she later formed the closest of friendships with after they fought their way through the iniquitous Holders and managed to get them to leave her alone. Two girls with unwavering loyalty that never failed to bring a smile to her face despite their own difficult circumstances. Two girls that vowed to be her shield and kept their word day in and day out. Two girls that never let her down.

Two girls she one day found in Delyth's home upon visiting, lifeless on the blood-stained floor, eyes vacant, light ebbed from them. The eyes that lost the capability to express true and profound love, to be a getaway to their own souls, dead. She sees them every day. The image of that harrowing moment continues to remain vivid in her head to this very second.

The moment she left the house where their departed bodies lay—her two best and only friends—she was screaming. Screaming silently to herself and screaming at people to punish the one behind the immoral executions. She watched them get dragged to the Pits of Death, several deep holes in a desolate area of the kingdom filled with the remains of her deceased people, and when she inquired as to why such a heinous act had occurred, the guards claimed the girls had it coming their way when they chose to disobey one of the rules.

Ivy has been alive long enough to know that Holders never need a reason to suddenly decide when to take a Powerless' life—not a proper one, anyway. There was nothing about rules that caused her friends' deaths, nothing about misbehavior. No, it was simply that man—that awful justification of a living being.

As the image of the killer takes shape in her head, she feels a surge of raw anger shoot through her and her grip on the knife tightens. She knows him well. Many people in Arya do. What sickens Ivy the most is how quickly word of him slaying her friends spread like wildfire yet Holders continue to greet him with kindness as if he hadn't done it. Murder is still indecent in this kingdom, is it not? Ah, right. The crime is only deemed unacceptable when it's a Holder who's lost their life. She scoffs at the thought.

As her anger intensifies, so does her temper. Ivy slams the tip of her knife into one of the filthy kitchen walls of her dilapidated house and gradually drags it down, leaving a mark. But in her mind, she replaces the wall with the slayer's neck, and the vivid image of it slit and bleeding brings a small smile to her face.

Gozar Agulto, I'm coming for you!

——..○ ☽ ▢ ☾ ○..——

"Welcome to Day Zero of Amulet Academy!"

The announcer's gravelly, booming voice brings the crowd of students to immediate silence. Normally, an announcer would be jovial and welcoming when greeting them but the man standing straight before the entrance of the new academy is neither of those things.

Both of his large hands are behind his back, feet brought together, head raised slightly, and an austere expression planted on his oblong face. This isn't a test but the young schemer knows she must approach it as such. The students that are shivering at the mere sight of the announcer have already failed.

"I'm certain you already understand just how problematic the Outsiders have gotten," the man carries on. "Arya needs additional Holders protecting it and that's where you come in. But right now, none of you are ready yet. However, don't worry. That's what this academy is for."

He pauses to gaze around once again. "Are you ready to see what it looks like?"

After his words, there is a sudden feeling of jubilation in the crowd of students, as if they are both firmly on solid ground and levitating all at once. Despite the fact the academy hasn't officially begun, she can't miss the chance to make an unforgettable appearance. There is no such thing as commencing her plot too early—the quicker, the better, in fact.

"You must take your training very seriously," the announcer calls out again in a warning tone. "The safety of Arya will soon be resting on your shoulders. Plus, the Royals worked hard to set up the academy. Each one of you must make sure to show your gratitude to them."

The mere mention of the Royals elicits a deep sense of irritation in Ivy. Aside from Gozar Agulto, no Holder will ever be able to anger her as much as the Royals do. She holds the view that they, along with their predecessors, are the primary cause of the suffering that takes place in Arya. They hold the power to change the unforgiving rules and ensure equality in their kingdom yet they choose not to.

It is evident that they relish their sovereignty and the control it affords them. The Powerless are free to starve and drown in the filth of the streets, free to meet their end in some freezing field with cold steel running through their intestines, so long as the Holders indulge in their lavish parties and fine foods. Then again, with ethereal faces and Amulets so powerful, of course, every Holder idolizes them.

But all this will change once it is revealed that one out of the three Royals has been deceiving Arya.

As the plotter glances around, in search of a familiar face in the crowd, her eyes come across a person she's been dreading to see since she stepped foot inside Arya again three days ago. At the sight of the boy, her nostrils immediately flare and her face scrunches up in disgust.

Alvin!

It is not surprising that Alvin would be present in a place where he could garner attention. Ivy hates the effects he still has on her. Despite her efforts to move on, just the mere sight of him drags her back to the past—back to when he would enter her bedroom in the middle of the night and touch her in a way that would cause her to recoil, in a way she could never speak about because she knew no one would ever believe her words over a Holder's.

She mentally shudders at the memory. If only Adora gave her some guidance on how to not let such people get under her skin.

Her feelings whenever her thoughts wander to her adoptive brother are not exactly ones of terror. Undoubtedly repugnance. Anger. Maybe, even a bit of despair. Despite Adora warning her never to let her rage get the better of her, she can't help but envision herself gradually running a knife across the boy's neck, watching with a satisfied grin as he doubles over on the floor with agony.

And how is the rest of her adoptive family doing? Did they celebrate her departure? Did they discuss how relieved they were once she ran off, at risk of getting herself killed?

On Day Zero, students are allowed an hour to explore and familiarize themselves with the academy, their teachers, and their classmates. But none of that is on Ivy's agenda. Her sole purpose is to make it clear that she's back to seek retribution against her enemies and justice for her people. Anything else that does not align with her goal is irrelevant. She's steadfast in her resolve to fulfill this aim and she's prepared to go to any lengths to do so.

The office, a large chamber for the chosen headmaster located close to the main doors, is the first stop once inside the institution. There, students collect a piece of paper each consisting of information regarding where their classrooms and who their lecturers are.

"Hey! You over there!"

It's only been two seconds since Ivy stepped inside her classroom when a voice behind her calls for her attention. A very dissatisfying classroom. There is nobody in here she knows, and although that's not entirely a bad thing, having a few familiar faces witness the hell she's about to break loose will go a long way. Ivy pauses in her tracks and turns, coming across a middle-aged guard approaching her with haste. The man scans her head to toe before giving a nod of what seems to be confirmation.

"Yes, you seem to match the description."

She frowns. "Match the description for what? What's going on?"

"There's been a slight change," the guard informs, leading her out of the room and toward another at the very end of the hallway. "For whatever reason, Athena Takao wants you in the same classroom as hers."

"Athena?"

"Yes. What other Athena Takao do you know?" He rolls his eyes mockingly.

At first, Ivy feels conflicted regarding the situation at her fingertips. On one hand, she's repelled by the fact that an adolescent child possesses such immense power that even the school guards are willing to behave like her loyal dogs and comply with her demands.

On the other hand, Ivy feels a sense of renewed hope upon realizing that her encounter with Athena yesterday did not go in vain. There is just something so comforting and rewarding about being in the same classroom as someone she knows well—someone she was formerly good friends with and now despises to the core. Someone is going to be there to watch her scheme go down before spreading it around and she prefers it to be someone as narcissistic and boastful as Arya's Golden Girl.

Before she steps inside, Ivy takes a moment to inspect the door. 108. Mr. Abalos. She's never heard of the man before and wonders for a moment if that is a good thing or not.

She carefully examines her new classroom as her pulse flutters in her chest for a brief period, suppressing a shiver at the notion of Alvin being one of her classmates. Aware that Athena and her adoptive brother were previously romantically involved, Ivy believes the likelihood is high. Again, it's not that she fears Alvin but the sheer sight of him seems to do well at stoking the fires of her animosity.

With a certain degree of fear, she admits her uncertainty about her capacity to remain composed if she were to share a class with the aforementioned boy.

Fortunately, Alvin is nowhere to be seen. But another person whom she least expects comes into sight. In a moment, Ivy stops walking in response to the familiar girl. With her beautiful honey complexion, neatly groomed eyebrows, and heart-shaped lips, the Gochueze girl hardly appears identifiable yet the pendants she's wearing and the scar of a somewhat half-moon give her away immediately. Clover Hermione.

What is she doing here?

Clover remains fixated on her two necklaces to notice Ivy make her way to an empty seat at the very back, farthest to the right.

She can see Athena and Jade whispering among themselves, unable to take their eyes off of her but this time, Ivy is too preoccupied with someone else to care much about what they may be saying. The door swings open and a man, possibly in his early thirties, walks inside. Without a word, he picks up one of the writing materials at the front and neatly puts down a name on the board.

"Call me Mr. Abalos," he announces, his voice sharp, almost strident. "For the first thirty minutes, you'll be in here with me, getting to know one another and such. For the last thirty minutes, you'll be given the opportunity to look around the academy, be familiarized with your surroundings, classmates, and future classrooms. Don't hesitate to ask questions if you have any."

Ivy slightly tugs on the strap of her dirty brown satchel bag as she examines the classroom for the second time. A fair-skinned boy has taken the seat next to hers, leaning against the black soft plastic, his long index finger playing with the pendant around his neck. He mutters something incoherent and scoffs as his hands suddenly clench. Ivy wonders for a second if someone is forcing him to be here.

Aside from Athena, Jade Lavender, Isagani Abadiano, a Gochueze boy she's not surprised to see in a place like this either, and Clover, a face she's yet to get used to looking at, there's no one in here she knows. But this is good enough for Ivy, especially with the way Athena and Jade still haven't stopped peeking at her.

"I want to learn about each of you," Mr. Abalos proceeds, his short portly body pacing back and forth as he speaks, "but who in the world cares about your favorite foods and such? Most certainly not me."

His words earn a few cackles here and there. Ivy remains quiet and still, silently counting the seconds until the next step of her plot begins. To her, Mr. Abalos seems more like the type of man a mother would warn her children to steer clear of, someone who preys on the weak—although to be fair, that's almost every Holder.

"I'm more intrigued to learn about the powers you possess. That is the reason this academy exists, in the first place, is it not? Let's get right into it. Please, take out your Amulets, so we can begin."

Exhilarated chatters fill the room as students shuffle about, either reaching into their pockets or bags to bring out the requested item.

Most of them, however, are already wearing their Amulets. According to Holders, it's common sense to have your pendants with you wherever you go, preferably around your neck, so everyone knows what your status is. This often reminds Ivy of the time Athena accused her of seizing her Taupe Amulet. It was the same day she decided enough was enough and fled Arya as soon as the opportunity came.

It's not difficult to depart this kingdom. No, not at all. Arya has four gates yet only three of them are ever kept locked. Someone can always exit through the fourth gate whenever they desire. Before she fled, Ivy often wondered why this was so. Holders are so keen on keeping her people imprisoned—why then did they make it too simple to leave?

She got her answer on the fourth day of her departure, the day she awoke from the ground of the wild, a patch of cold mire pasted to her pounding forehead, parched, starving, and worn out with a wounded leg that mercilessly continued to throb with anguish every second. It wasn't the longest she'd gone without food but it was easier to hope for some nourishment in a kingdom filled with barbaric bastards than a forest with nothing but trees, dead grass, and undergrowth.

They leave the gate open to mock her people—to make them believe even for just a second that they can have better luck outside, that all they need to flee from the torture is to simply walk through the exit. But surviving the wild is challenging—impossible, even. Perhaps, if a person planned to stay out there for merely a few days or a few months, they could endure it. A few months isn't what the Powerless are in need of, however.

Arya is positioned in an area where the nearest kingdom is so far away. It's surrounded by a greenwood where some Powerless are often taken out to work and then a vast water known as the Ocean of Miren where a ship is to be taken to sail across. Yet before even getting to that point, paying good jewels for a ship to await your arrival is a must—oh, and of course, you must be a Holder to aboard.

On that fourth day, Ivy was certain she'd die then. In fact, a large part of her began to regret everything—angering Athena which resulted in her getting framed for something she did not do, speaking back to her parents when she clearly understood that would land her in trouble, allowing her rage to get in control of her actions, suddenly growing brave and thinking she could live a better life elsewhere, and running away out of impulse.

That is until she met Adora, a woman who gave her a reason to continue living. Only through Adora was she able to manage three whole years in the wild, and that is purely because the woman had a certain powerful Amulet with her.

Still, the wild is no better than this kingdom, nor is any other kingdom out there as they are all the same. The Powerless have tried numerous times. Leaving Arya only kills them slower.

Mr. Abalos makes sure to take his time glancing from one student to another. In time, his hooded eyes land on the only student seated with a bare neck.

"Hey, you!" He points a finger at the indifferent girl, seething inwardly at the failure of everyone following his simple orders. "Are we going to have problems, young lady? I've dealt with disorderly people like you so don't think for a second that I am intimidated by this unruly act of yours."

All fifteen pairs of eyes goggle at Ivy in complete disbelief. She is now the center of attention as the educator makes his way to her seat. Ivy's invisible grin broadens. Having everyone—especially Athena since she is such a distinguished being now—believe she is, even now, the same vulnerable little girl as she was years ago is one of the most essential parts of her plot. Only then can she strike when least expected. And if she plays her cards right, even the queen is sure to get thrown into the equation somehow.

"I'm going to ask you this once and I expect an honest answer," the man says again, now standing right in front of the silent girl. "Where is your Amulet? Everyone else has got theirs."

It's only been a few seconds and the man is already glaring. Ivy looks up, her surly eyes staring into his interrogating ones.

"But what if I haven't got an Amulet, Mr. Abalos?"

Several gasps cram the room in an instant, her classmates and even the man himself taken back by her response. Regardless, Athena's arrogant and contemptuous stare remains the same, as though she has been yearning for this exact moment and is elated with the results.

Although she urges herself not to look at her, Ivy's attention skips over to Clover. Only a second goes by before Clover's eyes expand. The realization must have hit her. They stare at each other for a moment, and Ivy can't help but wonder if Clover is recalling the past where she practically left her for dead.

"Are you that dull-witted?" Mr. Abalos screams out, earning a loud chuckle from Athena. "This is an academy for Holders. Holders! Who told you you could be here? Who?!"

Ivy doesn't respond, bringing the man to sigh and quiver with frustration. "Oh, for crying out loud. This isn't the first time I've seen something like this occur. At the previous academy I taught at, a desperate Powerless snuck in and pretended to be one of us. He didn't get far. How could he? The Amulet he had around his neck looked faker than anything I'd ever seen. How utterly humiliating to do such a thing. But I have to say. . ." He sends Ivy a contemptuous glare. "You're a lot more foolish than he was."

"What Mr. Abalos is implying. . . Is it true?" Isagani Abadiano questions. Ivy can see he's trying not to burst into laughter at the thought of a Powerless sneaking inside a place she clearly doesn't belong.

"Of course, it's true!" Mr. Abalos cries out. "The Powerless will do anything to run away from their fate. Such cowards they are."

"And such pig-ignorant people they are, as well," Athena adds with a sneer.

Mr. Abalos lowers himself to Ivy's height, raising the volume of his voice as if he isn't already loud enough and speaking in such a mocking tone that makes it seem Ivy is nothing but a mere child. "You need to be in possession of an Amulet to be a student in this academy. It's mandatory. I'm very certain that was obvious from the very beginning."

It was. I suppose I just like to stir up drama.

"What's your name, young lady?"

Upon hearing this question, Ivy straightens up while her uninterested face alters into a dour expression. "The name's Ivy. Ivy Pearls!"

word count • 4488

03 | THE INCRIMINATED

CHAPTER THREE — THE INCRIMINATED

"WHY do the Powerless do this?"

Twelve-year-old Eun looked up from her paper to face Athena who'd spoken. "Do what?"

"Fantasize about living a prosperous life that they clearly do not deserve," Athena said, sitting up from the mattress and setting her own paper aside. Not much of it was done, which wasn't surprising seeing as she had zero concerns for her education. But why would she when she had the power as one of the king's favorites to make the lecturers pass her, regardless of her scores? "Yesterday, I witnessed a man get dragged out of his home and executed in front of his family. I don't know what he did but he was a Powerless and that's enough for me. Yet the wife kept on screaming about how unfair it was."

Eun glanced away from her then, pretending to go over the school questions on the paper. She did not do well as a liar when looking straight at the person she was lying to.

"That's just how they all are," Jade half-attentively said, staring at the pair of earrings Athena had just gifted her. The earrings, a spectacular shade of light blue, were glamorous and exorbitant—so, so exorbitant. She loved high-priced things. And yet, a small frown rested on her face.

Eun understood without even having to inquire that the cause for her hesitance was the fact the gift came from Athena herself. Over the months of being in this friend group, she'd come to notice Jade's consistent expressions of annoyance whenever Athena opened her mouth to boast about anything, as well as the frequent taunts Athena would throw her way, which Jade repeatedly claimed she was alright with despite how chagrined she always appeared to be. Jade loved gifts but not when they came from the same girl she was so envious of.

"I just find it so absurd," Athena carried on. "They came into our world with no Amulet and expect to be treated equally, as though we're all the same. How foolish is that?"

Eun paused, soaking in her friend's words. "So, you believe the man deserved the execution?"

"I believe the Powerless should just stop behaving as if they deserve better. They really don't." Athena got up from the mattress and skipped over to where her chiffonier sat, picking up the diamond bracelet that rested on its flat surface. "This," she pointed to the jewelry with a small chuckle, "is worth more than all of them combined. We Holders were kind enough to let them stay in our world. That should be enough for them considering how meritless they all are." When she finally took notice of the saddened expression etched onto the younger's face, she frowned. "What? You don't agree, Eun?"

Eun opened her mouth to speak but the words stayed stuck at the back of her throat. She was aware that what she was currently doing was improper. She shouldn't have been here in Athena's room, sitting on Athena's bed, eating Athena's food, gossiping with Athena's friends. She knew the day of truth would come one day and Eun could already picture just how enraged Athena was going to be once she found out.

But she was enraged. Anytime Athena opened her mouth and talked about her people in such a harsh manner, Eun couldn't help but allow the irritation to prick at her, to allow despair to ravage her face. Although she was frequently around Athena and her friends, who were all Holders, laughing or eating with them, dressing up or studying with them, rarely did she like any of them. But in order to ensure that her body would continue to be free from all the physical torture, she needed them.

Yes, she was using them all, toying with their minds, deluding them into thinking she was one of them. No, she did not feel guilty for it. They were far worse than her, the way they behaved was far worse than what she was doing. She wasn't certain who the voice belonged to but a faceless woman in her dreams frequently told her that it wasn't wrong to try to save herself from the Holders' claws—to write herself a different story.

Maybe, this wasn't the best way to do it, but it was all she had at the moment.

——..∘ ☽ ▢ ☾ ∘..——

Silence. Complete silence.

Students turn to each other, loud whisperings arising. Judgment fills their eyes but not a single being is as captious as Athena herself.

Then, it is silent again.

Ivy.

Ivy.

Ivy Pearls?

Aside from Athena, Jade, and Clover who remembers her clearly, confusion engulfs their minds. While the three girls ponder over how Ivy made it back to Arya alive and why the sudden change of name, the rest of the class tries to recall where they've seen her face before.

With a surprising number of seven-hundred-and-fifty-million citizens, Arya is no doubt the largest kingdom in the Land of Thegn, so needless to say, having to recall a face that was last seen three years ago is not so easy. On the other hand, from being Athena's friend to her attention-seeking adoptive parents working for the Royals themselves, Ivy can't exactly deny the bit of popularity she had before she fled. It was something, albeit possibly not of the positive kind. Over the years, attention became one of the many things she dreaded. It still is.

"It's you! Angelo Calinao's daughter," Mr. Abalos recalls, a dazed look of bewilderment crossing his stubbled face. "You're back? How. . . How are you still alive?"

With legs crossed, Ivy leans back, a proud smile playing on her lips. Only after she steals a quick peek at Athena, taking notice of her former friend's abrasive expression, does she finally understand the girl's objective. So, this is why Athena wanted her in the same classroom. Not just to keep an eye on her but to be present during her downfall. Ivy can already tell what the arrogant girl is thinking. "I don't know why or how she's back but I'll show her that choice was a grave mistake." She can already picture Athena running about and filling every ear with a retelling of how this moment went down. She can already hear the gossip.

Mr. Abalos' baleful tone when he begins to speak again draws Ivy's focus back to him. "Miss. Calinao, you can no longer be a student at this academy. I don't know how you thought you could get away with lying your way inside." His face scrunches, undoubtedly revolted at the fact a Powerless is sitting right in front of him.

The corners of Athena's eyes crinkle in a smile. "I think I've figured it out," she says while their lecturer starts his way towards the door. "You were never gone, were you, Eun? You fled from your home but you stayed in the kingdom, you stayed hidden." She raises a brow when Ivy does not respond, "I'm right, aren't I?" and gives a lopsided grin. "Oh, Eun. You should have just stayed hidden."

"Perhaps, she missed us." Jade cackles, her dark-red painted lips forming a disparaging smile.

"Perhaps, she did." Athena half-shrugs. "After all, she left the only place that fed, clothed, and sheltered her. All for what? Freedom? Please! There's nothing nice in this world you pigs deserve!"

"Hey, Athena!" Eventually, a fourth student cuts in, her big doe eyes staring at Athena with a look of disapproval. "That's not very nice."

Yet upon taking in her altercating classmates' ridiculing reactions, the displeasure is quick to fade into regret.

Ivy scoffs lightly at the sight of this.

A Holder is either vain or a coward.

Even after every mocking word that left their twisted mouths, the smile on Ivy's face remains. They expect her to quiver, to break. They expect her to fall to her knees and plead for mercy. But the days of listening to Ivy Pearls weep are over, the days of watching terror flare across her face, of watching her writhe on the ground, of watching her inhale and exhale shallow breaths, rigid with agony. Perhaps, the woman from her dreams wasn't so wrong, after all.

Just after Mr. Abalos finished ordering a guard to call the headmaster to discuss Ivy's expulsion, the room erupts in clamorous gasps. The sudden noise brings the man's attention away from the door straight away, and when he too comes across the item that caused the confoundment, his perplexed eyes expand.

"What in the world?!" he thunders.

Ivy can imagine the beating of his heart picking up pace, threatening to rip through his chest, after all, around her neck is an Amulet she just pulled out and put on. However, it isn't simply any Amulet. It does not take anyone long to recall where they've seen the necklace before. The priceless golden oval-shaped diamond pendant is hard to forget.

"That looks exactly like the Amulet the queen possesses!" Jade points out in a flash, abruptly rising from her seat. "So, that's why she was so afraid to show it before. She stole it!"

Ivy postures forward, resting her arms on her desk. She doesn't fidget, her feet don't shuffle, and her smile does not falter. From the looks in her foes' eyes, she can see it's all beginning to aggravate them; her phlegmatic demeanor, those taunting responses, her unwavering self-assurance, unlike Eun Calinao, unlike the little girl that was so easy to manipulate three years ago. "Is that really what you believe?" Her eyebrows raise, feigning surprise. "That I somehow managed to find my way inside the palace, a place that is so heavily guarded, without being caught and seized the Golden Amulet from the—"

She isn't given a chance to finish because the next thing she knows, a hand grabs her hair and yanks her out of her seat. Ivy's body meets the floor with a loud and painful thud! and when she looks up, Mr. Abalos' enraged round face is glaring back at her. This time, she stays silent, does not bother getting up, does not bother fighting back. Adora did teach her how to but she sees no point in wasting her energy now.

"I don't understand your objective here, Eun, but you've just made yourself your worst enemy!" he shouts. "I won't allow you to disrespect Queen Matilda like this. Enough is enough!"

A dozen responses run through her mind but Ivy holds her tongue. She needs to let them think they're in control, underestimate her. Mock them, just as they mocked her people.

Then comes the familiar bitter taste of blood, along with a jab of pain where Mr. Abalos struck her cheek with his palm. The strike almost doesn't hurt, and whether that may be because of the prolonged agony she had to endure or the brutal training Adora put her through, Ivy isn't certain. Did she anticipate the attack? Of course, she did. She'd be a fool not to. Holders tend to strike first and deal with consequences later.

The man turns to the students that have encircled themselves around the two of them and orders in a barbed tone, "Get Headmaster Huang in here now!" Holding both of Ivy's arms together with one strong hand, he hastily reaches for the Amulet around her neck with the other but Ivy doesn't allow him. Once the opportunity presents itself, she brings her head forward with her mouth wide open, sharp teeth targeting the desperate man's fingers and not missing. A loud yelp slips past his lips.

Headmaster Huang steps inside the classroom just in time to witness him striking another blow to her jaw. "And what is the meaning of this?" With a darkened expression, he rushes over, still yet to notice the pendant that started the commotion. "Mr. Abalos, would you like to tell me why you're attacking a student?"

"Headmaster Huang, Eun is the real villain here!" Athena quickly butts in. "Mr. Abalos was only trying to get back something she stole. Call Queen Matilda now. Let her know her Amulet has been seized."

Puzzled, Headmaster Huang slightly sways his hand back and forth, motioning for the man to step away from the girl. He obeys and, in an instant, the headmaster's short, large body takes his place in front of Ivy who's got a hand over her bleeding lips. "Just what have you gotten yourself into, young lady?"

"Call your queen," ignoring the several death glares and bewildered looks, Ivy responds with disdain. "I am being terribly accused of something I did not do."

Jade scowls. "You still dare to act all arrogant?"

"Why not?" Ivy throws her head back in an exuberant laugh. "I haven't been caught committing a crime of any sort. You do understand that you can be punished for such horrid accusations, correct?"

"Only if they turn out not to be true." The small chuckle that leaves Athena's mouth next is mirthless. "Oh, give it up, Eun. Everyone here knows you seized Queen Matilda's Amulet."

"Hand over the pendant," the headmaster's demanding voice follows, his small chubby palm taken out. "Or else, I'll have it taken from you by force. Do not start unnecessary drama."

Ivy pauses. Despite the sharp pain the cut on her bleeding lips brings, her grin is the biggest they've ever seen. As she gradually makes her way up from the floor, she holds up a finger. "Arya's tenth rule, if more than one person claims an Amulet belongs to them, solid proof from each must be shown before action is taken."

Purloining another being's Amulet is just as big of an offense in this kingdom as attempted murder. If found guilty, the crime gets you years behind bars. Yet when it comes to the queen's golden pendant, it's instant execution. Ivy knows this. She knew what she was getting herself into even before she stepped inside Arya.

It was established as a key regulation that if any Holder ever loses their necklace, they are to notify an authority right away, and nobody ever fails to do so. Years ago, however, the Powerless devised a tiny little ploy regarding this rule. Some of them would march up to those in charge and protest the loss of their pendants.

They always made sure to be especially vocal about it, always made sure that, at least, everyone who lived in their area was aware of their issue. This way, if anyone were to ever question them about where their Amulets were, they could sulk about how they lost them and how the authorities never managed to find them again.

But once the Royals eventually discovered this strategy, they added a condition that anyone reporting their missing necklace must have at least three other Holders affirm that they indeed had an Amulet, to begin with. These Holders were to be seen donning their own pendants for the sake of verification.

"We already know the Golden Amulet belongs to Queen Matilda!" Isagani insists.

Ivy ignores him and turns to Mr. Abalos, instead. "You said you wanted to learn about our powers, did you not? Well, we're wasting precious time. Why don't we have a little. . . presentation before Queen Matilda arrives?"

They want to snag her by the neck and strangle her to death. Yet, at the same time, they also want to see her make a fool of herself, just as her people have previously done during their own attempts to take down the Royals. They know what presentation means. And Ivy knows Holders are unflappable in the face of opposition.

When she sees them hesitating, her smile broadens. "Arya's eleventh rule," she says, "you cannot stop someone from proving that an Amulet belongs to them."

"Unless it's clear that it belongs to a Royal!" Athena urges.

"Nowhere does it mention that bit," Ivy informs matter-of-factly, then turns to the men again. "Well?"

There's another small pause before Headmaster Huang finally exhales and his shoulders drop, as though in utter defeat. "Take your seats, students."

Athena gasps. "You can't be serious."

She, Jade, and Ivy are the only students left standing as the rest of the class sit, some a little more enlivened than others, especially Isagani who's shaking in his seat with such thrill as though he's finally gotten the gift he's been begging for. As their lecturer carries on with his glaring, Headmaster Huang exits the room.

With the door wide open, they can all overhear the man ordering a guard to have Queen Matilda brought to the academy straight away. Now, Ivy's the one shaking with thrill. Internally, of course.

"Y-you can't be serious!" Athena repeats, slamming a foot against the floor like a child, a helpless anger simmering in her, nearly consuming her. "Can't you see how strange this situation is? Eun is a Powerless.

Everyone knows that. Who in their right mind would pass their Amulet over to her, especially one that looks so similar to Queen Matilda's golden pendant? Can't you see she's just wasting everyone's time?"

"Well then, explain how she got the Golden Amulet in her hands, to begin with," the same doe-eyed girl from before responds, as though she's gathered some newfound courage to speak again.

Athena's face contorts. "It's fake."

"Who in their right mind would bring a fake to an academy?" another student pipes in with a scoff. "Or, even worse, order a presentation with it?"

Athena's mouth stays open, at first, surprised that they're even considering giving Ivy a chance despite everything they know about her. "She's a Powerless," she insists again. "I know because she posed as a Holder when we were younger, tried so hard to fit in where she didn't belong."

"Let us see it for ourselves, Athena," a third student responds. "A Powerless can become a Holder, you know. Things could have changed."

Athena scoffs, gives a bitter laugh, and though still tensed, though her glare has yet to leave her face, she replies, "Alright then."

Ivy fixes her gaze on Athena's black narrow eyes. If she was still as wide-eyed as her younger self, she would hope to spot the same altruism Athena had for her before news of her Powerless status got disclosed.

The troubles truly began when one of Athena's friends from back then asked her to show off a magic or two. Of course, this was at the time Ivy was still falsely claiming to be a Holder. Athena came to her aid right away, although only for a little while. She told the girl Ivy was simply too shy to comply with the request yet went on to inform everyone that Ivy would be taking part in the Talent Show the following week.

When the day of the Talent Show arrived, Ivy had no other choice but to fabricate a sickness but she'd already reached her limits and the lie was insufficient to alley Athena's suspicion.

"You befriended a Powerless," people would tell Athena mockingly. "Are you that blind?" And Athena did not take the insults well.

More than half of Arya is sightless of what is in front of them. The Royals lie to Holders every day in an effort to increase their loyalty but Holders are too stubborn and dim-witted to accept this. Ivy may loathe the Royals but she has to confess it is quite impressive how they have the entire kingdom wrapped around their fingers—Holders are duped into carrying out their wicked biddings and the Powerless coerced.

"Why don't we get this presentation started already?" Headmaster Huang says once he enters the room again. "Queen Matilda is on her way. This is your last chance, young lady."

Ivy shrugs. "I'm ready."

Mr. Abalos hesitantly steps to the side as Ivy begins to make her way to the front. She runs a thumb across her lower lip, wiping off the blood that's still smudged on it. The conniver halts in front of their teacher's desk and looks up to face her classmates. The same look of interest can be seen in their eyes, all of them waiting for her to either humiliate herself or disprove their claims regarding her purported Amulet.

Athena shouts, "Just hurry it up already."

My pleasure.

"First, I will select a target for my presentation," she explains. Ivy looks to the left and then to the right before choosing to approach the boy who is seated next to her. She knows nothing about him, thus unaware of what his abilities are. But that just makes this all far more electrifying.

Disregarding the boy's apparent turmoil, Ivy places a hand on his broad shoulders. She can already feel her Amulet begin to glimmer its bright, golden light as soon as her palm comes into physical contact with the boy, and so can she clearly visualize everyone's faces of bewilderment. Glowing, after all, is a feature of Amulets that indicates the functioning of a power.

A fake Amulet is not supposed to glow.

Ivy redirects her attention to her hand, which is still resting on her target's shoulder. Golden rays of light radiate around her palm as though it's become the sun itself. The power she is utilizing tells her that the boy endows Invulnerability. When the gleaming finally dies down, Ivy knows she's ready.

Phase three.

She takes her hand off the boy's shoulder and looks around again. When her eyes settle on the glass vase sitting beautifully in a corner of the classroom near Mr. Abalos' desk, Ivy scrambles towards it. She picks up the fragile item from the floor and, with as much force as her arms can bear, brings it toward her head. The raucous sound of the vase shattering into a thousand glittering fragments pierces through their ears, each sharp silver jabbing into the schemer's skin and falling to the floor. But afterward, when all the pieces have fallen with a loud, grating clang! not a single indication of damage appears anywhere on her face.

"Invulnerability?" Ivy's target gasps. "That's my power. Invulnerability. Did she—?"

The class is left in a trance as Ivy takes a little bow of contentment.

"Power Absorption," Mr. Abalos chokes out.

"Actually," Ivy immediately corrects, pleased with their expressions, "the ability I just performed is called Power Replication. You see, when I made physical contact with my mark, a replication of his power was sent to my body, therefore, I was automatically able to do what he could do."

"You thief! You liar! You wretched little thing!" Mr. Abalos proceeds in an accusing tone, pointing a stubby finger her way. "You did steal the queen's Golden Amulet."

Ivy can't miss the chance to deride him for his ridiculous response then by, of course, stating a fact that everyone is already aware of. "Only the Holder of a certain Amulet can access the powers of that Amulet. Please, Mr. Abalos, if you're going to argue with me, at least make sense."

She knows the man merely ranted nonsense as a result of his brain struggling to make sense of what she just performed. Everyone else in the room is most certainly feeling the same way, as evidenced by the fact that their mouths are wide open and their eyes have expanded. "Or... Are you suggesting that perhaps, you Holders got the facts all wrong?"

"Don't put words into my mouth, Eun!" Mr. Abalos yells. He turns to face the headmaster, his eyebrows furrowed with concern. "Please, deal with this senseless brat."

A small amused scoff leaves Ivy's mouth. Her? Senseless? For simply proving them wrong?

Not even the elderly man knows what to say. He rubs his short beard as he continues to stare at the girl, puzzled, curious, impressed, and embittered all at the same time. "Where did you get that Amulet from? Are you suggesting that our queen is not who she says she is? That is a bold claim."

"I am not obliged to answer any of your questions, Mr. Huang. If any of you still cannot see the truth even after what I just performed, then I worry for Arya. Clearly, none of you are smart enough to protect this kingdom."

Before the headmaster can enunciate a reply, the door opens and a guard's head pokes inside.

"Queen Matilda is here."

word count • 4054

04 | THE LION'S DEN

CHAPTER FOUR — THE LION'S DEN

WHEN the announcement that young Matilda Azura possessed the Golden Amulet came, Holder women and young girls were the only ones that rejoiced. The rest wept.

Centuries ago, the Golden Amulet was something that was only rumored to exist—a necklace that would surprisingly bring the Land of Thegn eternal serenity and happiness with its tremendous powers. But that was all it was during then. Just a rumor frantic people made up with not a single piece of evidence to defend the idea, therefore, not many believed it. According to tales Ivy often heard when she was younger, the Amulet would, in time, be handed to the one person who could elevate not just the Kingdom of Arya but the entirety of Thegn to grandeur. At such a young age, Matilda Azura was already next in line to be queen.

None of this, however, concerned the Powerless. Even if the rumors were accurate, the pendant would not have any impact on their horrid lives. Holder men thought it was a man who would possess the Golden Amulet. They did not think a woman could manage such potent abilities. But what could they do, anyway? Absolutely nothing. There was no point in demanding a change once the owner of the pendant had been chosen.

According to these Holders, the one who possessed the Golden Amulet was a god.

Matilda was repeatedly acknowledged for any notable occurrence that took place. Someone, at last, got the job of their dreams? It was all thanks to the great Matilda. A lovely baby successfully delivered? All the gratitude went to the oh-so-wondrous woman.

As time passed, people began to perceive her as a divine figure, someone to seek out in times of hardship. In academies, teachers would educate their students on all matters pertaining to Amulets and never fail to bring up their queen.

"Although all pendants come in different shapes and colors, there are quite a lot that grant the same abilities. One thing that sets the Golden Amulet apart from the others is its distinctiveness—it's the only one that grants powers no other Amulet is capable of," they would say. "It's what makes the queen special. She's in possession of powers no other Holders can perform."

Ivy wonders...

"Queen Matilda is here."

...Just how Arya will respond once they learn their queen has been deluding them all this time.

Mr. Abalos frowns. "So soon?"

"It turns out she was already on her way to the academy before you requested for her." The guard gives a half-shrug. "She's starting her academy evaluation now."

Ivy makes no effort to conceal the sneer her lips have formed.

Phase four.

"Where is this child?" the celebrated woman's aggravated voice sounds outside of the room. "And what is this about the Golden Amulet?"

Headmaster Haung widens the opening of the door for the queen and Ivy's posture straightens upon hearing the woman's voice again. "Please, make this worth my time. I've heard of other bored, fat-headed Powerless children fake things just for attention. It's displeasing."

The prominent woman enters the classroom but without delay, no one fails to perceive the Golden Amulet hanging around her neck.

"W-what is going on?" a student cries out. "I thought there was only one."

"My Amulet. . ." The queen's puzzled voice trails off as her eyes stare at the pendant around Ivy's neck. Of all the drama she's had to face over the years, this one truly takes the cake, she thinks. "Ah," she sighs, "another Powerless pretending to be a Holder? And is that Angelo's daughter I see? How adorable. I think the fact that you're somehow back surprises me more than that Amulet you've got."

"Eun isn't pretending to be a Holder, Your Majesty," Headmaster Huang states behind her. "The Amulet around her neck is real."

Queen Matilda chuckles. "You don't actually believe that, do you? I thought you were better."

"We watched her perform a power," another student Ivy does not know blurts out.

And right then and there, the color from the woman's face fades, her expression dulled. "Are you. . . Are you diddling with me?" she demands but from the uneasy tone of her voice, Ivy can tell she already knows the answer to that. Why in the world would any Holder ever lie about something as serious as this?

Queen Matilda grips her elegant red glinting a-line gown that's got its end scattered on the floor. As she makes her way to the guard who has yet to leave, the gown whirls about her, and her tall heels clang against the pristine marble floor. "I want three more of you in here. Now!"

"Yes, of course, Your Majesty!" And with that, the guard is off.

When she turns to face Ivy once again, the woman's monolid eyes flare with fury. "You and I are going to have a very long chat, Eun. Maybe, I'll go easy on you if you come with me willingly."

"I suppose the guards are to escort me to the palace?" Ivy rises from her seat. "They're really not necessary but I understand your doubt." Of course, she will accompany the woman voluntarily. In fact, for her plot to succeed, being in that palace is a must. It is the only way she can bring both the woman and her husband out in the open for a more appealing outcome.

But not before she turns to her classmates again. She must be certain that they are all fully aware of what is going on. "Think about it," Ivy says. "I was able to access one of the Golden Amulet's powers. What do you think that makes me? Think about it."

"You best keep your mouth shut if you want any chance of getting out of this alive!" Queen Matilda hisses, reaching forward and grabbing the young schemer by the arm.

"But, Your Majesty, we must know what's going on here," Headmaster Huang urges. "How is a Powerless girl able to access the powers of your Amulet? It doesn't make any sense."

"That's what I'm going to find out. You need not concern yourself over this matter. The Royals will handle it." The woman's teeth grind just as the door opens again and four guards walk in. "You're quite daring, aren't you, Eun? You could have just come back in peace, apologize to your parents for leaving and the pain you caused them, and have a chance of returning to your old life. Instead, you decide to stir up trouble. Well, let me tell you this. A Powerless liar like you won't go far. Just how many of your people have tried to overthrow me? A lot. And how many have actually succeeded? None. You're no different from them."

Ivy slaps the woman's hand away and cocks her head to the side. Maintaining her composure seems to irritate the queen even more. "You pretending not to be so apprehensive has just become my favorite sight."

Queen Matilda's hands fist. At first, it looks like she's about to blow—her eyebrows have curled into a glower, her lips are quivering, and her diamond-shaped face has turned scarlet. She exhales, though, and forces a smile. "I won't allow you to get to me, Eun. I never will."

Ivy pauses just in front of the door and turns to look at the woman once more—the same woman who nearly imprisoned her three years ago when Athena claimed she'd stolen her Amulet without evidence, the same woman who never bothered to look into her friends' murders, the same woman she watched spit on a Powerless nine-year-old pleading to spare some food for his dying mother, Queen Matilda, a woman who has grown to become her greatest foe.

"Oh, I think I already have."

Outside the academy, Ivy is led to a white carriage. Seeing the four horses tied to their ride causes her to halt in an instant before whirling around to face the guards behind her.

"I need to get my horse."

Taking note of the frowns that are quick to appear on their faces, Ivy sighs. "My horse, Snow, was my ride to the academy. I need to make sure she's okay. She means a lot to me."

It was after three long years of training and plotting that Adora gifted the animal to her. "This way, you won't be lonely," she told Ivy. "Snow will not disappoint you."

One of the guards, a wrinkled round-faced middle-aged Aryan man, chortles. "Coward," he utters. "You dare challenge the queen herself, and now, you won't even see it through. Why are you making such pathetic excuses now?"

"This isn't a trick!" Ivy retaliates, immediately reaching forward and grabbing hold of the guard who'd spoken by the arm with pique. "Just send one of your men to the stable next to the academy. I kept her there. I'll willingly come with you, alright? But I won't leave her."

"Listen, you senseless little thin—"

"Just go get the horse!" Queen Matilda grits her teeth, cutting the guard off.

The man's shoulders slump but he lets out a defeated sigh seconds later and nods to the two guards standing beside him. The two of them nod back and head toward the stable.

"She's white!" Ivy calls after them. "With a black saddle that's got Snow imprinted on it. She should be at the very back!"

"Alright, come on now." After grabbing her arm while opening the carriage door, the round-faced man shoves the girl inside before she can protest any further. Ivy rolls her eyes at the brutal force. It's not surprising. Holders are far too aggressive, especially when they feel threatened.

All her worries are soon to fade once she espies the horse just as requested.

The ride from there to the palace is almost silent.

───..∘ ☽ ▫ ☾ ∘..───

Only when they step foot inside the throne room does Queen Matilda feel she can breathe again. Ivy can see the look of relief all over her face as she's ushered further inside.

"Eun Calinao!" the woman barks. She may have been furious back at the academy but at least, she made an effort to contain it. Now that they're here, however, she knows she doesn't have to do that anymore.

Seated upon squared, padded, high-backed thrones behind her standing tall and lush figure are her husband, King Titus, and their eleven-year-old son, Prince Tobias adorned in lavish attire with their robes shimmering, rings sparkling, and crowns radiating a brilliant glow. A guard called them in earlier.

"See what you've gotten yourself into now?" The woman's grin is more sinister than ever and Ivy can't help but wonder what sort of torturous punishment she's got planned for her.

"I haven't been arrested," she reminds the queen, although she's sure that won't do any good. "And you have no reason to do so either. I have not broken any rules."

Queen Matilda takes a step forward and jeers, "I do not need a reason to throw you behind bars."

"Wouldn't you like to ask me a few questions first?" Ivy suggests with a teasing smile. "Perhaps about where I got the Amulet or who gave it to me or why I've come back. Ah—perhaps not. After all, you already know the answers to all those questions, don't you?"

Queen Matilda looks at her family, her eyes a telltale sign of anxiety and the skin between her drawn-arched eyebrows wrinkled. "You two should step out." And then, her focus shifts to the guards standing by the door. "So should you. This is between me and Eun. I'll have it figured out myself, no worries."

"No, no, no. They should stay."

The taunting look on Ivy's face causes Queen Matilda's heart to skip a beat, a dozen more questions appearing in the woman's already troubled mind. The expression that crosses the queen's face is immediately familiar to Ivy—those pleading, dilated eyes, the slightly quivering lips, her clenched fists. It's fear—complete and utter terror, an expression Ivy has been so eager to see on her.

Queen Matilda's heart is racing, her head wheeling and her eyes see nothing but darkness, her ears ringing with the enraged cries of a million people. Her skin is crawling and her bones rattling, her muscles screaming of a dread unknown.

It's a glorious sight that Ivy would pay good jewels to see every single day.

"Your family should have your back, no?" she presses. "Your Amulet did supposedly get seized."

"By an idiot who doesn't seem to realize the deep grave she's dug herself." The queen's eyes squint, hands fiddling with the crystal bracelet around her right wrist. "Darling, don't you see?" she says to her husband, a forced smile plastered on her lips. "It's just another Powerless wasting all our time. I'm sure you don't want to be here for this. Perhaps, you could take Tobias out for some fun. He's been a bit bored lately. Haven't you, love?"

"I effortlessly accessed one of the Golden Amulet's powers."

Ivy refuses to beat around the bush any longer. She knows what Queen Matilda is trying to do and she can't allow her to be successful. "Performed it, as well," she adds, "in front of my classmates. You can ask them. I'm sure they're still back there, quarreling over what they saw."

"And how would you have been able to do that?" King Titus raises an eyebrow. "Tell me, Eun, how did you manage to steal my wife's Golden Amulet?"

"I didn't." Ivy shakes her head slowly. "I didn't go anywhere near the pendant your wife has."

"So why, then, was I informed that you did?"

Ivy's chin raises, her words leaving her lips in a confident tone. "Your wife knows how to lie her way through anything. She's been doing that for the past twenty-seven years."

"Don't believe anything this scoundrel says!" Queen Matilda growls, placing a hand on the man's arm. "The truth is, Eun found a way inside the palace, inside my chamber, seized my Amulet, and replaced it with a replica so I wouldn't notice. This," she reaches for the pendant around her neck and yanks it off, "is a fake, and she's unfortunately still got the real one with her."

"Why are we wasting time, then?" King Titus exclaims. "Why haven't you had it taken from her yet?"

"Oh, she tried." Ivy chuckles, her mind reeling back to the carriage they were in and the countless attempts the woman and her guards made to snatch the pendant from her.

Queen Matilda trembles again. She knows how to lie, yes—her mother taught her, ran her through several possibilities, and showed her how to get through each one of them. But none of those possibilities included a Powerless escapee returning to the kingdom with the one thing that could throw her off the throne, throw her out of this world. "If you didn't steal from me, where, then, did you get that Amulet, Eun? We all know you're a Powerless so don't bother lying about your status."

King Titus does not wait for her response. He waves his hand, motioning to the two guards that have been silent yet gripped, and barks an order. "Take the Amulet from her!"

"Try as you may, you won't find the Amulet on me," Ivy warns. "Knowing that there'd be desperate people trying to steal it, I hid it."

Queen Matilda pauses. Replacing half of her fright is single-mindedness. Yes, she tried to take the pendant but the Golden Amulet has one power she was never told of. The ability to keep itself hidden. Ivy made sure it stayed invisible throughout that entire ride.

"Where did you get it?"

"You know where. You just don't want to admit it, is all. You're... too afraid."

"You know what?" the woman suddenly snickers. "This is good. This is very good. If it was someone else in your position, perhaps, I would be afraid. But no, it's just you, Eun, a Powerless good-for-nothing, so help yourself out there while you still can. I know you're not cruel or foolish. You're only angry. Is it still those two friends of yours?

They're why you're doing this, aren't they? You just want vengeance on the one that slew those girls. I assure you throwing your life away isn't the way to do it."

Ivy smiles. "It fills me with great joy to see you so desperate."

"Eun, you still have a chance at getting out of here unpunished if you do the right thing," Queen Matilda threatens but the dread continues to lie underneath. "You're surrounded. I can have you killed in a matter of seconds and no one will even care. Hand the Amulet over. I won't ask nicely a second time."

"Why should I do as you ask?" An exasperated sigh leaves the younger's mouth, eyes narrowed and nose crinkled. "So, you can replace it with the fake pendant you've got and continue to delude the kingdom?" She chortles, throwing her head back in amusement. "Oh, Matilda. We both know killing me is the last thing on your mind. You'd have to first find a way to force me to replace my name with yours."

King Titus' head tilts and his brows furrow. He rises and gives Queen Matilda a puzzled look. "What is going on? Why does another being have your Amulet? A Powerless one, at that."

"Love, she's just playing around. All these words coming out of her mouth, they're false." Her mouth has gone dry now, cheeks flushed, and jaw clenched. "Let's not drag this any further, Eun. You seized something that clearly was not yours, so hand it over. Now! This is your last warning."

"You know what? You're right. As much as I am enjoying this little banter, we shouldn't drag it." Ivy simply nods, placing her hands on her waist. "But no, I won't hand it over. Yes, I'm certainly not foolish. But cruel? Don't test me. You're not getting what you want. Not this time."

Her response leaves the queen frozen in her spot, not just taken off guard by the audacity Ivy has to speak back in such an outrageous manner but feels the hairs at the back of her neck raise in alarm as well, as though her spine is being raked by invisible fingers. The subsequent nostalgia blinds her for a moment. Ivy can see in the woman's dark eyes that Queen Matilda is finally recalling the past.

"Thinking about her?" The schemer's eyebrows raise quizzically. When she takes notice of the king's deepened puzzlement, she clarifies. "Your wife is well aware of who it is I'm speaking of. She treated her elder sister the same way she's treating me now. She's trying to take something that never belonged to her, to begin with. For the second time!"

King Titus opens his mouth to speak but the woman does not allow him to get in a single word. The memory of her past struggles with intransigence is more than enough to incite her and she does not wish to cope with it again. After all, the past ought to remain in the past. When she realizes she has no other choice, she breaks out of her trance and waves a hand for the guards to approach.

"You will hand that Amulet over, Eun Calinao!"

Ivy shakes her head. "I don't think so."

"And how do you plan on getting out of here with this palace filled with my men?" Queen Matilda cackles, disregarding her husband's bewildered state. "Please, Eun. Do yourself a favor and stop embarrassing yourself. I thought I could convince you to snap out of your witless state but I'm certain I speak for everyone when I say this conversation has gone on for far too long. You've refused to behave obediently, so now, you've left me no other option but to imprison and punish you severely."

Ivy sighs, collectedly caressing the Golden Amulet that's all of a sudden reappeared around her neck. The mere sight of it causes Queen Matilda to gasp lightly, her eyes lighting up with excitement. "Once again, you're not getting it. Of course, I have to have an exit plan before stepping inside the lion's den."

But the queen is unwilling to hear any more of it. "Lock her up. And take the Amulet."

"Time Pause."

"What—?"

The world freezes, as though turned into a motionless photograph, Queen Matilda standing with a pointed finger, her face frozen in a bewildered look, her men near Ivy, arms outstretched, ready to grab onto her, and King Titus and his son sitting in their thrones behind the woman, the king leaning forward, brows furrowed, mouth open and the boy staring straight at his mother, concerned. Though he's young, he understands. He knows what this accusation could do to his mother, to his family, to him. Ivy dashes out of the palace with great speed, met with hundreds of immobile people, animals, and things here and there once she's outside, including her own horse.

Colorful sculptures, that's what they all look like, unable to move, think, feel. This is the kind of stillness that even a feather would fall straight down without drifting in any direction, the wind dead, grass straight and silent, the leaves ceased to rustle, dangling more as if painted there. Even the rumble of the vehicles is absent. Motionless all because of the power she instituted.

Not her own, of course.

Ivy was shopping in the market a few days ago when she overheard a certain round-faced middle-aged Aryan guard telling his friend all about how he'd used Time Pause to escape an awkward circumstance. That was when she decided he would assist her. Best of all, he wouldn't even be aware of it.

She spent two days roaming about Arya with half of her face covered, collecting information about the man. The only thing Ivy learned that actually piqued her interest was that he was an academy guard, so, she began to ask around about the forthcoming academy he was training to work at.

In order for Power Replication to be effective, Ivy has to be in direct physical touch with her target for a good five seconds. Throwing a fit about how much her horse meant to her and grabbing the guard by his arms while pretending to be furious helped her with that. Plus, Snow is meant to be her getaway ride.

Ivy hops on the animal, and once she is certain she has a nice head start, she mumbles to herself. "Time Play." And just like that, the kingdom is brought back to life, each individual going about their own way, doing about their own thing, unaware of what just occurred.

Ivy tugs on the reins to put light tension in her horse's mouth. The moment she has Snow's attention, the girl softly commands the animal to advance by gently squeezing it with her legs. "Ha!" Snow scrambles off.

At this time, Ivy can hear the queen's shrill voice behind her. Following Queen Matilda, who has already mounted her own horse, is a large number of soldiers galloping after her. All at once, they scream for anyone to stop Ivy from riding any further.

"Good," Ivy mumbles again.

They are acting just as she expects and wants them to. At present, a tremendous number of people have surrounded them, trapping her and Snow in a circle. Before glancing back to see how far off the Royals and their men are, Ivy gives the area a brief scan. Unfortunately, the person she's searching for is nowhere to be seen.

The next thing she knows, her arms are grabbed and her body yanked off the animal's back, a swarm of Holders already shouting in her face all at the same time. Ivy is once more left astounded and impressed by how well the Royals have control over these Holders. All of them are still in the dark about what is happening, yet they've chosen to side with the Royals. Perhaps, it does make sense why they would act in such a way since the Royals are well-respected, but Ivy is still of the opinion that they all possess a fair amount of foolishness.

"Everyone, step back!"

They obey, each person moving aside. Queen Matilda shoves her way through the crowd until she is eventually in the middle, standing before the reviled girl.

Ivy sneers. "Took you long enough."

word count • 4132

05 | Villain of the Story

CHAPTER FIVE — VILLAIN OF THE STORY

FIVE YEARS AGO11TH SEPTEMBER 1998

EUN never really understood just how much every bit of her people's workaholic days should have been more appreciated until The twelfth of September arrived. Certainly, rights to many things, such as rest, could have been given to them, yet when a brutal Powerless Tournament commenced out of nowhere for entertainment, every one of them yearned for the better days. Yes, they certainly paled in comparison to Holders. Their torturers made sure to tell them that every day. But did things have to get this far?

"Psst! Eun, come quick. Something's happening."

The day before, she was awoken by an unexpected commotion coming outside of her bedroom. Eun idly left her bed and trudged to the small window a few feet away. She often made sure it was closed before falling asleep—those flies were a tremendous menace at night.

The night sky was aglow with bright lights, the pale crescent moon shining a silvery claw. As the occasional barking of faraway dogs broke the silence, Eun looked up at the blanket of stars that stretched to infinity before gazing down. Sighting her two best friends, Benecia Patel and Delyth Nguyen, on the other side of her window was not what she anticipated. Unless given a cleaning job at night, those two were never allowed to leave their homes during such a late hour. Neither was she. It was one of the rules of the kingdom they'd grown accustomed to.

Meanwhile, Holder children would consistently boast about certain night jamborees they'd taken part in everywhere they went. Eun was well aware of how it felt to hear another person exclaim about how astounding and better their lives were, after all, she attended a school where the majority of the students were Holders.

And, as an after-school activity, she was to cleanse the inside of the building with the rest of the Powerless children that'd been forced into the job, as well. Her parents often spoke of how fortunate she was to even be attending an academy, at all. Very few people of your kind have a right to education, they would say. Time and time again, Eun refused to heed their words. Benecia was the fortunate one. She got to be home-schooled.

"What's going on?" Eun questioned in a hushed tone from where she was still standing after coming to realize seconds later that dogs weren't the only ones ruining the peaceful silence. Was this another jolly Holders were hosting? Why did these people insist on doing such a thing in the middle of the night?

"You might want to come see this for yourself, Eun." Benecia gulped with a drained look, her usual animated voice edged with fear. Only when she glanced over at Delyth and noticed the girl fiddling with her fingers did Eun's heart begin to pound.

With both girls there on the ground to catch her, Eun managed her way down from the window. Whatever the girls had come for must have been consequential enough to risk their lives being out here. That thought alone caused Eun's body to go cold with dread. Delyth swiftly grabbed her arm before she could utter another word and dragged her away from the house, Benecia following closely.

The nearer the girls got to what Eun speculated was their destination, the easier it was to perceive boisterous sounds of cheering. As much as she hated for it to be true, Eun knew her previous jolly assumption was the only thing that could explain whatever was going on. Parties Holders threw never ended well for the Powerless. Holders were found to be much more brutal under the influence of alcohol.

"What have you led me to?" Eun queried again, yet neither of her friends gave a straight answer. "This better be worth it!" she hissed, already picturing the wrathful looks on her parents' faces once they found out she'd snuck out. The punishments would be severe and in no way was she ready for them.

"It's best we don't get close," said Benecia. "We don't want to get involved in this."

"Involved in what?" demanded Eun once again.

"During work, we overheard a Holder talking about an event happening tonight," Delyth replied. "An event that's got something to do with us. This won't end well but if we can figure out what they're planning this time, we may have time to warn the rest."

Eun winced at the idea. "Remember the last time we tried to do that?" Her friend was often buoyant and heartening and she loved her for that—it was one of the only things keeping her going nowadays—but this time, it was hardly enough to convince her that they could pull this off. And if they got caught, things would go from bad to worse, except unlike last time when they were given several whips as warning, it'd be instant executions, no questions asked.

Eun could still feel the stinging pain from the hits. She was always down to help her people but not when it'd go in vain regardless and cost them their lives.

"That's what I said too," Benecia mumbled.

"That was back then. We should be over that," Delyth urged. Yet during their run, she was frequently seen wincing and pressing a hand against her stomach from the pain. Delyth had gotten it worse than the two of them combined. "We can't let the Holders get away with whatever it is they're planning."

"Stop acting so brave all the time!" Benecia urged, her tone harsh but concerned. "You don't always have to be a hero, Delyth. Sometimes, you just have to admit that there's nothing you can do."

"But there is something we can do!" Delyth shot back, more persistent than before. "There's always something we can do."

Benecia's lips quivered, as though she had something else to say but forced it down her throat.

When her two friends finally came to a halt, so did Eun, all three of them hiding behind trees in the tiny woodland they'd just entered. The night was alive, the roar of the crowd and music thrumming straight into their eardrums. With a glass of wine in one hand and their Amulets swaying this way and that, Holders moved their bodies like there was no tomorrow.

It would have been beautiful—perfect, even—if not for the fact they were here for the sake of lives that were at stake. Eun wasn't sure how many times she'd wished she could be one of them. How wholly incredible it would be to dance her problems away. One night. That was all she yearned for. Just one night of the Powerless finally throwing their own jamboree without getting put to death for it.

"Why did you bring me here?" came another question, Eun's voice thick with distress.

Before either of her friends could give her an answer, the music came to an abrupt stop. Several whines sounded, angry shouts to bring the party back to life coming next.

One Holder stood tall on top of a boulder, holding his glass of red wine high and calling for everyone's attention. Once that was obtained, the man roughly cleared his throat.

"We did not just come here to dance. That much, you should understand. We're Holders, are we not?" he began, instantly receiving nods from the audience. "We deserve more entertainment, do you not agree? And, what's more entertaining than watching a bunch of incompetent Powerless beings battle?"

It was easy to remember the man as diabolical Gozar Agulto, one of the main guards of the Royal Palace and a fearful but over-appreciated man in the kingdom. People often gossiped that he would make a better king than King Titus, and though both men were great friends, it wasn't difficult to understand that Gozar agreed with the gossip. He was born for extraordinary things—to be a leader, he'd stated more than once.

"What day is it tomorrow?" the man questioned out loud before bringing his glass to his lips.

"September twelfth, I believe," another man replied.

"Right!" Gozar snapped his fingers with an elated sneer. "I now declare that every September ninth, a series of battles will be held, in which Powerless beings will fight each other to the death for our entertainment."

"He's drunk!" Delyth hissed.

"So, what if he's drunk?" Benecia scoffed. "This was bound to happen. Admit it."

As the cheers from Gozar's sudden announcement eventually died down, a new voice of a woman spoke. "But hold on a second. Should you not receive permission from the Royals first?"

"Shut up, woman!" Gozar jeered as he unsteadily got off the boulder. "We all know Titus would enjoy this just as much as us if not even more. There's utterly no need for permission."

Eun gradually slid down to the ground, trepidation fluttering in her stomach as she peeled her attention away from the loud conversation.

"The Royals always allow him to do as he wishes. This will be no different."

Delyth gasped lightly. "We must warn the others. We can at least try to defend ourselves."

"What's the use?" Benecia cried out. "In the end, they always find a way to get what they want. If it's a gruesome fight they desire, a gruesome fight they will get. The best thing we can do now is find a way out of this kingdom. Find a way to escape once and for all."

"Then, let's do what we've always been best at doing," Delyth responded with determination, turning her head from one girl to the other as her hands fisted. "We hide."

——..○ ☽ ▫ ☾ ○..——

PRESENT07TH SEPTEMBER 2003

One of the Royals' men tugs her up from the ground and, barbarously choosing to disregard the small bruise on her left cheek from falling off her horse, the man's muscular arm grips onto her jaw, forcing her to stare at the Royals that are glaring back. Ivy side-eyes the guard, and thanks to the familiar ruffled black hair, prominent high cheekbones, and squared jaw, it doesn't take her long at all to recognize him.

The one and only Gozar Agulto.

Ivy instantly feels a stab of anger. Don't touch me! Get away from me! she wants to yelp but refuses to allow her hatred to have the upper hand. Right now is not about Gozar Agulto—she has yet to start her little plot against him. No, right now, she must focus on what is more crucial. Adora cautioned her to constantly keep in mind what her people needed and what she wanted. Athena Takao and Gozar Agulto are her wants—the two people whose demise she'd feel gratified by but wouldn't benefit her people as a whole.

At the same time, Ivy can't help but wonder how, even after all this time, this repulsive man is still nothing more than a guard—a follower, rather than the leader he so confidently claimed to be numerous times. How could he be born for great things when he's still struggling mightily to elude the Royals?

By now, the crowd is whispering amongst themselves, mouths falling open, hands flying to chests, some of their eyes bulging, and others blinking rapidly, unable to comprehend the sight before them. They've, no doubt, noticed the Amulet around Ivy's neck. When Queen Matilda hastily reaches for it again, Ivy closes her eyes. The Golden Amulet is no longer visible once she opens them.

"Take her back to the palace!" the woman hisses.

"No, not yet." The king calls out behind her, raising an arm to stop the guards. "Matilda, you're still yet to explain to me what is happening. This is all so puzzling."

"I've already explained, my love." But even though the queen's voice is soft, there's a hint of irritation buried behind it. If someone else dares question her, she might just explode. Trying to conceal her apprehension with a small smile, she ushers Gozar to begin moving again. "And we will not let her go unpunished."

"Matilda is afraid~" Ivy sings mockingly as Gozar drags her across the ground toward the horses. "She's afraid of the kingdom learning her secret." The guard's movement is, however, slow—or, at least, not as quick as he should be, and when Ivy looks up at him, she can see the glint of hesitation in his eyes.

"What is she on about?" King Titus interrogates.

The woman gives an exhalation of frustration. "I-It's nothing, darling. Eun is just sick in the head."

"I suppose this is the part where I let everyone be aware that I accessed one of the Golden Amulet's powers," Ivy carries on, making sure her voice is louder this time. "Do you really think I'd be able to use its power or make the Golden Amulet hide itself if I was not the owner of it?"

That's when Gozar halts, the crowd stops whispering, and King Titus and the rest of the guards freeze in their spots. Ivy just grins. Her entire body aches from the way Gozar was brutally dragging her but she pushes the pain aside. She knows she's got them now. She's got their full attention.

Anger flares across the queen's face when she realizes this too, her hands clenched, knuckles whitened, head filled with hisses that snake through like tendrils of smoke, a colossal rage surging through her chest. "This girl right here is a thief!" she blurts out, attempting to take matters into her own hands. "However, I'm glad to inform you that she isn't as intelligent as she is valiant. She seized my Amulet and had the audacity to attend an academy with it, thinking with her mindless head that I would not find out."

Ivy would speak but why interrupt the woman in the middle of digging herself a bigger grave?

"We all know this is something the Powerless love to do—pose as Holders, as us! But they never succeed. And neither will this little girl. The Golden Amulet isn't invisible because she made it so. No, it's hiding itself because it knows it's in the wrong hands, because it knows it's been taken away from its rightful owner." She pauses once the crowd begins to mumble again, as though trying to pick up what they're saying now. "I owe you all a massive thank you. You just helped me capture a vicious criminal, one that's threatened me, my family, my people, my kingdom. These ungrateful Powerless will never learn but hopefully, after Eun receives her punishments, they'll know better than to carry on with this thievery nonsense."

"Right, right, right." Ivy chuckles under her breath, wondering just how many people can see through the woman's fake smile. She would clap to ridicule her if not for the fact Gozar is still gripping onto her skinnier arms. "Make me the villain of the story."

"Keep that mouth shut! You've been caught, Eun." Queen Matilda demands. But on the inside, she's pleading.

Ivy has never heard her use that tone before. It makes her shiver with pride.

How did this so-called miraculous woman survive with her secret for this long? No, a better question. How did she deceive the kingdom for this long? Surely, there is no way she could have endured her unbearable private affairs alone for years. She must have had help.

Ivy glances at the king next. In all honesty, the man doesn't seem to be entirely certain of what is going on. Ivy can sense that a part of him wants to believe his wife. Regardless, the other part of him is beginning to rethink every little thing Queen Matilda has ever told him.

Although their son isn't present, Ivy's mind shifts over to him. Prince Tobias couldn't have been helping his mother, either. Yes, the boy is not at all pure but Ivy doubts he possesses the skills to protect the queen and keep her confidential matter hidden for so long. After all, Queen Matilda's secret ought to have already eaten her alive long before she married and gave birth.

So, who is helping her?

Queen Matilda would have needed solid proof that the Golden Amulet undeniably belonged to her. She would have needed to persuade Arya. How did she accomplish it? How did she manage to perform all those wonders that deemed her a god? During her younger years, even Ivy herself witnessed some of the miracles and believed the woman. It was Adora that finally opened her eyes and showed her the truth.

Once an Amulet emerges for a child or is passed down to a Powerless, altering their impermissible status and deeming them Holders finally worthy of respect, their full names are automatically engraved on the necklace as a way to symbolize that it belongs to them now. Unfortunately, for some unknown reason, the names constantly stay invisible, making it impossible for everyone to see.

"How can we tell which Amulet belongs to whom?" people often wondered. "What if a person claims an Amulet belongs to them when in fact, they stole it from someone else?"

All these queries ceased coming centuries ago when a woman rose with a statement that she could see all engraved names on the pendants. The theft of seizing a Holder's Amulet was quite simple to pull off during then yet as years passed, it became increasingly difficult to commit. The worst penalties were served.

Not a lot of people held this remarkable ability to see inscribed names, and those who did were seen as extraordinary beings in the eyes of many Holders. These unique beings could not only see imprinted names but held the power to allow others to view them too by making the names visible for a number of seconds.

While Holders rejoiced in this, the Powerless, on the other hand, perceived it as a curse. To get away from penalties, wicked chores, and their generally harsh lives, they would often seize a Holder's Amulet and claim it as their own. With this special power only a select few Holders possessed, the Powerless beings were again compelled to reveal what their true status was.

Many years after the first woman with this momentous gift was born, the Holders realized there was one other way to determine who the real owner of a certain Amulet was. The abilities of a pendant could only be employed by its actual possessor. If a thief stole an Amulet, they would be unable to use its powers as it wasn't their name engraved on the necklace. From then on, it was announced that during every Amulet Assessment, all Holders were to showcase at least one power of their pendants as identification that it, indeed, belonged to them.

"Take Eun back to the palace and have her locked up," Queen Matilda orders again.

But this time, nobody moves.

"I said—!"

"We heard you," Gozar cuts her off. "But I think we'd like to hear from Eun first."

Ivy scoffs lightly at his words. The man can't stand her. She is nothing more to Gozar than a worthless, fragile target. That was all Benecia and Delyth were to him as well when he took their lives. Ivy knows the sole motive behind his insistence that she is heard is because Queen Matilda might just be a step closer to losing her position. And if Arya begins to believe her husband assisted her with this crime, he will lose his too, which gives Gozar an opportunity to take over. Ivy cannot let that happen.

That is why she's set aside another plan made just for him.

The guard lets go of her arms, allowing her to finally move freely. "The Amulet you currently have with you is nothing but a fake replica of the real Golden Amulet—a thing you have used to delude this kingdom," she states proudly, walking toward the woman as she does so. "You cheated all your Amulet Assessments. It makes sense, actually. You used your power as Queen of Arya to keep the assessments away from that fake pendant. Genius, if you ask me. But it's come to an end now, Matilda."

"You don't know what you're talking about!" Queen Matilda attempts again before her glare shifts to the mumbling crowd. "And if you really believe her, then there must be something wrong with your heads as well. I have proven myself many times. But this little girl comes along out of nowhere and all of a sudden, all I've done for Arya is no longer remembered? Can't you see she's filling your heads with this story?!" she continues to thunder with rage. "This is the thanks I get? Really?"

"Then, how do you explain—?" a commoner begins.

"Ivy must be a witch!" Queen Matilda shouts. "Or must be in cahoots with one."

Ivy raises her eyebrows at the sudden accusation. She has to admit she wasn't expecting those words to fall out of the woman's mouth.

Then again, the queen is sinking into a puddle of desperation. "The witches are a myth," she says calmly. "You sound like a child."

As the mumblings grow louder and the number of judgmental looks increases, Ivy takes this time to scan the throng in search of a particular man—the same man she struck a bargain with on the first day of her return. Perhaps, the man might not be needed after all since Arya seems to be siding with her but Ivy wants him here just in case—just to show everyone one final proof and end the dispute once and for all.

"Alright, alright. I understand your hesitation." Queen Matilda exhales, her chest rising and falling with each sharp breath she takes. "This little girl comes out of nowhere and shows you that she can access the powers of the Golden Amulet, which is impossible because it belongs to me. I understand why you would believe her but please!" Now, she's pleading. Ivy almost expects her to fall to her knees and begin weeping. "That Amulet belongs to me! I, myself, don't understand how a Powerless idiot like her managed to pull this off—I don't understand how she managed to get my Amulet in her hands but I'm telling the truth. It's mine!"

Her? A god? All Ivy sees is a pathetic woman.

"Y-you know what?" another one of the guards speaks suddenly. "Queen Matilda is right. She's done a lot for this kingdom even before she was crowned queen. We shouldn't believe this girl just yet. Besides, how can we be certain that this isn't all staged? Did she really use one of the Golden Amulet's powers? I don't know. I wasn't there. Were you? So, how can you be certain?"

Ivy can pick up some of the things they're saying now. It's not good. "It seems many of you have gotten that I performed said power in front of a class," she reminds. She knows better than to allow their twisted way of thinking to bring her down. And if that man she made a deal with can get here, all will be well.

"This is something that should be resolved in private for now," King Titus says. "We will get back to all of you with answers as soon as we can, I promise. But for now, we will take Ivy back to the palace and figure out what in the world is going on." He snaps his fingers at Gozar, and although he hesitates at first, Gozar reaches in and takes hold of Ivy again.

Where is that man?!

Before the guard can begin tying Ivy's arms with the rope they brought along, a certain boy has already squeezed his way through the crowd of people and is now standing under the nose of the king. Ivy is quick to acknowledge who the boy is. It is the same student who served as her target during her presentation back at the academy. The boy raises an arm, bringing more attention his way. The words that roll off his tongue causes everyone to pause before they begin to mumble amongst themselves once again. Even Queen Matilda appears a bit shaken as well.

"I hold the ability to see engraved names on Amulets."

For Ivy, his bold words are relieving to hear. However, the queen, on the other hand, is not as pleased. She stomps over to the boy yet he does not quiver in terror as Ivy expected him to.

He's quite courageous.

"You dare call me a liar?"

"No," comes his response. As one of the Holders, he knows the queen cannot lay a hand on him. "But if you're telling the truth, then you have nothing to worry about, Your Majesty. Correct?"

Very courageous!

"Give everyone a greater reason to trust you," the boy adds, "because we cannot deny what our eyes have witnessed and what our ears have heard today."

"What have you come here to do?"

"I will look at the Amulet and show everyone whose name is truly printed on it," the boy answers, then turns to Ivy and holds out his hand. "Please."

Queen Matilda looks ready to reject the notion but it is not her decision. Ivy smiles and closes her eyes, the Golden Amulet reappearing around her neck. She takes it off and hands it to the boy.

It is finally the moment of truth.

word count • 4249

06 | OFF WITH HER HEAD

CHAPTER SIX — OFF WITH HER HEAD

"ENGRAVED on this is the name: Ivy Pearls!"

It suddenly becomes silent for a brief period of time. Apart from Ivy, who is twirling about in her head, everyone else has conveyed looks of terror and bewilderment. Surely, it can't be. The woman they've trusted for years has been deluding them? No, impossible! They would have been able to see through her lies.

All those miracles she performed were real. They'd witnessed them all. How was their queen able to exercise abilities that no other Holders could if the boy's audacious claim was true and the Golden Amulet belonged to someone else? She was able to access another Holder's abilities, something only the Golden Amulet's true possessor could accomplish.

The woman utilized the special pendant's wish-granting power to make it rain when the plants were on the verge of extinction, to request for unlimited food so that the kingdom would never have to face famine, and to provide a treatment for a fatal disease. All of her requests were granted by the Golden Amulet without fail. They witnessed it happen. They did.

Did they?

No, they did! And because they are certain they did, each one of them raises their fists and shakes them in the air, insisting the boy give them the real truth. And by truth, Ivy knows they mean a version they'll be satisfied with—a truth that doesn't paint them as fools.

As evidence to support his claims, the boy erases the name's invisibility on the golden pendant and displays it for all to see. Sure enough, it's Ivy's name printed on it—her current name, not the one people still know her by. "An engraved name cannot be faked! Every single one of you is aware of this fact," he calls out. "This Amulet belongs to Ivy Pearls, whether you like it or not."

King Titus makes no attempt to silence the roaring mob. Neither does his wife. She stands firmly planted in place, staring at the ground with a faint expression of humiliation and dread, allowing the irate shouts to pierce through her ears. Ivy wonders if she's beginning to look back on everything. Is the woman beginning to regret carrying out her mother's wicked plan? Is she at last beginning to feel like a fool for believing she could live the rest of her life without anybody finding out?

Ivy hopes the memories are haunting her. She hopes the queen's head is muddled with every detail of the past, of every wound she inflicted on her half-sister, of every cry that left her victim's mouth, pleading to be let go.

Queen Matilda eventually lifts her head. Not only are the Holders shouting, but the Powerless as well have stopped what they were doing and are demanding an explanation. How dare that woman torture us for our status when hers is precisely the same?—they must be thinking. She dashes forward and takes hold of Ivy's arms, unwilling to let the girl go without a thorough simplification. "You ran into Adora, did you not? Tell me this instance! Did you?"

"Oh, so now, you're willing to say her name." Ivy scoffs and forcibly shoves the woman away before facing the crowd instead. She can sense that the Powerless are torn between feeling more incensed that someone who shares the same status as them is a major cause of their suffering and more relieved that the woman they loathe so much is this close to losing her position as queen.

"It was Adora, wasn't it?!" Queen Matilda is still insisting. "H-How is that possible?"

You thought she was dead, didn't you?

"If you are a Holder and beautiful, you have it all," Adora told her once. "Some of these Holders, they claim to have worked hard for their success but we all know it's because of their capacities and outward appearances that they've achieved anything. Talent is irrelevant to anyone."

Adora was a Holder but according to her corrupt parents who had her locked up for most of her life, her face gave anyone who looked at it nightmares. Her mother blamed her father, claiming she got the dreadful appearance from the pig-looking man. Nobody could know she'd been coerced into marrying him. Nobody could know that such a vile thing was her daughter.

But her father insisted on the contrary, Adora told Ivy. He asserted that the looks came from her—she was the reason their daughter turned out the way she did. One night, a heated argument sparked between them and he left for the tavern in a fit of rage—and ended up doing something that became his secret shame. He slept with a Powerless woman.

Queen Matilda's biological mother was a pitiful woman who was later strangled by his antagonized wife when she found out what he did months after Matilda was born. And even though she was humiliated and furious at the fact her spouse betrayed her trust, she was in no position to leave him. Not when he had power. Her parents would not have forced her to marry him if he was not powerful in some way. But Adora's mother could not deny what a beauty Matilda was. A shame the Powerless woman passed her awful status to the child.

"So, what if Adora handed her Amulet to Matilda?" the man suggested. "Do you realize Adora possesses a pendant everyone has been talking about? If Matilda got it in her hands, think of the many things she could achieve."

Many declare day after day that these unique necklaces not only grant powers but ensure freedom. Even after her own Amulet materialized, Adora's persistent terror only ever increased, so she knew that wasn't the case. If the proverbial sayings are accurate and Amulets really do ensure freedom, then she never would have been confined to her own squalid bedroom, grappling to survive her family. Or, at the very least, what used to be her family. In time, they developed into ruthless animals waiting to finish her off when the time was right.

During her time spent with Adora in the forest, Ivy learned of how her teacher maintained a little mirror in her chamber. Every time she looked at it, she was forced to see the dark purple bruises painted all over a face she hardly recognized, the unkempt black hair that her younger half-sister had purposely cut in different lengths, the swollen dark eyes she could hardly open without wincing in agony every now and then, her bleeding chapped lips that stung from every little touch, and the revolting gap at the bottom of her left ear where her father had yanked her earring out in a fit of rage.

Adora informed Ivy that she made it a point to check her appearance in that little mirror every day since it served as a reminder of how crude the kingdom was. Now, whenever she needs to get motivated, Ivy forces her mind to go back to the images of her teacher's horrid state, of her friends' lifeless bodies, and of every Powerless she's witnessed getting beaten and executed.

Freedom? Pfft! Right.

"Matilda once said something about having a sister who passed away from an illness," Ivy starts, ignoring the death glare the woman is sending her way. "But the truth is, her half-sister was locked away with only two options—give up her Amulet and finally be free from the torture or be stubborn and continue to rot away in her bedroom." Ivy makes sure to be extra loud when she says half. She wants everyone to know that the two women did not entirely have the same parents. In Arya, half-siblings rarely ever get along.

"Of course, Adora knew she would not be free from the torture if she gave up her Amulet. Would you ever give up your Amulet?" the girl barks and immediately, heads begin to shake. "You want to know what Adora did using that clever mind of hers? Using one of the wishes the Golden Amulet grants, she created a fake replica of the pendant and gave it to her sister. All these years, your queen has been deluding you into believing she possessed the actual Golden Amulet. How foolish do you all feel now?" And when the crowd goes silent again with shame, Ivy believes for a second that she's done it.

"You shouldn't feel foolish just yet," King Titus says abruptly, before the crowd's wrathful chanting can resume. "Matilda has passed all of her Amulet Assessments. How could that be if she possessed a fake necklace? Please, answer me that, Ivy Pearls."

"Because, as Queen of Arya, she's got a different kind of power," Ivy responds. She readied herself beforehand for any inquiries that might be made. "Your wife undoubtedly paid the Head of the assessments off. I've learned that they're good friends. The Head must be a part of all this manipulation. He knows Matilda doesn't possess an actual Amulet." She pauses for a moment and turns to the woman who is still quivering in her spot. "You were the one that selected him to be the Head, were you not?"

"And do you have proof of this claim?" King Titus questions with contempt. "Do you have proof of anything you've just uttered?"

"Yes, I have proof." Ivy gestures toward the Golden Amulet the boy beside her is still holding. "My engraved name on that pendant is my proof, and it should be more than enough."

The people around them continue to yell accusations of fraud at an ever louder volume. Ivy isn't the least bit surprised when a swarm of them charge forward to attack the woman only to be stopped by some guards and other Holders who aren't ready to believe their queen deceived them all these years. Perhaps, the guards are choosing to protect her because as of right now, they still owe her loyalty.

But Ivy cannot comprehend the reasoning behind the rest who have already placed themselves in fighting stances or spread their arms as though they were wings big and strong enough to shield the queen. Why do they continue to hold onto the notion that Queen Matilda is blameless? How can they be so confident that Ivy's statements are untrue, that the boy made up the engraving, regardless of the evidence right in front of them?

Nevertheless, Ivy does not worry. With intrepidity, she raises her own fist and opens her mouth once again. "Forcing someone to hand over their Amulet is a crime!" she hollers, and is met by a mixture of enraged cheers and juvenile boos. "It is illegal to misrepresent your royal position to a whole kingdom. What kind of hypocrisy does that display from her? She's still here, why?"

"H-Have you all lost your minds?" Queen Matilda finds her voice again. At first, it's unsteady with fear but the more she speaks, the bolder it becomes. "Have every single one of you forgotten how much effort I have put into making Arya the best? We're the wealthiest, we're the strongest, and IT'S ALL BECAUSE OF ME!" She pounds the palm of her hand against her chest, nearly suffocating on her fury. "THE FACT YOU'RE STILL ALIVE IS BECAUSE OF ME!"

Some of them are sure the woman is going to explode. Her eyes have turned red, a vortex of outrage and bitterness swirling inside her. Her words cause several people to pause, and when she begins to scream again, her voice sounds strained. "I have done more good than any one of you here. Even you can admit that."

"That isn't the truth!" Ivy urges with clenched fists. "You haven't got a single good in your heart."

None of you do.

"Is this the type of being you want to be listening to?" Queen Matilda calls out again, a silent desperate plea for Holders to come back to her side. "A Powerless ne'er-do-well who doesn't respect the Royals and makes up lies? Eun Calinao is a thief—one who refuses to heed the rules of the kingdom all because her friends were killed. Deservingly so, might I add. That's all she is! Eun Calinao, a worthless little thing."

At the sound of this, Ivy grits her teeth. But when she realizes what the woman is trying to do, she swallows down her frustration. No way will she allow Queen Matilda to get to her. Not now.

"Just like every other Powerless child who blames us for every little thing, Eun decided to commence a fight. How valiant she is—I must admit—to directly target the Royals. Whoever filled her brainless head with false promises and fabrications of being able to take down the Royals should be immensely ashamed of themselves." Queen Matilda shakes her head with astonishment lingering in her bloodshot eyes. "But of course, this plan won't work. It won't work because I trust every one of you to be smart and see through the lies.

"No one should forget about how I held this kingdom together. I have liberated many people over the years and have helped families more times than you can count. How, then, are you going to listen to this wretched girl and demand your queen be imprisoned solely based on a fabrication she made?"

Once again, it's you, you, you. Ivy scoffs. Everything is always about you, isn't it?

"And Ivy is forgetting one more thing," the woman suddenly adds. She takes a little pause to catch her breath before carrying on. "Something she didn't want any of you knowing, otherwise, she would have brought it up. Before Adora fled the kingdom, she slaughtered our father and four guards in cold blood."

And deservingly so.

"What does that have to do with the Golden Amulet?" Ivy queries with raised eyebrows.

"This special Amulet works differently than the rest. That's already been made clear," the queen begins again, much calmer this time. "It's to be used for good, and good only, so imagine the penalty Adora received when she became a killer. She had her engraved name erased and lost the pendant permanently. Yes, I admit I did not possess the Golden Amulet first—Adora did. But when she committed this heinous crime, it was passed down to me."

"So, why then did you not report her when you still had the chance?" a commoner questions from the audience. "We were informed that your father died from a chandelier suddenly snapping and crushing him to death." A series of raised fists and approvals are heard next.

Queen Matilda sighs, her right hand resting on her chest as her face forms a fake pitying look. She sucks in another sharp breath to ready herself—to explain the truth, they may think, to lie her way out, Ivy knows. "I will admit it right now. Neither my mother nor I wanted the kingdom to know Adora was gifted with the Golden Amulet first. She was a shame to our family. Everything about her was humiliating from the way she dressed to the way she behaved. She was just so improper that I could hardly tell people she was my sister.

"I hated my father for so long for sleeping with another woman, for the pain he caused me and my mother." She choked out a sob, her saddened gaze falling to the ground. "A-And there was something wrong with Adora. She was sick, a psychopath jealous of the bond I had with my mother. Therefore, we promised her that if she departed the kingdom permanently, we would stage the killing as an accident. That is how Adora ended up living in the wild. It was a much better punishment than prison."

Ivy searches the crowd, her eyes flashing with terror for a moment when mumblings arise, every Holder deliberating over what Queen Matilda just said. A mixture of fear and anger claws up her throat, heart dropping at the nerve-racking sight and lips almost beginning to quiver at the fact they are even thinking about it. After all she went through to give them this proof, they still foolishly choose to side with the Royals and deny the truth.

Perhaps, her plan isn't as perfect as she believed. She underestimated the love these people have for their Royals, underestimated their loyalty, their stupidity.

It is time to attempt another tactic.

"Matilda wasn't lying when she said I am angered by the deaths of my friends." She raises both of her hands slightly as if to surrender, wondering what other strategy she can use to fight the chaos of her aggravation. "I know you don't want to hear about two Powerless girls right now but believe me, they did a lot of good for this godforsaken kingdom and, of course, they had to lie about their status just to get around. In fact, they even crafted two fake Amulets—"

"Where are you going with this, Eun?" Queen Matilda asks with a roll of her eyes. There's still a tear under her right one. "We don't want to hear about your friends, you're certainly right about that."

"Shut it!" Ivy folds and unfolds her hands. Resentment clouds her thoughts. Breathe, she tells herself. Breathe, Ivy. "Everything was going quite well for them. . . until someone called them out on their lies. They weren't well-known but some of you should remember the names Benecia and Delyth." Do not let her get to you. "As soon as the truth came out, their lives went downhill. Nobody—not a single soul—cared to ask for further proof of their status. No, as soon as you saw that they couldn't do magic, you deemed them both Powerless.

"So, why in the world are you thinking about letting this woman go?" Her gaze rushes back to the queen, who is in the process of whispering to one of the guards, perhaps ordering him to detain her. "Her position as Queen of Arya should not mean anything—it isn't proof, it's a title. She can't use the Golden Amulet and she doesn't have her name imprinted on it. What more do you idiotic cowards want?!"

"I SAY OFF WITH HER HEAD!"

Ivy is immediately taken aback by the abrupt, sharp, and harsh words. As more people join in on the chanting, Holders and Powerless beings altogether, her shock can only intensify. Ivy's heart thumps with dread at the possibility of the chanting being for her only to sigh with relief once she pieces two and two together and understands it is for Queen Matilda instead. The scene before her leaves her baffled. She's never seen such a great number of people of various statuses on the same side.

Yet this is not exactly what she wants. It isn't what she came back to the kingdom for. While she told the story of Benecia and Delyth, a small naïve part of her—Eun, young and foolish—believed it would dawn on Holders that what they are doing to the Powerless is illogical. Rather than that, Holders have taken it as a way of claiming that all Powerless beings, including their queen, do not deserve a life in this kingdom—or anywhere, in fact. Yes, she thought foolishly. Of course, Holders aren't going to change over the course of minutes.

What are her people meant to gain from this, though?

Her shoulders almost drop with defeat when a number of guards begin to shoo the crowd away from the scene, insisting they go back to whatever they were doing beforehand. But people keep coming back and their vexation continues to grow with each passing second.

"What do we do about her, Your Majesty?" a guard questions, pointing at Ivy.

Before King Titus can give an answer, a commoner screeches, "Leave her be! Queen Matilda is the true liar here. Punish her instead. Hang her. She deserves to be hung!"

"Execute me," Ivy speaks, "and you get an uproar."

"You're getting an uproar, either way, Your Majesty," the same guard presses, glaring daggers at the girl. "You cannot accept this sort of disrespect. You cannot let this go. She must be punished."

"At least, have the Golden Amulet taken from her first," another guard urges.

"But you can't." Ivy scowls at the suggestion. "It belongs to me. That has been proven."

"The boy could have been lying—"

"What for?" Ivy folds her arms. "What reason would he have to lie for me?"

"You shut that mou—"

"Silence!" King Titus hollers with a raise of a clenched fist before he takes a pause, going over his only two options. His wrathful eyes scan the area and land upon several glares sent his way. Finally, the man lowers his arm and turns to face his queen who's still struggling to control her rapid breathing. "Leave her be."

"What?! But—"

"Do not question my decision," the king says. "Leave the girl be. We'll get back to her later.'

As a small, weary sigh leaves her mouth, Ivy watches the guards tentatively head back to their horses. In an instant, another crowd forms around her, each of them throwing one question after another, pleading that she tells them more about the Golden Amulet and Adora. But Ivy is not interested in doing any more talking, so rather than that, she turns to the boy still standing there and takes out her hand.

Understanding what she wants, the boy places the Golden Amulet on her palm, and as he's doing so, a number of arms from the crowd suddenly reach forward in an attempt to grab the pendant. Ivy knows they'll never leave her alone now but at least, they'll always be willing to listen whenever she has something to say.

"Thank you. . . for earlier." Choosing to ignore them all, Ivy nods gratefully at the boy. "You really saved me back there. . . uh, sort of."

"Hmm."

Ivy awkwardly clears her throat in response to the dry comment and turns to go.

"Wait!" the boy calls out suddenly, bringing Ivy to a halt. "I just want to ask something."

"Yes? What is it?"

"How were you planning to get out of that situation?" His face seems to recoil as the words roll off his tongue. "Did you really start drama with no plan to end it nicely?"

Ivy sighs. "Even you think I'm a fool. Of course, I had a plan. There was. . ." She stops for a moment, pondering silently to herself over whether telling the boy is an intelligent move or not. Ivy would agree that it isn't if not for recalling something Adora informed her during her training. You need to have a team.

"There was a man I made a deal with. He's in possession of the same ability as yours, which is why I was counting on him to show up and prove to everyone that this Amulet had my name engraved on it. He didn't show, unfortunately."

"Possibly because he grew a brain at the last minute and decided it was best not to get himself involved," the boy taunts out of nowhere, the unexpected tone of disdain catching Ivy off guard. "I don't even know what I was thinking when I did what I did. I suppose, in the heat of the moment, I only focused on my hatred for the Royals and the fact you are innocent. . . But you're not innocent. No, not at all. You're just like the rest of them."

"What are you on about?" Ivy scoffs, folding her arms with a look of disbelief. Perhaps, it really wasn't such a smart decision to answer his question. "I am innocent. That was proven."

"The only thing that was proven is your ownership of the Golden Amulet. That's it! But underneath all that justice for the Powerless junk lies a girl desperate for power." His tone turns sardonic. "Be honest, Ivy. That's the only reason you did all this, isn't it? For the power."

"Where is all this coming from?"

"Oh, forget it." The boy scowls, turning his legs to walk off. "Once a being receives an Amulet of their own, they're bound to turn arrogant and cruel. You don't really care about the Powerless. You're just obsessed with Queen Matilda." With those last words, he saunters away, leaving Ivy in a bewildered state.

What just happened?

Obsessed with Queen Matilda? In what way did she show that?

Ivy draws herself back from going after him. It is possible he misunderstood her intentions. The only thing that puzzles her, at the moment, is why. The boy is a Holder. Why would he care so much about the Powerless beings? Why did he sound so against his own people?

Is it possible he—?

The young plotter shakes her head immediately, shoving the forthcoming question to the back of her head while watching the boy fade away amongst another small crowd of commoners who are still gathered together, whispering about the incident that just occurred. No, it can't be.

With the Golden Amulet in hand and an insistent look pasted on her face, she turns around and wanders away.

07 | Adora's Teachings

Chapter Seven — Adora's Teachings

Three Years Ago 18th September 2000

ADORA is a dirty rat.

Despite her profound respect for the woman, who'd, in time, come to serve as her mentor, Eun couldn't disregard the thoughts that rang in her mind. As she gazed upward, her back aching and her hands clinging to a broomstick bestowed upon her by Adora, she was met with a sight that evoked both discomfort and curiosity. The floor, covered in grime, prompted Eun to cough from the dust that filled the air. She wondered how the woman had survived this long in such filth.

Adora, drawing upon the skills acquired during her childhood in the kingdom, ingeniously fashioned brooms out of plastics, hairs, and corn husks. These broomsticks were their sole cleaning implement. The absence of cutting-edge house-cleaning tools, a privilege enjoyed by those residing in the kingdom, occasionally presented a formidable challenge when it came to maintaining cleanliness in their abode. Nevertheless, Eun had been a housemaid long enough to know how to make use of the only appliances Adora owned.

"Good morning, Eun."

Eun whirled around at the sound of the low, barely audible voice, coming face to face with the woman who stirred awake. "Is this how your day always starts?" she inquired, primarily out of curiosity, but partly with mockery.

With one side of her body resting on a tattered white mattress and her arm supporting her head, Adora let out a soft chuckle. "You must be used to waking up so early, huh?"

"Anything to avoid getting a b—" The girl, in the midst of her discourse, suddenly halted after realizing what word was about to fall out of her mouth.

Despite her departure from the kingdom, the remnants of her habits persisted.

"Here, you don't have to worry about waking up so early, Eun. Nobody's going to hurt you. Not anymore," Adora stated in an assuring tone. "And you most definitely don't have to worry about cleaning. That is no longer your duty. Besides, Eun, I'm a collector. The accumulation of items over the years has made the cabin appear cluttered but it is not the floor itself that is dirty."

Despite the tiny space, something a housemaid for wealthy Holders like Eun wasn't used to, Eun refrained from complaining. This was still an improvement from her previous situation.

"Well, since you're already awake, Adora," she said, waving the broomstick in her hand.

"Ah, alright, fine."

As a housemaid in the kingdom, Eun's daily routine was filled with a multitude of tasks. From the moment she woke up in the morning, she had quite the to-do list that demanded her attention. Breakfasts were often rushed, leaving little time for leisurely meals. Sometimes, she would even forgo it altogether, as the Holders she served were known for their impatience.

The straw woven mat Adora owned helped with cleaning. It was taken outside and beaten while Eun diligently swept the floor. Later on, herbs would be sprinkled throughout the rushes and mats to keep the stench away. With the presence of the Golden Amulet, Adora was able to maintain a certain level of adequacy in her living conditions.

This invaluable item often provided her with essential survival items that she would lack.

"Do you still have more of that lye soap left? The walls are worse." Eun called out from inside the shack, hoping Adora was nearby to pick up her request. Lye soap was made from the ashes of trees and shrubs, mixed with lard. The Golden Amulet provided the lard, while Adora found everything else from searching the area.

Eun was still yet to learn how the Golden Amulet truly worked. Even now, she was in a daze ever since she learned Queen Matilda had been fooling the entire kingdom with a fake necklace.

Oh, how satisfying it would be to disclose the truth in front of everyone and show the Holders their precious queen wasn't who she said she was. Nothing said vengeance better than that. But after the horrors she'd witnessed, Eun could never see herself inside Arya again.

"If you became Queen of Arya, what would be the first thing you'd do?" Adora quizzed, the lye soap in hand.

"I would change the rules, of course," came the younger's response, pondering to herself why Adora had posed such a sudden query. "Rules that will deem Holders and Powerless beings equal."

The woman hummed softly as she shifted over to the walls. "What sorts of rules would you make and how would you ensure that everyone followed them? Holders won't be happy, at all."

"It doesn't matter if Holders are happy or not. If the thought of living in peace with people of a different status truly dissatisfies them, then, they can leave. Who's stopping them?"

Eun watched as the woman cracked a wider smile. Is this a test? "And, well. . . I don't want to be as cruel as the Royals are," she mumbled, stroking her chin as she further contemplated the question. "One of the rules I would make is that not a single soul is authorized to mistreat another just because of their status," she explained. "Whoever breaks my rules will be thrown behind bars." Eun grinned proudly at the woman. "How does that sound?"

"Would there not be a rampage?"

And in an instant, her face fell. "You make a point, but frankly, it doesn't matter what happens or what rules are made. There will always be some people that won't like it. If push comes to shove, those who insist on starting a rampage will be cast out of the kingdom." She paused again, studying the woman's face. Despite her scruffy features, she could still see her smile hadn't faded yet. "Is this. . .? Is it finally time to commence my training?" The broom slipped through her fingers as excitement began to bloom within her. "Is it time I learn more about the Golden Amulet? Oh, please, say yes, Adora."

Yes, Adora had indeed seemed quite strange to her a few days prior. The woman's account of what the truth was sounded illogical. But when Adora showed her the Golden Amulet and even performed an astonishing ability using the pendant, Eun understood her entire life had been a lie. Queen Matilda had been a lie.

She wasn't even deserving of the title "queen".

Rather than answering Eun's question, Adora threw another one her way. "You remember the Spawn of Slaves days, correct?"

Eun nodded. "I learned about it in history class."

"And do you remember the specifics of what happened?"

Eun pressed her lips together, the elation gradually dying. Her shoulders slumped and a small frown found its way onto her face. Why was Adora asking her to recall such a thing? "Of course, I remember. Who doesn't? It was one of the saddest times in history. . . Well, at least, for our people." She often had to remind herself that she was born after those horrid days but if she had been before, her biological parents abandoning her would have made so much more sense.

During those years, there was a significant rise in the number of suicides among the Powerless. This trend caused great concern among

Holders, not primarily due to the well-being of the Powerless themselves, but rather because of the rapid depletion of their workforce. In response, the Royals at that time, King Darius and Queen Aqua, implemented a prohibition on such actions. However, this rule proved ineffective in deterring the Powerless from disregarding it once they lost everything to live for.

So, the Holders decided... What better way to fix their problem than to compel Powerless women to engage in reproduction? While the men were subjected to arduous labor, the women were gathered for the purpose of producing more workers for the Holders. Of course, it was expected that the Powerless men would be the ones engaging in intimate relations with the women, after all, only in this way could the best outcome be obtained. Nevertheless, a significant number of men dissented from participating in this endeavor. As a consequence, several of them were subjected to execution.

Holder men, driven by a perceived lack of alternatives, took matters into their own hands. Eun shivered. Despite numerous instances of sensual violence and abuse, none of the men faced consequences. The Spawn of Slaves era served as the backdrop for the notorious reputation of King Darius and Queen Aqua, who emerged as the cruelest Royals to date. The two of them brought a different diabolical side to Holders.

Eun, knowing she could never live with the thought of being the result of sensual violence, grappled with the realization that countless other children shared that fate.

"Now, do you remember how Aqua passed away?"

Passed away? Eun grunted indignantly. She had detested that phrase ever since the deaths of Benecia and Delyth. "A Powerless slew Aqua." She may not have been physically present during that incident but because it was such a significant and widely discussed occurrence, Eun could still recall every little detail of it.

Aside from the Spawn of Slaves days and Queen Matilda's proclamation of possessing the Golden Amulet, Aqua's death was the most shocking event to occur. Not only did it instill terror and hatred among Holders, but it also ignited a sense of courage within her people. The demise of this woman, whose actions were unforgivable, had served as a powerful testament to the potential capabilities of the Powerless.

"The arrow came out of nowhere," Adora mumbled, displaying a sense of satisfaction that grew every time she recalled that moment. "The Powerless celebrated that day."

Eun chuckled. "Well, how could they not have? Queen Aqua was a remorseless woman."

"Eun, tell me how it all went down."

The girl halted in her tracks, sending her mentor another look of confusion. "What?"

"Tell me how that Powerless man successfully carried out a plan and had a Royal slaughtered."

"Must I?"

Adora didn't respond, so Eun took her silence as a yes.

"Well. . ." As the child spoke, she grabbed a clean cloth from the basket set at the side of the room. "When the Spawn of Slaves days commenced, a multitude of mixed beings were born. Among them was a set of twins—one twin was born a Holder, while the other was a Powerless."

It stunned Eun to the core that even twins could receive such different fates. What further intensified her surprise, however, was the abhorrent treatment the Holder twin subjected his Powerless brother to.

Eun got down to wiping the tables with the cloth she'd picked out of the basket. She sought solace in the mundane act of polishing furniture, momentarily distracting herself from the somber narrative she was recounting. Perhaps, the reason why cleaning worked so well in calming her down was because cleaning was all she knew. While

Adora attentively listened, Eun washed the basins and cleaned out the chamber pots.

"I remember the Powerless twin was named Jin Sol," she continued, her eyes following every movement of her hand as she shifted the cloth left to right. "I didn't bother with his brother's name, though."

Over time, Jin grew disillusioned with the treatment he and his people endured. Recognizing the need for change, he embarked on a calculated plan to disrupt the status quo.

Jin's meticulous approach to planning involved a deliberate avoidance of written records. It was a strategic decision driven by his astute awareness of the potential risks linked with leaving traces of his intentions. By relying on his superior intellect, Jin sought to outmaneuver his brother, who may have possessed an Amulet but lacked the same level of intellectual acuity.

But central to Jin's plan was the implementation of both torture and murder. Prior to targeting Aqua, he cunningly captured his own brother, coercing him into relinquishing his Amulet. He did not do this so he could become a Holder and make life easier for himself. No, the purpose of the act was to enable him to assume his brother's powerful persona and facilitate the deception required to mislead others into believing that he was his brother rather than himself. And, in the end, he eliminated his brother to get him out of the way.

Eun shifted to the three wooden benches at the back of the shack. "Jin's brother worked as a guard for the palace, so, with his brother's Amulet now his, Jin was able to effortlessly enter and leave the palace whenever he wished. Days later, it was revealed that his brother was dead. Everyone believed it was Powerless Jin who'd met his demise when in actuality, it was his brother who'd lost his status as a Holder the moment he gave up his Amulet." She exhaled as she wiped down the candlesticks next.

As a guard in his brother's stead, Jin was frequently entrusted with weapons for protection, and exploiting his position, the man found it easy to pilfer a bow and a supply of arrows.

During the return of King Darius and Queen Aqua from their diplomatic visit to a neighboring kingdom, the attention of the crowd of Holders was fixated on cheering their beloved monarchs. Jin managed to go into the perfect hiding spot and took aim, unnoticed by the distracted onlookers.

Using her mouth, Eun made a sound of an arrow plunging into a body. "Whoosh! It was a perfect aim. He got the woman on his first try."

"Except, it wasn't such a perfect hiding spot, was it?" Adora raised her eyebrows knowingly.

Eun nodded. "Right."

At the precise moment, a Holder discovered him in the act and promptly reported his transgression. But Jin did not deny what he'd done. In fact, some speculated that even if he hadn't been caught, he would have admitted to his deeds. His intention was to ensure that those without power were aware of the considerable effort he had invested in eliminating the queen. He sought to convey to his people that despite their apparent isolation, they were never truly alone because they had each other.

Eun swiftly brushed her thumb across her eyes, preventing tears from cascading down her cheeks.

What a hero that man was.

"Eun, why do you think I wanted you to tell me that story?" came Adora's next question.

"To torture me?" Eun responded teasingly.

Adora sighed. "You want to create a plan to take out Matilda and her husband, don't you? That is why you want me to train you so badly."

"Then again, I can't see myself ever stepping foot inside that kingdom again," Eun added. "Wouldn't I be executed for fleeing?"

Adora stopped what she was doing and placed both hands on Eun's shoulders. "Matilda wouldn't dare have you executed once she sees you've got the Golden Amulet."

Eun suppressed another shiver. She wasn't sure how to feel about an object she'd loathed her entire life being the only thing keeping her alive.

"You want to be just like Jin, don't you?"

"Perhaps."

"Well, you can't."

Eun frowned and froze at Adora's response.

"Child, your training commenced as soon as you began answering my questions."

Eun's eyes expanded. "Really?"

"Yes, really. And I had you tell me that story so I could give you rules to abide by," Adora carried on. "Once you assume the role of the new Holder of the Golden Amulet, it is imperative to understand that taking the life of another being is strictly prohibited. The Golden Amulet possesses the power to administer punishment for such a wicked deed. So, no, you cannot do exactly as Jin Sol did."

But that doesn't mean I can't help my people as he did.

Adora raised a finger. "Rule number one. You must have a plan. A solid plan, Eun. You must plot it all out, make sure you know what you're doing, just as Jin knew what he was doing." She raised a second. "Rule number two. You must be ready for the consequences. Not every plan runs smoothly so, you must prepare yourself for the great penalty if your plan was to ever fail. It's not that I think you won't succeed, Eun, but you're going down a dangerous path, child, and some things are sure to go wrong."

"I don't even know if I'll go through with this," Eun grumbled. The slight faith she had in herself before crumpled like fragile sandcastles, eroded by the relentless waves of negative thoughts that crashed upon the shores of her mind. "As I said earlier, I might not even go back to Arya."

But Adora knew she would. Her conviction in Eun's abilities was unwavering, rooted not only in her faith in the younger but also in the purpose that brought them together. The Golden Amulet, the catalyst for their meeting, guided Adora to Eun because Eun was destined to stumble upon the weapon she would use to prepare and go into battle with Arya. Well. . . That is, if Eun didn't allow her fear and worries to get to her.

Just as she'd done.

"What's number three?"

A third finger raised. "Rule number three. Well, I've already said it. Unless it was self-defense, of course, never resort to killing nor any other criminal acts. By doing so, you'd be lowering yourself to their level."

Eun shook her head. "I wouldn't want that."

"No, you wouldn't." Adora agreed with a nod. She picked up three basins and threw one over to the younger. "Let's go get some water down by the river. We're still yet to do laundry."

"Ugh!" Eun whined as she stared at the colorful basin in her hand, earning a small chuckle from her mentor. "Doing laundry is the absolute worst. It's such backbreaking work."

While Eun and Benecia had worked as housemaids back in the kingdom, Delyth suffered from the revolting role of a laundress. Sure, they washed clothes from time to time but it was never as bad as Delyth had it. The poor girl would frequently complain to her friends about how increasingly onerous her job was. Having to clean and dry all the linens and garments within households, Delyth's hands were immersed in water day after day and would become dry and cracked.

She also had the privilege—whether she liked it or not—to intimate knowledge about the bodily functions of those she served, as she often had to deal with scrubbing bloodstained sheets. This aspect of her work, although unpleasant, was a constant reality that Delyth and several other girls she worked with had to endure.

"Rule number four," Adora suddenly brought up, bringing Eun's attention away from the horse that walked along behind them. "It is important you do not attempt to carry out this laborious task alone."

"What is that supposed to mean? Jin Sol didn't have any help."

"That's because Jin Sol wasn't planning to take down the entire kingdom, just the Royals themselves," her mentor reminded. "The man simply wanted the Spawn of Slaves days to end. You, on the other hand, want Holders to actually respect your people. You realize how near-impossible that's going to be? Plus, you're still just a child. You're going to need help, Eun, whether you like it or not."

"I suppose you're right, but—"

"And you must have a Healer on your team," the woman added before Eun could finish her thoughts. "You're going against millions of Holders. It'd be impossible for you not to get hurt. A Healer will be there to mend your wounds, however big they may be. Have it be someone you trust."

A name had already sprouted in Eun's mind. The Healer she was thinking of was an unnatural Holder whom she recalled being one of the kindest men she knew in Arya.

"This brings me to my fifth rule," Adora said, making a turn. "You must understand that your people aren't perfect, either."

"Why would that be a rule?" Eun mocked.

"Because you tend to make them seem like they're so perfect themselves." Her mentor shrugged. "Yes, Holders are much worse but the Powerless can get pretty venomous, as well. I know a couple who've done horrendous things. Take my half-sister, for example." She came to a stop and turned to face the girl.

"Is this about Elaine Chao?" Eun accused almost immediately.

"This has absolutely nothing to do with Elaine," Adora insisted. "It's just that I've noticed whenever I bring up a certain bad thing a Powerless did, you tend to overlook it. Sometimes, you even try to justify it. Yet, whenever we're on the topic of Holders, you've got a lot to say. I understand where this behavior is coming from but hold your people accountable, too. Remember that just because they're abused doesn't give them the right to abuse others."

The younger exhaled sharply, redirecting her focus toward the ground. She wasn't even sure why she'd brought Elaine up. Thinking about that woman and what she'd done always brought a blaze of pain. Even up until this moment, Eun wasn't sure whether or not it was an error in judgment to align herself with Elaine. Perhaps, it really was indefensible what she'd done to her own daughter.

Then again, who's to say the child's demise wasn't imminent, regardless?

Elaine Chao, a victim of the Spawn of Slaves era, was unable to bear the thought of her child enduring the same torment she'd encountered. The physical strain endured. The relentless beatings for minor infractions. The coerced sexual servitude to the Holder men the moment she was deemed the right age. Elaine would take her own life before subjecting her own flesh and blood to such horrors. And that, she did.

But not before smothering the child with a pillow prior to the day she turned one.

When the same troubling thoughts as before came to mind again, Eun's physical stability faltered, causing her knees to give way. Before she knew it, she was on the ground. Despite the discomfort caused by the dirty and tiny hard objects that poked her skin, she chose to remain in that position, with the palms of her hands resting on her lap. "You know, I always used to wonder. . ." In an attempt to articulate her thoughts, she began, but her voice momentarily trailed off, as though carefully considering her words. "What if that's what my parents wanted to do to me? What if the idea had come to their heads, even if just once? To get rid of me."

"That is a terrible way of thinking, Eun."

"Well, you know what?" Eun persisted, adamantly refusing to meet Adora's gaze for fear of succumbing to further distress. "Entertaining such thoughts actually provided me with a bit of solace. It means they loved me... It means they sought to shield me from the brutal fate that awaited me. Thinking like this was... I-It was so much more comforting than believing they'd simply abandoned me because they didn't want me anymore."

She didn't want to believe she'd been discarded.

Eun dragged a hand over her eyes, the unshed tears staining her sleeve. "I suppose this is part of the reason why so many of our people understood why Elaine did what she did... because frankly, sometimes death is much better than the cruelty we face. In the end, one needs more courage to live than to kill himself."

Adora crouched down before Eun, swiftly enveloping the young girl's upper body with her arms and squeezing her gently for a little while. To Ivy, in that precise moment, it felt like an encompassing sensation akin to the embrace of wings. The warmth emanating from Adora's arms enfolded her like a comforting blanket.

"A Powerless said this to me once," the woman spoke with a consoling tone. "To live is to suffer. To suffer is to find some meaning in the suffering." When she broke the embrace, Adora tenderly brushed a thumb against Eun's cheeks, accompanied by a slight smile that illuminated her entire face. "Rule number six. Confront the dark parts of yourself, Eun, and work to banish them with compassion and forgiveness. Your willingness to wrestle with your demons will cause your angels to sing."

"You're awfully wise for a woman who had to live in the wild alone for years," Eun said, which prompted the woman to laugh once more as she rose from the ground.

"Come along now." Adora picked up her basins from where she'd dropped them. "We've still got some water to fetch."

word count • 4112

08 | The Smell of Death

CHAPTER EIGHT — THE SMELL OF DEATH

PRESENT 07TH SEPTEMBER 2003

"ARE you ready?"

Ivy will never forget the heartrending state her lecturer was in during this moment.

Three years ago, when she first stumbled upon the suffering woman's shelter in the middle of the forest with a bruised leg, Ivy was more than ready to begin her days of living in the wild alone. Now, the adolescent can't help but laugh at herself for thinking so irrationally. Despite possessing many skills, none of them are fixated on survival. Without Adora around, her body would have already rotted a long time ago.

Yet, no matter how proficient Adora was, the woman was hiding something. However, during this moment—a time that Ivy can't seem to ever get out of her head—Adora couldn't hide the truth anymore. The woman looked sicker than ever. Worst of all, she hadn't been eating as much over the last couple of months, and it showed. Adora was unhealthily underweight with her skin sagging and bones protruding, offering knobbiness and sharp angles that made her look frail and weak. Her hair appeared thin and lackluster, and her eyes had a pinpoint look to them, glass, bright, pinched, and dull.

Ivy can still remember rising from her knees, dashing inside the shack, and coming back out with a basket filled with medicinal herbs. She can remember beseeching Adora to tell her what was wrong—to tell her why her condition was getting worse.

"Surely, you won't die on me, will you?"

And Adora chuckled when the young girl asked this, not seeming to notice her puzzled eyes glistening with unshed tears, a shimmering pool of unspoken sadness.

"Are you ready, Ivy?" she asked again after letting out a harsh cough that was sure to have hurt her brittle chest.

Struggling to suppress the anger that built up within her, Ivy's hands balled. "You're doing it again!" she wailed. Tears cascaded down her cheeks in a river of sorrow and frustration, each droplet a testament to the depths of her despair. "You're avoiding my question. Stop doing that!" But now that she's calmly riding Snow back to the torn-apart house she resides in, recalling the past, Ivy regrets having raised her voice. Even if the anger was there just for a short while, she regrets ever feeling that way toward Adora.

"I will answer your question but first, you must tell me how prepared you are."

Adora's words did not sound promising in the slightest but Ivy had already reached a desperate point, so, not another complaint fell out of her mouth after that.

"It's been three years, Ivy," the woman carried on, trying valiantly to sit up straighter but failing. "How prepared are you to carry out your plan?—to bring the Holders down and justice to your people?"

"More than ready, Adora." The adolescent exhaled sharply, ignoring the hammering of her heart. "It'd be even better with you by my side."

Adora let out a sigh, a hand gently resting on her chest as she lightly swayed her head from side to side. "Well, I'm not prepared for what's next. I fear for you. It pains me to say this, Ivy, but my time. . ."

My time. . . Ivy shuts her eyes, putting her faith in Snow to take them to where they need to go. Adora never finished her sentence but she never needed to. And the next thing she recalls is throwing herself to the filthy ground, her teary eyes growing more disconsolate by the second. Adora was sick—seriously sick—but what did she expect? Her mentor was a woman who was forced to make do with whatever the wild and Golden Amulet had to offer all because her envious family had chased her away.

That day crushed her then. And it still does.

How could she be so foolish? Even after all the hints of her mentor's sickly state thrust in her face, the coughing, the frequent pauses and sudden confusion, the way her eyelids would droop, heavy with weariness, the weight of her immediate exhaustion even after the littlest activity threatening to pull her into a slumber from which Ivy felt she might never awaken, even after all that, she still chose to look the other way in denial. She refused to acknowledge the fact that the only Holder who ever accepted her, regardless of her status, was leaving. Permanently. During her plotting stage, Ivy constantly dreamt of standing beside her mentor after ultimately achieving her desire for justice. That wasn't going to happen now.

But that moment was also the day Adora finally admitted the truth to her. Ivy wished her mentor didn't tell the story while on the brink of death. She could hardly concentrate on the words that left the woman's mouth for her attention was all on the blood Adora was coughing out.

"I was already unwell long before I met you, Ivy. Living in the wild hasn't been rainbows and cupcakes, after all," Adora rasped. At this time, she was holding the younger's hand but let go as her shoulders dropped. Her stamina was waning, Ivy could see that. "Sure, I've been away from people who have only ever wanted me dead but I've had to suffer alone for a long time. I've been out here for twenty-seven years. The Golden Amulet gifted me Snow to reduce my loneliness. It's also one of the reasons you were able to find my tiny shack."

Even now, Ivy cannot believe it. Twenty-seven years. Nobody else can even survive one.

"The Golden Amulet is to be used for good, and good only," said Adora after swallowing hard. "I never did understand what my parents meant when they claimed we would all be in grave danger if the Amulet was to ever end up in the wrong hands. Neither did Matilda. All that girl wanted was to be a Holder—no, someone much greater than any other Holder. But after I wished death upon my father and had it come true, it all finally made sense to me. That wish was made in a moment of rage. I had no way of telling it would actually come true, therefore, the Golden Amulet was merciful and my penalty was light."

Penalty. This is something that has always terrified Ivy ever since Adora talked to her about it, no matter how much she hates to admit it. The Golden Amulet is the only pendant that serves its owners punishments whenever it sees fit. One of Adora's punishments was Old Age. Ivy was sure her mentor was around the age of seventy when she met her. Imagine her surprise when Adora admitted to her that she was actually in her thirties.

"I cannot stress this enough, Ivy," Adora told her during her training two years ago. "Do not commit anything that the Amulet deems wrong, especially killing."

Do not stoop to the Holders' level.

"Is that all?" Ivy raised her eyebrows with a puzzled smile when the woman stopped speaking. She watched Adora gently push the basket of medicine away, as though to say that nothing could heal her illness. "Light penalty? That doesn't sound too bad, Adora."

"It doesn't get any better."

The small smile on Ivy's face slowly vanished upon sighting the sorrowful look on her teacher's face. "What happened, Adora?"

"Before I abandoned the kingdom," responded Adora, "my sister poisoned me, hoping I would die so she could easily seize the Golden Amulet. I only ever found out after I'd fled."

Poisoning? The color drained from Ivy's face. If it was any other Amulet, what Adora's sister had done would have been such a nonsensical plan. But this was the Golden Amulet. Unlike the rest, it didn't disappear when the Holder of it died without passing it on. Instead, the Holder's name would be automatically erased and replaced with a new random name—a person deemed just as good or even better than the previous.

Matilda must have been hoping that person would be her.

"The Amulet promised me a cure, so I didn't concern myself over it. Woefully, in order for me to successfully leave the kingdom, I had to get through these four ferocious guards that would not let me pass. In the end, I slew them." Ignoring Ivy's flabbergasted expression, Adora carried on. "I paid a price for that cruel act, one of my punishments being Old Age and the second being to never receive the promised cure."

"Well, then... How is it that...?"

"That I'm still alive?" Adora finished for her. "The Golden Amulet kept me alive. I should have been dead years ago but I couldn't die. Not until I found a new Holder for this pendant."

"Me?"

"Yes, you." Another violent cough left her dry mouth followed by several spits of blood. Ivy recoiled at the sight but persisted in staying close with her mentor. Even from where she was standing, she could feel the woman's heart slowing down. "I understand your head is filled with plans for revenge, Ivy, and there's possibly nothing or anyone who's going to be able to stand in your way—"

"I don't see it as just revenge," Ivy cut her off with a wince. "No, this is so much more."

"Yes, I get that. Believe me, I do." Adora slowly nodded. "However, the path you are taking won't be at all easy. You're still just a child. I hate to say it, yet, you know it's true."

"I do."

"This is why one of my rules is forming a team." The woman lifted her shoulders for a moment, taking a long pause as though she'd forgotten what she wanted to convey. "I. . . uh. . . A-As I was saying, a team is there for backup in case anything goes wrong. It can't just be you against the kingdom, Ivy, let alone the entire continent."

"I understand."

"Good. Please, keep my rules in mind, Ivy."

The sweet smile on her mentor's debilitated face that has formed in her head pains Ivy's heart in several ways, bringing her back to her two beloved companions that were executed and every other Powerless who have had to endure the same fate. And during that very shattering moment, Ivy held both of the woman's hands tight as tears gushed down her cheeks, unwilling to let go.

Not even after Adora took her final breath.

"There, that's her! That's the girl!"

When the sudden enthusiastic voice comes into earshot, Ivy's mind is immediately driven away from the harsh and unpleasant memory. People have not stopped swarming around her ever since the showdown against Queen Matilda. In fact, as she's making her way to her shelter, a number of them are following. Ivy scoffs and rides faster. She's never liked the attention—but she knows attention is the only way to win.

At the outskirts of Arya lies a small village known as Angora, situated a mere distance from the kingdom's fourth gate—the very same gate that Ivy took to flee three years prior and enter Arya again just a couple of days ago. Within this diminutive village, amidst a collection of dilapidated dwellings, exists a small abode Ivy sought refuge in upon her return.

Exhausted, famished, and parched, she was fortunately welcomed by a man who dwelled inside. He's a Holder, so Ivy never trusted him. Regardless, she stepped inside when the man offered. He's been residing in that small space for years, each one more back-breaking than the last. All the man yearns for is a high-paying job that can keep him well-fed throughout the rest of his difficult life, and Ivy promised him just that. If he managed to turn up in time to show every eye that the Golden Amulet truly belonged to her, then she was sure to help him flee from his misery. But how can she trust him now when he couldn't even fulfill his part of the bargain?

It still stuns the girl to witness a Holder go through such arduous times. A Holder! When the man explained his struggles to her, she didn't believe him, at first. Holders don't suffer. They inflict sufferings. But then, she thought to herself: what would a Holder be doing in the poorest area of Arya? Everything made slightly more sense when the man revealed that he was actually an unnatural Holder.

In this world, there are four statuses—Powerless, natural Holder, mixed, and unnatural Holder. Ivy rarely ever thinks about the last two. To her, if you possess an Amulet, you are a Holder, and if you don't, you are a Powerless. Simple as that. But Yeblil loves to complicate things.

Centuries ago, the Royals that governed during then outlawed the transmission of Amulets. This meant no Holder was permitted to hand their necklace over to someone else, even when they were on the brink of death. Such a shame, Ivy thinks, since so many Amulets were wasted those years. After all, if a Holder dies without passing their Amulet onto someone else, their Amulet dies with them, never to be seen again.

Pendants spontaneously materialize for natural Holders before the age of seven. Unnatural Holders are those that were once Powerless but gained power after having a Holder pass their Amulet to them. Few Holders opt to transfer—many of them hold a strong conviction that the Powerless should stay Powerless. The fact that the man she is staying with doesn't fit the bar for attractiveness doesn't help, either.

Snow comes to a halt as soon as they near the front of the structure. Like every other house in this mostly deserted village, it appears to be on the verge of collapse. Unless tasked with guarding the fourth gate, hardly any soldiers make an appearance here. It's no surprise the village smells like death.

Ivy hops off her horse, prepared to bombard the man with questions as to why he failed to show, especially when she needed him the most. But immediately after she opens the door and peeks inside, her nose picks up an unexpected horrid but familiar scent of a certain liquid. It smells like death more than usual. Only then does she understand why he disappointed her.

Sprawled out on the stained hardwood floor is the man's lifeless body in his own puddle of blood.

Ivy scrunches her nose. At first, all she can do is stand there in disbelief and puzzlement. She isn't, in any way, close enough to the man to care deeply for him but it has been so long since she last saw a deceased body. All the feelings she's suppressed almost come crashing back.

Who would do this?

Ivy kneels down next to the dead, paying no attention to the blood that is smearing her clothing. With quivering lips and mystified eyes, the girl reaches forward and takes hold of the man's frigid hands. She's not going to weep for him—she didn't know him. And plus, he is a Holder. Even if he's unnatural, the man is still a Holder. She wonders if perhaps he did this to himself. But why would he? In contrast to the rest in the hamlet, to her, he was hopeful—he woke up with a delightful smile on his face that Ivy found strange and went to bed praying for a better day tomorrow. A person has lost in life when their heart grows hopeless, he told Ivy—and he never wanted to lose.

Ivy examines the entire body until she eventually comes across something that catches her off guard. The man's left hand is lying next to a button. Not just any button, however. It is the same diamond button that every guard wears on their suits, handed to them by the Royals as soon as they are given the job. Such a piece of expensive jewelry cannot be made anywhere else in the kingdom.

Ivy reaches for the item and picks it up with a frown. The man must have put up a fight, yanking the button off of the guard's uniform in an attempt to save his life. Nevertheless, she finds it incomprehensible that a guard would travel to this little, mostly deserted town merely to assassinate this helpless commoner. Why would such a thing occur? It isn't like the deceased man is a Powerless, either. While it's true that he wasn't a natural Holder, none of this makes any sense, whatsoever. Why would a guard kill one of his own peop—?

Ivy abruptly stops in the middle of her question when the answer comes to her.

Her. It is because of her.

Someone must have seen her with him. They must have believed that the man was aiding her with her scheme. It doesn't matter if one is a Holder or not, simply assisting another individual carry out a cunning plan to overthrow the Royals would be sufficient grounds for execution. Ivy wonders if it's one of the Royals that ordered this killing yet she wouldn't be surprised, either, if it was a guard that decided to take matters into their own hands and slaughtered the man in cold blood. If they feel their prized Royals are in any way under danger, many Holders are prepared to kill in order to protect them.

The man's body is still a bit warm. If Ivy has to guess, she'd say he was slain during the showdown. Pushing all possible notions to the back of her head, Ivy rises from her bloody knees, the diamond button slipping through her fingers. The image of the motionless man cannot leave her head now, not even as she exits the house and rides Snow out of the hamlet after giving him a befitting burial behind the house.

——..○☽□☾○..——

"I used to dwell in Arya as well... many years ago. Not possessing an Amulet is the reason you abandoned the kingdom, is it not? You must have been cast out... treated differently. Oh, believe me, I understand how that feels."

"You haven't got an Amulet, either?"

"I never thought it would happen but I received my Amulet just two days before I turned seven. How fortunate is that? Two days more and I would have been labeled a definite Powerless."

Argh! Ivy grunts and aggressively shakes her head, eager to shove aside the sudden memory of the day she met her mentor. Adora, leave me alone. You're distracting me. But it isn't just the fact the past sidetracks her, it's the deep ache in her heart that comes with remembering. And she knows her head only ever does this when she's exhausted or keen on taking her mind off of something depressing that occurred, such as the deceased man. But she doesn't need to think about Adora right now—she doesn't want the agony to show on her face, she doesn't want to be seen in a moment of weakness.

Ivy doesn't want to falter.

She can't be absent-minded in a kingdom where enemies who want nothing more than to stone her to death roam freely, where she'll be seen as puny and incapable of being the Golden Amulet's Holder if a single tear dare leaves her eye. So, she goes to the only place where she knows her weakness will not be derided.

"Y-You've come back."

And this time, despite Ivy's best efforts to hold back her tears, a drop manages to slip through and stains her cheeks. The last time this happened was four days ago when Adora died in her arms. Since then, Ivy has promised to never weep again but she knows she still has a long way to go.

Crestfallen, the young girl stares back at the Tuskeawanian woman standing by the half-opened brick door. In spite of the fact they haven't seen each other in such a long time, the woman doesn't look like she's aged a day. Ivy was afraid the countless tortures would ruin her face but, even now, the resemblance to her deceased friend is all there, bringing Ivy back to the cherished days Benecia was still alive, not happy, but well. Perhaps, Benecia is part of the reason it took her a while to come to visit. A lump forms in her throat at the thought.

"I-It really is you." The woman, Mrs. Patel, gasps lightly. She steps forward and cups the young girl's cheeks, tears brimming under her own sullen eyes as well. "I thought I was losing my mind when I overheard people talking about an Eun Calinao who'd supposedly challenged the queen. Oh, it's been far too long. I-I didn't think I'd ever see you again. None of us did."

Ivy sighs with relief at the sight of the delectation written all over the woman's wrinkled face. Benecia's family is her family. They took better care of her than her adoptive family ever did—perhaps, even better than her biological family but Ivy can't say she's entirely sure since she doesn't remember them at all.

"Come in, come in!" Mrs. Patel insists eagerly, grabbing Ivy by the arm and dragging her inside. "Everyone is going to be so delighted to see you, Eun." Her jaded dark brown eyes dance with delirium as they divert away from the girl and face one of the bedroom doors that looks like it's on its last legs. "You can all come out," she cries out. "Don't worry, it wasn't the guards as we thought. It's Eun!"

"Eun?" a younger frail voice sounds from the other side of the closed door. It is soon to open and a familiar head immediately pokes out with excitement. "Eun? Is it really you?"

"Engel." Ivy's eyes broaden at the sight of the little boy, allowing him to wrap his bony arms around her. One by one, two other thin figures pile out of the room, both of them sharing the same look of surprise as they wait for their turn to embrace the girl. Even though it's been three long years, none of them look any different or. . .bigger. . . than the last time they saw each other.

Mrs. Patel's face lights up for a moment. "This is the nicest surprise we've had since. . ." Her soft voice suddenly trails off as she faces the floor, instead. Her tear-stained cheeks are swollen and puffy. The hush that falls causes Ivy's heart to ache even harder. Of course, three years are not enough to grieve and forget the past, especially when it consists of losing loved ones, of knowing that they could have lived another day if not for some vile man. Ivy never goes a day without thinking back to her two dear friends and the bright futures they could have had ahead of them—at least, as bright as the brightest future a Powerless can get.

"I thought for certain that it was guards coming back to completely finish us," Benecia's elder sister, Astoria, chuckles as she unwraps her arms around Ivy's figure. "They haven't exactly left us alone ever since you fled. In fact, some of them believed we were hiding you."

Ivy instantly winces at the words. "I hope you didn't get punished because of me."

"They didn't have much proof." Astoria shrugs, a hearty laugh leaving her mouth. "But. . . Oh, why did you come back, Eun? Why did you come back to this death hole? It hasn't gotten any better since you left."

"Where I was wasn't any safer," she tells her, failing to keep her eyes from falling down to the young woman's exposed legs once something catches her eyes.

She pales at the sight of the dark bruises scattered all over her skin but once Astoria catches her staring, she is instant to switch the subject before Ivy can even question it.

"Please, don't tell me the rumors are true, Eun. What is this about you challenging the queen? Haven't you suffered enough?"

Ivy remembers then that even though the Golden Amulet is around her neck, it's hiding. After the many attempts that have been made to seize it, she can't take any more chances. "All I did was reveal the truth," she responds. "It's about time everyone learns what a manipulative liar Matilda is."

"So. . ." Benecia's aunt pauses. "She really doesn't possess the Amulet?"

"No, she does not." Ivy looks from one person to another until a sudden reminder sparks in her head. "Where's Mr. Patel?" she queries, eyeing each individual. "Is he still out farming?"

Engel doesn't waste a second to cry out, "He's been taken! Ivy, our father has been taken."

Mrs. Patel blanched. "Aldwin didn't take it very well when he learned about what happened to our daughter. He wanted justice, not just for Benecia, but for Delyth as well. If only he listened to us when we warned him there was nothing he could do as a Powerless."

"What did he do?" Ivy's eyebrows raise quizzically.

"He tried to slay Gozar," Benecia's aunt speaks with fisted hands. "I wish he succeeded."

"Attempted murder?" Disbelief transforms Ivy's face as she anxiously clutches onto the hem of her tunic top. "W-What was he thinking? Did he not understand that the punishment for that crime is execution?"

"Aldwin knew what he was getting himself into." Mrs. Patel lowers her head. "But Gozar, with his twisted mind, wants to keep Aldwin alive just so he can torture him now and then since he was the target. And, needless to say, the Royals accepted his request."

When she was with Adora back in the forest, Ivy did her best to leave the scorching agony alone as far as she could. In time, it consumed itself and left her with the task of moving toward happier spaces—toward the plan she spent days and nights plotting. Now, when she acknowledges the pain of others, her own reduces slightly, for, in that realization, there is a sense she isn't alone.

Wrath serves just as a protective barrier for suffering, much like a cornered soldier aimlessly shooting grenades, terrified for his life, lonely, and desperate. Ivy breathes in slowly. What if, in the end, nothing blows up? There are so many Powerless beings out there crying for help, such as Mr. Patel himself but what if, in the end, all her planning turns out to be in vain?

After minutes of Astoria insisting she made her food and Ivy denying her hunger, the young woman turns toward the kitchen. "Save your food for yourself," Ivy calls out after her but she doubts Astoria will heed her words. Her stomach may be grumbling but she's accustomed to going days without anything.

"May I ask one thing, Eun?" Benecia's aunt says. She waits for Ivy to nod before she carries on. "Why was it that when that boy revealed the Golden Amulet's true owner, it was Ivy Pearls engraved on it, not Eun Calinao?"

"Ah yes, I forgot to mention." Ivy brightens, feeling a flush of excitement. "It's no longer Eun Calinao." She hasn't had the finest chance to speak about the change of her name, not that it matters much right now. What people refer to her as or know her by is of little importance to Ivy.

"But why Ivy?" Mrs. Patel questions in the middle of her offering her a seat.

"The name. . . It represents eternity and fidelity," Ivy says. "Because none of them will be getting rid of me that easily and I will always stay faithful to my plan and my people. Plus, I for sure was not going to keep the name my adoptive parents gave me."

Mrs. Patel smiles warmly. "I like that."

Benecia's aunt sighs, plopping herself down on the dirty ottoman next to the one Ivy has settled on. "Well, a lot has happened since you left, Ivy. For instance, Mrs. Raven."

"Mrs. Raven? That sweet old lady?" Ivy recalls. "What happened to her?"

"It's a tragic story, my love." Mrs. Patel squeezed her eyes shut. "You remember her son was sick?"

Ivy nods at the question.

The woman proceeds, "Well, a few months ago, Mrs. Raven tried to steal some medicine for him. She got caught during the attempt, unfortunately. No Holder was willing to give her the medicine her son needed, therefore, her son passed away."

Ivy's downhearted eyes flash with horror. "How is Mrs. Raven doing now?"

The three cast a glance at each other with mouths bolted shut. Astoria exits the kitchen then and walks over to them with a small tray of cabbage, beans, eggs, and brown bread. A sad smile forms on her face. Having overheard the question, she places a hand on Ivy's shoulder after setting the train down. "There is no more Mrs. Raven," she calmly clarifies. "She's been long gone since her son died."

Ivy exhales heavily. "No. . . How?"

"Hung," says Astoria.

Not even the steady stream of liquid trickling down her face can cure Ivy's consuming resentment. "Those spiteful Holders."

"Yes, I agree." Astoria nods. "But, Ivy, she hung herself."

"Well, is that so shocking to you?" Ivy scowls, her lips trembling. "It doesn't matter if the deed was done with her own two hands, the Holders are still at fault. They've always been at fault."

This only fuels her anger and she does not bother holding it in anymore. At this point, what use does that serve? The throbbing agony and fury that fills her head once again remind her of her true purpose in returning. She can't leave her people to fight on their own. She can't leave them with the same horrid fate Mrs. Raven was dealt with. Her scheme needs to be done. And she will get it done.

No matter what it takes.

word count • 4946

09 | reuben kang

CHAPTER NINE — REUBEN KANG

FOURTEEN YEARS AGO

"WHERE is your Amulet?"

There it was. The golden question.

The young boy's quivering hand rose to his heaving chest in hope that the one thing his father so desperately desired had finally appeared. But fear was quick to strike him in the heart at the feeling of his neck being bare. Where was it? Where was that stupid Amulet? There was nothing the boy loathed more than being hustled—that, and the sight of blood. Despite his father's impatient behavior, the timing of the pendant's arrival was out of his control. The slight irritation he felt from the expectancy was finally getting to him.

"Where is your Amulet?"

The beating of the boy's heart quickened once he could practically sense the man breathing down his neck. He gradually peeled his eyes away from the small shelf of new toys his mother had recently bought him and faced the glaring man whose hands had already balled into fists and face become crimson with rage.

"I-I don't have it."

"Oh, you don't have it?" the elder hissed with thick raised eyebrows in a clear ridiculing tone. "You don't have it? This is about the hundredth time I'm asking you and you're going to give me that same pathetic answer?"

What else was he meant to say or do? Should he have called upon the merciless gods that refused to give him the Amulet his father so keenly waited for? Was that even how it worked?

Tightly gripping the child's arm, the man stared in silence as he listened to the younger wince in pain from the nails that sliced deep into his tender skin. Soft whimpers left his son's mouth. Slight blood was already dripping from the wound the man had made and the child could feel it.

"Nam-gil Kang!"

The sight of the angry woman standing by the bedroom door elevated the child's mood. It was as though she'd heard his forlorn cries all the way from downstairs, and without wasting another second, she dashed toward the two of them and shoved the man away from him.

"Is this still about his Amulet not appearing yet?" she screamed, rage rippling through her. "Reuben is five, for crying out loud. Five! He's still got two more years, Nam-gil. I have no idea what you're worried about. It will come."

It will come.

Regardless of his mother's uplifting words, Reuben Kang knew he would never believe it. At the young age of five, he'd already lost that hope. Perhaps, if the kids at school didn't harass him for it, things would be different. In a way, he understood why his father was so troubled. A lot of children his age that resided in the same area were already getting their own Amulets. Each of them never shied away from the chance to boast about their pendants nor the powers they granted.

"You know better than to speak to me in that tone!" his father growled, pointing a finger at his wife. "If not for me, neither of you would be living half as decent as you are right now, so hold your tongue."

"Why do you bother to keep me around then?" The woman scoffed. But Reuben understood she already knew the answer. Who else was going to keep the house clean, cook meals, and take care of the younger one? All his father knew how to do was go drinking at the tavern. Reuben would often hear him coming back late at night, drunk out of his mind. He hardly knew his father anymore. The man was becoming more and more unfamiliar as days passed.

Furthermore, his mother had been the one to lie about being a Holder, in the first place. That was how she got married to one. Her parents excelled in deluding those around them, and with the help of each other, commenced their own secret small business. They would spend as many hours as they could every day creating realistic-looking Amulets, and Powerless beings would pay good jewels to get a forgery. Of course, when the assessments arrived, these fakes were useless. But it felt sweet to walk around with a pendant adorning their necks and not have looks of disdain sent their way.

"What in the world was I thinking, getting involved with a worthless woman like you?" Rage ran red through the man's head. "If I'd known there was a possibility my own flesh and blood could end up as a Powerless, I wouldn't have even spared you a glance."

The words alone shattered the woman's heart—Reuben could see the disheartened look on his mother's face. Then again, what had she been expecting? For her husband to be different? For him to refuse the influence of every Holder who repeatedly claimed that possessing no Amulet was a shame? For him to look at her, a Powerless woman, with genuine love?

It was foolish to think in such a way—to hope. Reuben wondered why his mother still did.

Nam-gil leaned in forward with a sneer. "You best pray Reuben receives his Amulet before he turns seven, otherwise, I am leaving the both of you. Something I definitely should have done a long time ago, but consider this a chance, Nadiya. If you weren't my wife, do you really believe you'd still be alive?"

His mother swallowed hard. Reuben could see her fighting back the tears that threatened to break free. "We are not having this conversation in front of our son," she insisted. Regardless of the strangling agony that made her want to pound the wall, rip her own hair out, and even attack her husband all at once, there was always a bit of confidence that lingered within her. Maybe, that was why she still had hope after all this while, Reuben thought. Because it was the only thing keeping her sane.

Nadiya turned to face her child, bent down, and gently patted his head. She was a beautiful woman with her perfectly sculpted diamond-shaped face. That was the one thing his mother had going for her—beauty. Reuben often wished his looks came from her instead. Not that his face was something anyone would ever consider ugly—his father was a handsome man. He had people complimenting his appearance left and right. Reuben just hated the fact that anytime he looked in the mirror, the intractable man was the first person he saw.

"Why don't you go outside and play with the other kids, Reuben."

He wanted to reject the idea. How many times in the past month had he attempted to play with kids his age only to be shunned because he was different? How many times had parents pushed him away and screamed that he never came close to their children until his troublesome status changed? Reuben would rather find playmates in the other Powerless children struggling just as he was but his father had made it clear that that was prohibited.

Nam-gil scoffed at the suggestion, shaking his head while at it. "He doesn't have an Amulet. Who would want to play with him? It's better that he waits until he becomes a Holder before ever approaching the other kids again." A scowl formed on the man's face as he glanced away.

Without uttering a single word, Reuben speedily made his way out of the house. Day after day, his mother told him never to allow his father's harsh words to get to him. But he was weak.

Vulnerable.

Once outside, Reuben's ears picked up an audible conversation coming from two small children, of them a little girl his age who looked to be on the verge of tears and the other a boy a few years older who laughed and pointed. There was a small crowd of other children surrounding the two, either booing mockingly any time the girl's mouth opened to say something or cheering whenever the boy retorted back with a vicious insult.

Reuben understood what was going on and he wondered if it was best to approach the fight or pretend he hadn't seen it. Of course, he would feel guilty if he chose to leave the Powerless to fend for herself. He always did whenever he made such a choice. But Reuben was beginning to prefer the guilt over the wounds that would surely appear on his fragile skin if he was to ever get involved.

"Why can't I play with you?" the sobbing girl was insisting, her shoulders already slumped with defeat.

"How many more times must we repeat this? Look at you. You've got no Amulet yet!" the boy in front of her exclaimed with yet another eye-roll, proudly clutching onto the crystal part of the pendant that hung around his own neck. "Each one of us here already has ours, so you can come to join when you get yours too. Simple as that. Until then, stay far away from us."

Reuben prayed then that the girl would take the hint, understand that she was not wanted, and walk away. Instead, she pouted and urged further. "But I'm still five! What if I get it tomorrow? Why can't I play with you now?"

"Like I just said, when you get it, you can come join us. Until then, continue to be a worthless Powerless and stay away from us!" came the boy's harsh response. "What if you never get it? We'd have made a mistake inviting you to play with us, then. We can't allow that to happen."

"But—"

"Go away and don't bother us again!" The boy veered around and strode away from the crying girl with a pleased look as though he'd just done the entire world a favor. Applauding behind him, the crowd of children followed. Other Holders that had witnessed the little argument chuckled with amusement, some screamed for the girl to go back to her parents. Did she really think she would get her way by shedding some pathetic tears? they ridiculed.

Watching the girl cry her heart out tugged at Reuben's, making it even harder to walk away then. He wanted nothing more than to console her. Or maybe, they could cry together over their misfortunes. Even better, curse the Holders for their wicked ways. But was it smart to go to her, especially when his father had made a clear rule against it? To befriend her?

What if in a few months or years, the girl got her Amulet and he didn't? Her attitude towards him would be sure to change. Their friendship would have been a waste of time. He just knew it, after all, once a being received an Amulet of their own, they were bound to turn arrogant and cruel. It was just the way the world was. His mother taught him that.

"Hey! Wait up!"

He couldn't believe the words had come out of his own mouth, and only after the girl turned to look at him did he realize he was waving as well. To hell with his father's rule.

To hell with these Holders.

The boy raced over to where she was standing, his heart pounding with sheer excitement at the thought of finally achieving his number one goal—making a friend. "I heard what that boy said to you. That was so mean of him." He didn't dare put much attention to the looks of distaste Holders sent his way nor the derisive whisperings. Searching the girl's face, he found nothing but confusion and a hint of hope written all over it. "My name is Reuben. Er... Reuben Kang."

For a brief while, the little girl blinked rapidly as if struggling to grasp the reality that someone else was now finally speaking to her. She couldn't believe it. Someone was actually speaking to her. Eventually, she ran a hand over her wet eyes and took out the other for the boy to shake while her lips spread into the widest smile she'd ever formed. "I'm Cesaria Faun. It's nice to meet you, Reuben."

——..○ ☽ ▢ ☾ ○..——

PRESENT 07TH SEPTEMBER 2003

Frustrated narrow steel black eyes peer down at an Amulet lying on a large smooth stone table, a tightened reddened hand on either side of the cobalt blue pendant. The library, once modest and snug, now appears cluttered with antique books that were recently retrieved from their shelves dispersed all over the table and floor.

Reuben is doing it again.

Pining. Struggling to tamp down his wrath. Eating his heart out for his mother. Pondering over the absurdity of individuals losing their lives over something as foolish as Amulets. Yes, they grant powers. And so what? In some ways, this has become a daily occurrence for him. Pine. Struggle. Cry. Ponder. Sleep. Wake up. Do it all over again.

When his stomach grumbles, he breaks his gaze from the Amulet and turns to his hands, instead. They've always been so smooth, spotless, free of any wounds. But today, his hands are covered in bleeding cuts that sting whenever he touches them—and all because he chose to get himself involved. All because he finally emerged from his shell and decided enough was enough. Perhaps, that was a mistake. He's always hated the sight of injuries—blood, to be specific.

Ever since his mother's demise, he's made sure to be careful—to steer clear of anything that can do him harm. Aside from the state of his hands now, when was the last time he got hurt? When was the last time he bled? Reuben can't even remember. Today is different, though. Today, when he saw that helpless Powerless surrounded by three Holders that would not leave her alone, something just snapped inside of him. He had to intervene.

"Reuben, are you alright?"

The boy sighs and picks up the Amulet—his Amulet. He casts a quick glance towards the librarian, Mrs. Shaan, who's positioned beside one of the tall gray pillars. "I suppose." He's always known how to keep his aggravation in check but inwardly, he's seething. No matter how much he despises it, this is the world he lives in—this is the world he, and every other striving being out there, is imposed to bear with. "Apologies for the mess, Mrs. Shaan," he utters with a sheepish smile.

"Is there something, in particular, you're searching for?" Mrs. Shaan questions as she bends down and picks up one of the books on the floor.

Another frustrated sigh leaves Reuben's mouth. Although there's a lot on his mind—the academy, his living expenses, the number of jewels he currently possesses—his thoughts can't stop reeling back to what went down hours ago. "A book that properly discusses the Golden Amulet—where it came from, what its powers are, why Holders are so obsessed with it, why a girl my age seems to be the true owner of it."

All the books he owns centered around this special pendant are only tales, someone's imagination. Reuben needs something real, something that answers his questions, and he needs it now, especially after what he just did to help that girl.

Who was she, anyway? Many seem to know her. Eun-something, is it? Or, Ivy Pearls, according to the name on the golden pendant. He has never given these necklaces the same amount of attention as the other Holders do but Reuben has to confess that the confrontation has piqued his interest. So, all this time, Queen Matilda never possessed the Golden Amulet? This is the only drama he sees himself ever relishing.

His stomach grumbles for the second time, catching the woman's attention straight away. Mrs. Shaan frowns in bemusement, her large mink-brown eyes pensive.

"Have you not eaten yet, Reuben?"

He feels a sharp pang of humiliation at the inquiry. He's neglected his hunger for far too long, Reuben knows that. When was the last time he ate again—a meal big enough to fulfill his stomach, even if for just a little while? Two days ago? Despite that, he cannot let the librarian know. All she'd do is insist on feeding him and Reuben can't allow her to do such a thing knowing she's hardly got enough to feed her family.

"I'll eat as soon as I get home. I just need to find this book first."

But he won't because he's jobless. Since he began living alone, Reuben has only been able to earn his jewels by helping elderly women with tasks they can no longer perform on their own, such as going to the market. Yet that isn't a real profession—not one that pays much, unfortunately. And he needs one. Fast. That is the only reason he registered for the new academy, in the first place.

Mrs. Shaan nods yet there seems to be a tightness to it as though she's holding herself back from saying something else. She's doubtful. The vacillating look on her dark-skinned dimple-in-chin face speaks for itself. Regardless, she pushes her questions aside and glances down at the books Reuben's picked out. "The Golden Amulet, hmm?" she says, deep in thought. "And I suppose this has got something to do with that girl."

"I'm just puzzled, is all," Reuben tells her. "Queen Matilda doesn't possess the Amulet but that doesn't explain how she was able to perform all those miracles. Perhaps, there's something about the Golden Amulet we're missing or-or perhaps—"

"Reuben, please do me and yourself a favor and don't go investigating this," Mrs. Shaan says in a sharp cautioning tone with a pinched expression. "You know what happens to people who go too far. You're a nice boy. I would hate for anything to happen to you."

Reuben pauses, soaking in the woman's warning. "I'm already involved, don't you see? I was the one who revealed what name was engraved on the Amulet. Queen Matilda most likely loathes me but it had to be done. So then. . . I might as well just see it through."

"Queen Matilda's anger is all the more reason to stop what you're doing right now," Mrs. Shaan carries on, slowly picking up the scattered books and placing them back on the shelves. "I worry for you, Reuben."

"You don't have to worry. I'm invulnerable, remember?"

"How, then, did you get those cuts on your hands?"

Reuben mentally winces. He hates how stupid he was being during that fight with those unsparing Holders. "I. . . I wasn't wearing my Amulet."

Mrs. Shaan's eyes expand. "Well, why not?"

Reuben doesn't answer. He abhors Amulets—and he abhors how something he despises so much is the only thing ensuring his safety—but this is another thing he can't let the librarian know—a confession that can never leave his mouth. "I won't make that mistake again, I promise."

"W-Why wouldn't you. . .?" Mrs. Shaan starts again in a stammer but stops almost as soon as she does, peering intently at him. No Holder she knows of would ever think to take their pendants off, especially during a fight. But when it's clear Reuben doesn't want to discuss it any further, she hesitantly turns back to putting her books back in their rightful places. "W-Well, I'm sorry, Reuben, but I don't think I can give you what you're looking for. And not because I don't like this road you're taking. I just don't have a book that thoroughly explains the purpose of the Golden Amulet. All I've got is fiction."

"Do you think I'll find something in The Great Library of Findara?" he questions. "Perhaps, that should have been the first place I searched. It is the biggest library here."

Mrs. Shaan's full lips spread into a small smile but there's still a hint of concern in her eyes. "You can try. But just so you know, it wasn't until Queen Matilda revealed that she had the Golden Amulet that anyone knew it truly existed. The Golden Amulet may not be as potent as they think. It could just be an ordinary Amulet."

"But it grants powers no other Amulet endows."

"And so what?" The woman scoffs. "Anand Khatri was the first Holder with the power of Invulnerability. It was an ability no one had ever seen before. But as years passed, more Holders were born with the same power, including your grandfather. See what I mean?"

Reuben sighs. Perhaps, it was his great love for mysteries that pushed him this far but he knows the librarian is right. "You believe it's all a myth, don't you?"

Mrs. Shaan shrugs. "That may be because I read too much fiction. Yes, I know the Amulet grants extraordinary powers, not to mention it's the only pendant that's golden. But Arya is jumping to conclusions far too quickly. An Amulet that will bring eternal tranquility? Pfft!"

Reuben's lips part, showing his teeth in a buoyant smile. Mrs. Shaan is never afraid to speak her mind and he admires that about her. It was the woman's jaunty and warmhearted character when he met her at the market that drew him to her library four years ago. Perhaps, it is how similar Mrs. Shaan is to his mother that brings him comfort whenever he is around her.

"You can still try, Reuben," the librarian says. "I'd rather you didn't but if you really want to know, you can still search. I'm not stopping you."

"Mhm, we'll see."

The subject drops there. Mrs. Shaan leaves to welcome a new Holder who just entered, leaving the boy alone at the table to reflect on his difficult circumstances. Although still new, Amulet Academy has already been said to be the best one out there—the finest educators have been selected to teach there and a high number of well-trained guards to protect it.

Our future, they call it.

Reuben knows if he performs well, finding a nice, high-paying job won't be an issue. Yet, at the same time, he questions whether another, much safer would have been preferable. He despises the idea of getting physically harmed, not to mention his use of Invulnerability is not as effective as it could be. Why, then, did he choose to enroll into a school where the primary goal is to educate its students how to fight?

"The academy officially starts tomorrow," Reuben calls out to the librarian when she's alone again as if she doesn't already know this. "I may not come to see you as often."

"That's alright," Mrs. Shaan says, carrying a new stack of publications. "Just get home and eat."

Reuben leaves the small library with his new book of the week in hand. Only when he's halfway home does he get a sudden disturbing sense of being followed. Knowing that he can't risk it, he stops walking. If it's the Holders from earlier coming back to finish him off, then he can't allow them to find out where he lives. Reuben knows he would never hear the end of it.

But the boy is only left surprised when rather than the people he dreads, the Powerless girl he helped is the one standing a few feet away from him. He exhales in relief but stops himself from waving. There are too many people around—too many judgmental Holders. He'd only become even more of a target if he's seen being friendly with the enemy, and after what he just went through with Ivy and Queen Matilda, that's the last thing he needs.

Standing right where she is—not too close but not too far—the girl's bloody chapped lips separate, and she mouths a quick 'thank you' before turning and dashing off.

Maybe, the cuts on his hands were worth it after all.

10 | Son of a Killer

CHAPTER TEN — SON OF A KILLER

PRESENT 08TH SEPTEMBER 2003

THROUGHOUT eighteen years of her life, Ivy Pearls can't recall feeling as full and wonderfully alive as she presently does. Ever since she disclosed the most admired woman's cloak-and-dagger past, the young girl has been walking on air, savoring the sensation of contentment that envelopes her. High in spirit, her skin is tingling and her eyes sparkling. The additional gullible students who pause in their stride every now and then to glare daggers at her are of no significance to Ivy. Today, it seems as though the sun is kissing her rosy red cheeks in bright daylight and no judgmental student is going to disrupt this special feeling for her.

Not even her troublesome brother.

Ivy can still feel the repulsive boy watching her from afar as she saunters to her homeroom class with hands gripped onto her dark brown satchel bag. Mumble after mumble arises among students that can't take their eyes off of her but Ivy doesn't make an effort to pick up what they're saying. All she knows is that Arya is torn between disregarding everything they witnessed and believing their queen while recalling all the miracles she executed or thinking rationally and siding with the girl who's clearly in control of the Golden Amulet.

It's almost humorous for Ivy reflecting how significantly her life has changed throughout the years. From her intemperate classmates often getting physical with her to her contemptuous educators that would deliberately fail her and attribute her alleged stupidity on her status, there never was a time when Ivy didn't feel dehumanized.

Absolutely nobody took any action. But all of that is no more.

If it wasn't for her derogatory parents that demanded she went to school, Ivy wouldn't have bothered with her education. They insisted she was fortunate to have this privilege when not many of her people out there could attend yet the experience was anything but fortunate for her.

There is still not a single school just for her people. Any Powerless interested in learning are compelled to endure the torture of being under the same roof as Holders. Ivy used to think Holders would simply cast the Powerless away from their academies. Now, she understands that if it means getting their share of entertainment tormenting them, Holders are more than willing to make more space.

No, Benecia was the fortunate one. Her aunt, who was more knowledgeable than a Powerless generally would be, taught her at home. For years, Ivy yearned for that same luck. Benecia would sometimes invite her to join her home-schooling sessions as Delyth frequently did but Ivy was merely allowed outside for a short period of time and much of that time was spent working.

"Is this it, Eun?"

Ivy is instantly able to work out who the voice belongs to. Not just because she's tragically had to listen to it for years—an unkind voice that haunted her day and night, even after she left Arya—but because lurking beneath that wicked tone is dread, something the speaker attempts vainly to cover yet never succeeds in doing. No matter how almost-undetectable it is, the tremor in the voice always makes Ivy shiver with satisfaction.

"What is it that you want now, Athena?"

Athena grimaces as she steps closer—but not too close. In her eyes, Ivy is still nothing more than a disease. Three other scowling girls stand behind her as if they are some form of backup. This is one of Athena's habits that Ivy picked up on the first month of their so-called friendship. Athena enjoys having people near during her arguments. This is so I'd have someone to cheer me on, she told Ivy once. But Ivy is also sure that these people are around in case something goes wrong and Athena begins to lose. In fact, she's sure that this is the primary—if not the sole—reason.

"This is why you came back to the kingdom, isn't it? For the admiration." Maintaining a crossed expression, the girl folds her arms. Her voice is loud, immediately causing heads to turn. "Tell me, how did you change the queen's name to yours? Or what, was it that boy? He's on your side, isn't he? You planned this together?" To Ivy, the anger and bitterness in her tone are almost as pleasing to hear as the dread.

"That would make sense," Jade adds behind her, "considering she did use him as her target for her presentation." Her hooded eyes flicker with elation. "We've got you now, haven't we, Eun? That boy was in it. He lied to everyone about the engravement. The both of you lied. Tell us, what did you promise him in return?"

"Or maybe," a student who's stopped to watch the bickering utters with a roll of her eyes, "just maybe, Queen Matilda isn't the honest queen we all thought she was."

"You take that right back!" Athena hollers with a new swell of rage. Ivy wonders whether she should feel pity or disdain for the way Athena conducts herself as though she were Queen Matilda.

"I'm starting to think you're all blind and deaf!" the student fires back at Athena. "The boy showed us proof. He made the name visible and every eye saw Ivy Pearls engraved on the pendant. Fools, that's what you all are."

Athena's round lips tighten as her scorching dark brown eyes stare daggers at the student. "You have no right to address me in such a manner!" She pauses and only after a few seconds have gone by with Ivy silently cackling in the background does she get a better hold of herself. Regardless, the venom in her voice is still yet to die down. "Do you think Eun is some sort of savior? That's why you're so bold all of a sudden?"

The student's lips quiver for a moment. The longer Athena stares at her with the same diabolical look she's well known for, the more she seems to tremble and sink further down.

"I still remember where you live, Sylvia," Athena mentions. "Would you like me to pay you another visit?"

Sylvia's confidence departs right then and there, and in a flash, she turns and speeds off.

"Goodness, you're all the same." Athena scowls, her stare gradually turning back to Ivy. "You pretend to be strong but it doesn't take much to break you." A series of depraved snickers follows.

"Is it so hard?" this time, it's Ivy that speaks. She sniggers softly as soon as Athena's laugh dies and her eyes switch back to the enraged look it previously had. "Is it really that difficult, Athena? To realize that you made a mistake?"

"Adora should have come here herself, then," Athena splutters, stubborn to a fault. She won't leave until she sees even just a sliver of the girl Ivy was three years ago. Regularly remembering the old times when Ivy would burst into sobs at the slightest provocation does no good in satisfying her anymore. Eun Calinao was a lot more fun to toy with, and the notion of not being able to elicit that same emotion leaves her heart hammering with a mixture of horror and fury. Ivy's calm demeanor is beginning to provoke her more than anything else. "Why did she send a lowlife? If she came and told the story herself, I would believe it."

"We both know that's false. You're far too engrossed with the Royals to believe anything that is said against them."

"That isn't true!" Athena urges.

Ivy continues to speak with increasing disdain. "Keep acting this way, Athena. You're merely proving I'm winning." And with another naughty grin stretched wide, she saunters away.

She lost everything, over and over. She began afresh with nothing over and over. Her enemies seized every opportunity to employ their subtle blades over and over. Yet, with the aid of her people's suffering and Adora, Ivy learned a little each time, keeping those mental notes her teacher gave to her safe and sound.

Perhaps, it isn't such a bad thing that things didn't go exactly as planned yesterday. "You learn more from losing than winning," Adora told her once. "You learn to keep going." And so Ivy turned every excruciating punishment she endured over the years into lessons—another chance to use the tiny fragments of light etched into what was left of her brain. Fragments that, in time, would unite to become what she aims to be in the future.

Only after she nears her classroom does Ivy come to yet a second stop. Another pair of legs are standing right under her nose. She glances up, mentally shaking her head with irritation at the thought of another student coming to fight with her. When her eyes finally land on the girl, it takes Ivy no more than a second to recognize the student's fine features. It's the doe-eyed girl from her class with that same look of slight fright. She can't recall what her name is—if it was even ever mentioned.

"I just came to apologize." The adolescent whips out a hand in a flash, offering Ivy to shake it. "I-It's Poppy Winters."

But Ivy only grumbles in response and slightly pushes the girl aside to enter the room.

"I-I just came to apologize for yesterday," Poppy repeats. "That's all, I promise."

Ivy takes a brief scan of their surroundings before a scoff leaves her mouth. "Ah, I get it now. You're only acting all courageously because neither Athena nor Jade is here to judge you. Quite pathetic, if you ask me."

Poppy becomes outraged by the remark as an instant of raw frustration rushes through her. "I just felt sorry that you were judged terribly by everyone, regardless of the fact the Golden Amulet really did belong to you. But fine. You don't want my apology? So be it."

For a second, Ivy wonders if her tone was perhaps a bit too harsh. Then, she remembers the girl is a Holder. Yes, Adora told her to form a team but she did not come here to pardon and make friends. Furthermore, how is Poppy's delicate character meant to push her plot forward? Silently, she watches the girl rush to her own seat set in the middle of the classroom.

As Ivy makes her way towards her designated seat at the rear of the room, the door swings open and a fresh influx of students pile inside. Of them, a Tykkian boy of considerable stature catches Ivy's attention. With his shoulder-length hair neatly gathered into a small ponytail, save for a few strands artfully left loose in the front, he takes a seat adjacent to Poppy. Ivy remembers having seen him the day prior, although, like the majority of every other individual, she hardly knows much about him.

"Morning, Ga-Eul." Poppy waves.

"Seems like we're early," the boy notes. Not even Mr. Abalos has arrived. "By the way, Poppy, I've been meaning to ask. How's your Healing coming along?"

The boy's voice is loud enough for Ivy to hear him, and when she does, her posture stiffens and her muscles grow rigid. Healing? She gradually turns to look at the two, bug-eyed.

So, the power Poppy possesses is Healing?

"You must have a Healer on your team. It'd be impossible for you not to get hurt. A Healer will be there to mend your wounds, however big they may be."

Ivy was wrong to cast Poppy away so hastily—she can see that now. The same girl she believed would be too delicate to assist her is the exact Holder she needs to better her team, or so as Adora informed her.

Poppy glances down at her Amulet and sighs. It's a pink crystal point necklace with dainty light silver flowers wrapped around the top of it. "Still on level two," comes her response.

Ivy winces mentally. The level falls short of the requirements for a plan as grandiose as hers. Then again, what was she expecting from a girl that is still so young?

The higher the level, the more potent Healing becomes. At the pinnacle of this ladder lies the ability to resurrect deceased bodies, such a power that could prove invaluable to Ivy in numerous ways. Nevertheless, the question arises: is it smart to add an inexperienced Healer to her team? No, absolutely not. It is only best she takes her time and keeps looking. Poppy is one out of thousands of Healers.

Besides, Ivy already has two other Healers in mind.

When the door opens this time, the rest of the class saunter inside, along with Mr. Abalos who's clutching onto a cup. As the ring of the bell sounds for the second time, the man cautiously closes the door with his foot before heading to his desk. But not before he shoots Ivy a troubled look mixed with a bit of fury.

"To be quite frank with you, I haven't had much time to plan out a lot of things," the man starts. Ivy apprehends his words instantly. She's the reason he hasn't had time to do a thing.

The best part is, Mr. Abalos isn't the only one. Ivy's classmates are disturbed. They can barely focus. Ivy imagines each of them is replaying the rumors over and over again in their heads. She knows an abundance of questions is roaming about in their puzzled minds. They appear unable to keep their eyes off of her, either.

Ivy turns to look at the boy sitting beside her, who hasn't been able to stop staring ever since he walked inside—the same boy who disclosed the Golden Amulet's true possessor. He's quick to glance away when he realizes he's been caught. She's surprised that he's willing to sit next to her, even now. There are two extra seats still yet to be claimed, far from the one Ivy chose for herself. Why doesn't he move then, especially knowing that some people believe he helped her? Or. . . Doesn't he know?

Mr. Abalos clears his throat. After finally snapping out of his inner thoughts, the man stops his pacing and folds his arms. "If you're certain of what your abilities are, every single one of them, raise your hand high."

Seconds later, more than half of the class shoots their hands up in the air. Mr. Abalos nods slowly, tapping the upper part of his left raimund boot against the floor as he ponders over his thoughts. "Alright," he carries on. "If you understand how to use all of your abilities, raise your hand high."

This time, only a small number of students have their hands up. Being one of them, Ivy can hardly contain the small sneer that has developed on her insolent face as soon as she realizes that the man is primarily inquisitive in her answer. He wants to know if she understands how to precisely utilize the Golden Amulet.

And, of course, the answer to that is no. Adora did not have time to teach her every single ability. Her training was spent more on learning how to fight and deal with Holders' deceptive tactics. The only reason she raised her hand is to give her educator a little scare.

"T-That's good to know," Mr. Abalos splutters, his gaze shifting away from Ivy once again.

Why must you make your interests so obvious? Ivy leans against her seat and watches the man take a few steps forward. Adora warned her of every possible danger that comes with possessing the Golden Amulet, one of which being people striving to seize it. Would Mr. Abalos attempt such a thing? Ivy wonders.

He does give the impression of a sick thief. Despite the current tranquility, Ivy is aware that a day will come when her enemies begin carrying out their threats. Finally coming to terms that their queen does not wield the Golden Amulet is one thing. Accepting the fact it instead belongs to a little girl like her, a girl, is another—and impossible, especially for men.

"This year's Talent Show is just around the corner," Mr. Abalos says. He smiles down at Athena. "And as the winner of last year, Athena Takao has been asked to be one of the judges. How thrilling is that, Athena?"

Athena only nods slightly. She would be giddy like a child if not for Ivy and her stunts.

"I strongly encourage every single one of you to take part in it," their educator proceeds. "It'll boost your chances of becoming greater. As preparation, we'll have a little class presentation. You'll each be given a turn to come up and present one of your powers. This is so you ca—"

The door opening cuts the man off. A guard pokes his head through the small space of the slightly opened entryway, his focus directly on Mr. Abalos.

"Headmaster Huang would like to see you."

"Me?" the teacher raises his eyebrows in confusion as he points to himself. "What for?"

"I wasn't informed." The guard shrugs.

Could it be about me? Ivy doesn't want to behave as though every little thing their teacher does revolves around her or the Golden Amulet but when it comes to the man, she really can't be certain. Didn't Mr. Abalos say a thing or two about reporting her to the headmaster to discuss her expulsion yesterday? Is he still planning to go through with that idea? Ivy wouldn't be surprised if he is. They don't have a compelling basis to expel her but they don't need one.

Amulet Academy is no longer of great significance to Ivy—at least, it wasn't until she learned that a woman she's been searching for works as a lecturer here.

"Is it alright if you stay here and watch my students while I'm gone?" Mr. Abalos asks the guard, to which he receives a minor nod back in response. While the guard enters the classroom and takes a seat behind Mr. Abalos' desk, their teacher exits it.

"So. . . What are you currently working on?"

"Nothing at the moment. We were about to have a class presentation when you walked in," the girl sitting behind Poppy is the one who answers.

The guard sits back against the desk. "Well, in that case, while you're waiting for Mr. Abalos to come back, why don't you take this time to properly introduce yourself to each other? I doubt you got the chance to do so yesterday considering someone started drama." He eyes Ivy gingerly.

"Introductions don't matter," says Isagani.

"Oh, but they do matter." The man sends them such a look that makes it seem as though all their lives depend on acquainting with each other. "How else are you going to work well with one another? There are dozens of competitions in this academy, which I'm certain you already know about. Some of these competitions require you to team up with your homeroom classmates and compete against the other classes."

Ivy frowns slightly. Why does this man have so much regard for something so little?

"I overheard Headmaster Huang speaking in his office and it seems he's got very important business to discuss with your teacher. I think it's going to take a while," the guard says, earning a small scoff from Ivy. It feels as though this man cares about introductions more than the class does. "Just tell the class the basics: your name, what you work as at the moment, how many powers your Amulet holds, and. . ."

His voice blurs for a moment as Ivy's focus lingers on one of his suggestions. How many powers your Amulet holds. . . It seems Holders have reached a new level of competition. Two days ago while aimlessly wandering about Findara, she came across two little boys debating over who had superior abilities.

The much younger boy asserted that quantity was always preferable to quality. The other, who Ivy thought to be his older brother since they shared a similar appearance, pointed out that it didn't matter how many powers an Amulet bestowed just as long as a Holder was skilled in utilizing them. The bickering would have escalated into an actual physical altercation if not for the woman that intervened in time.

What Ivy wants to know is why the younger was so insistent on the importance of the quantity each necklace bestows. Which Holders are out and about, filling the ears of little children with more disruptive lies about what they must be or do to achieve perfection in their lives?

"I'll pick who goes first!" the guard lets out a childlike cry, bringing Ivy back to her classroom. His eyes skim through the students while gently rubbing his chin. For a moment, they land and linger on Ivy but the man is soon to shift his attention elsewhere. Eventually, he halts at the student seated at the very back as well, just on the other side of where Ivy is sitting. "How about you there? Introduce yourself."

Ivy has to lean forward against her table and cock her head to the right in order to get a good look at the anxious oval Japanese face the guard chose. He's quick to swallow hard as soon as all eyes fall on him.

"Uh... Hiroshi. I-I'm Hiroshi."

"Just Hiroshi?" the guard says once the boy has made it clear that he isn't saying any more than his name. "Ah, don't be shy. At least, tell us your family name."

Ivy isn't sitting near him yet she can still precisely imagine just how hard and fast Hiroshi's heart must be pounding. Speaking must not be his strong suit.

"It's Sol!" the guard declares out of nowhere, taking everyone else by surprise. "His name is Hiroshi Sol. Now, allow that to sink in."

If not for the memory from when she was still with Adora that forms in her head, Ivy would never have gotten why the name is of any importance. It's Athena that rises from her seat first and accusingly gestures at the boy.

"You're the son of Jin Sol!"

"Jin Sol?" Jade gasps. "You mean to say that one of our classmates is the son of the man who killed our previous queen? Well, no wonder he seemed so anxious. He's related to a slayer."

Now, it's Ivy's own heart that's pounding. Flabbergasted with a mixture of joy, she continues to stare at the trembling boy. The son of the man she hopes to emulate in the future is only three seats away from her. Oh, how Adora would have loved to hear about this. It's clear to see now just how much Hiroshi resembles his father. How didn't she see it before?

Whether it's because of the loud whisperings that finally got to him or the snide looks cast his way, the boy jolts up from his seat and races to the door. Ivy is sure she caught sight of his eyes swimming with tears. This is a personal attack from the guard on the boy. The menacing smirk on the man's face makes it clear.

"Simply because he's the son of the man who slew Queen Aqua does not automatically define his character," Poppy urges. "Why should it matter? And why do you care? Why bring it up?" She gives the guard a dirty look. "You're here to watch us, not stir trouble."

"But it's a good thing he brought it up," Jade contends. "We need to report this to Headmaster Huang and demand he gets kicked out straight away. They really shouldn't be allowing anyone inside this academy. First Ivy, now him? Knowing what his father did, I don't want to be anywhere around that boy."

What his father did! Ivy opens her mouth to say but closes it almost immediately. For now, all she can concentrate on is the sniggering guard and why he would do such a thing, to begin with.

word count • 3998

11 | Justice or Vengeance

Chapter Eleven — Justice or Vengeance

Queen Matilda

AS soon as Queen Matilda's feeble body hits the crystal floor, a searing agony lashes across her lower back, much like the throbbing sensation in her forehead, which she earlier bashed. She curls up in a corner, arms wrapped tightly around herself, seeking solace in her own embrace, a physical defense against the encroaching tides of fear and anxiety. In front of her, the cause of her current aching state, is her husband.

"You have ten seconds to start speaking the truth before I have you beheaded!"

A rivulet appears in the dust on Queen Matilda's face. She daubs it away with her sleeve. "And here I thought you were on my side." She wants to appear anything but fragile and afraid, especially in front of her husband yet her thoughts are careening through a maze of worst-case possibilities, each one more terrifying than the last. Panic has hijacked her rationality.

"You didn't really believe that, did you?" King Titus scoffs, tapping his foot impatiently. The air crackles with tension as his jaw tightens, muscles twitching with every repressed urge to strike out, his eyes blazing with fiery indignation. "The odds are against you, Matilda. If you keep this secrecy up, your end will be just around the corner. Maybe, if you admit the truth, your penalty will be much lighter."

"I have admitted the truth!" the woman shrieks. She attempts to hold back the seething torrent of tears that have been building up since the moment the interrogation began. "The Golden Amulet previously belonged to my half-sister but it was later passed down to me after she committed those crimes." Her voice calms as she stares into the glaring man's eyes with a pleading look. "That is the truth, my love."

"And how do you expect me to believe you?" A look of great regret sweeps across the man's face. "Ivy has proof of her ownership. You do not. Why do you think I never took the Amulet from her?" At first, he paces, each stride a testament to the restless anger pulsing through him. Then, with heavy steps, he walks over to where the queen sits against the wall and reaches down for her hair. "Tell me right now, Matilda. The truth only. Did I get married to a falsifier?"

"I've already explained myself." Queen Matilda's voice cracks, emotions breaking through the façade of strength, as if misery has chipped away her armor, revealing the frailty beneath. "I cannot do this anymore. I don't want to sit here and allow a child to destroy my good name but what else can I do? Even my own husband doesn't believe me." She grabs hold of his arm and sinks her nails into it. "I did not lie, my love. I did not lie. I've told nothing but the truth from the very beginning. What evidence do you have that I lied?"

"Ivy is evidenc—"

"No!" Once again, her feelings become jumbled and her insides tight. She waits, wide-eyed, heart in mouth, hoping. As much as she hates to admit it, she needs a hug, even if it is just in the form of words. She needs soothing like a child, like the way her mother used to comfort her when she was much younger. She needs someone to tell her everything is going to be okay, that she's going to come out of this okay. "I'll prove it."

King Titus balks at the idea. To him, his wife sounds nothing more than a desperate woman using every tactic she can think of. Say he gives her a chance to prove herself and she uses it to flee instead. He can't allow that to happen. He can't allow a potential Powerless who may have deluded the kingdom to flee, especially with no punishments.

"Do not worry about how I will accomplish it." Once her husband's grip loosens, Queen Matilda swiftly slaps his hand away. "I'll do it. That's all you need to know. I'll do it and have you see that this girl has got you fooled. I speak only the truth, my love. I'll make you regret even doubting me for a second."

King Titus takes a step back. "I'm looking forward to it then." And he really means it. If it turns out that the woman he's been sleeping in the same bed with, the woman he's been dining with, the woman he's been ruling Arya with, the woman he has a child with, is truly a Powerless, the man will never forgive himself.

The door opens and a guard steps inside. He's flushed for a second, almost afraid he walked into something he shouldn't be witnessing. When King Titus motions for him to proceed, the man clears his throat and points a finger behind him. "Someone is here to see Queen Matilda."

"It must be my mother." The woman smoothes out her crumpled gown before reaching for where her favorite red heels lay. Afraid his wife would use the heels as a weapon, King Titus made taking them off her feet his first priority before commencing his interrogation. "She informed me beforehand that she'd drop by for a visit," she carries on, casting a cursory glance at the man who's standing tall and mighty with folded arms. Her attention then diverts over to the guard. "Take me to her."

"Yes, Your Majesty. Right, this way." After a bow, the guard pulls the heavy doors open, and waits for the woman to approach him before exiting the Throne Room.

She is led to the great hall, a rectangular room that is entered through a screens passage at one end and has a large bay window on one of the long sides. Queen Matilda's eyes shift over to the elderly woman standing just below the minstrels' gallery above the screens passage and her eyes instantly soften. It's been far too long since she last saw her. She can't contain the euphoric joy bubbling within her, the relief that ripples through awakening a reservoir of childlike wonder.

"Mother," the queen breathes out, disregarding the searing anguish in her feet as she rushes towards the woman in heels. She is quick to embrace the elder, her last remaining reserves of willpower to contain her tears shriveling away. "I've failed. I'm sorry. I'm so sorry."

Her mother casts a glance at the guard, shooing him away with just a slight nod. Once she's certain the man is entirely out of the room, she gently pushes her daughter away. Queen Matilda's gaze holds a distant longing. Her eyes reflect a vast expanse of feelings too complex to be contained within a single tear and for that, anger coils in her mother's stomach. "Are you really crying because of that little girl? I can't believe it." She scoffs. She does not hide the bitterness in her tone. "You've done far worse things, Matilda, but you're really going to allow her to put you down? Ah, maybe, I was wrong to think you could do this, after all."

"And here I thought you'd learn to stop being so acidic." Queen Matilda looks at her mother from the elderly woman's powder-white hair to her teetering legs. "You're too old to still be in a fit of pique."

"And you're old enough to have outgrown such ludicrous immaturity!" her mother snaps back, her jaw tightened. But underneath the rage that continues to ripple through her is despair weighed down on her like an unyielding boulder. "I'm not just some woman, Matilda. I'm not someone you can easily trample over. I'm not your enemy either—"

"And I'm not treating you like one. Is it that you feel I've drifted too far from you? Is that the cause of your behavior? Remember that I asked you to move in and live closer to me. Remember that I pleaded for your aid when I most needed you and you turned me down. Do you remember that?"

"Oh, don't play the victim, Matilda. Power has gotten into your head. How quick you are to jump back to treating me like your mother when you're in trouble."

"Yet, you're back," her daughter points out instantly, proud. "You've come back because you miss me just as I have missed you. You knew I didn't mean it when I said such harsh words."

But the irritated look on her mother's face does not go away. Anger wells up in Queen Matilda's chest. She's tried to be patient but it's clear her mother is never going to let her bitterness go.

"You know what, Mother? I don't understand this behavior. You're the one who told me that I needed to do whatever it takes to rise to the top. You're the one who taught me never to let other people stand in my way. I had to concentrate in order for this plan to work, that's what you said. It's all you. You! I followed your teachings, your steps. I did everything you asked."

"Matilda—"

Yet the woman does not allow her mother to get a word in. She takes a step forward and brings her voice to a whisper. "Believe me, you're not the one who gets to be angry. Because of this failure of a plan you constructed, we might meet our end soon. But how do you want to be remembered, Mother? As the woman who raised the greatest queen or as a coward who allowed the past to be her downfall?"

The elderly woman draws in a sharp breath, casting Queen Matilda an icy gaze. But not a second goes by before a mirthless laugh leaves her mouth. "My, oh my. I really did raise a killer, didn't I?"

"Well, you sure didn't raise a quitter," Matilda states proudly. "I know what you want in life, Mother. Don't ruin my chances at a happy ending and I won't ruin yours, how about that?"

The other doesn't respond yet telling from the woman's quivering hands grasping onto the white gown she is wearing, Queen Matilda knows her mother understands.

"Now, Ivy claimed it was Adora who gave her the Golden Amulet but that can't be true. Adora died a long time ago. I made sure of it. Ivy has to be lying."

"What if she's not?" Eventually finding her voice again, her mother suggests. "The Golden Amulet is known to perform miracles. Adora killed her father using it, after all. What if the Amulet kept her alive?"

"You think she may be alive even now?" the younger asks, yet without waiting for her mother to answer, she puts her hands on her hips and glances down at the floor as a new idea sprouts in her head. "I'll have some guards search the forest as soon as possible until they find her body, whether alive or dead. Oh, this is something I should have done a long time ago. I will not allow Adora to continue to haunt me and ruin the good life I've built for myself."

Queen Matilda forms a fist, glaring daggers at nothing specific. "All I need to worry about now is getting the Golden Amulet back from that thief. More people are starting to believe her, Mother. Can you believe that nonsense? Even after everything I've done for Arya, they're choosing to side with her."

"I'm surprised the guards still listen to you, Matilda."

Queen Matilda grunts under her breath as her forehead puckers. Some of them still do. The rest, as the king himself, are demanding proof of her ownership of the pendant before deciding whether it is best to trust her. Right now, she's hardly the queen. She no longer wields the same amount of influence as she once did.

But she's stubborn, born to hang on, to win, and fight for what she believes in. Confidence is the queen's inner golden caramel, a sweetness she is convinced is powerful and gracious. Fear and defeat are not an option and the woman is willing to do whatever it takes to save her own life.

Even if it means taking another.

——..∘ ☽ □ ☾ ∘..——

As soon as the bell sounds, Ivy shifts her chair back as relief warms her from within. If not for the unnerving stares her teacher sent her now and then, the lesson wouldn't have been as unpleasant. There is just something so sinister about the look in his eyes that left her a little on edge. No longer angry nor confused, a part of Mr. Abalos seems to have accepted he was fooled by the same woman he had such high regards for.

No, the look in his eyes was more like... hunger.

Did she put her life at risk? For certain, she did. Danger has been knocking on the young girl's door since and she invited it in as soon as she stepped foot inside Arya again. Ivy wonders if her teacher's hunger is just a strong desire to see her beheaded. If so, he would only be one of many, but if any of these people wish for war, she's more than ready to give it to them and come out victorious. With the Golden Amulet by her side, none of them would have even the slightest courage to touch her.

"Before you all go," Isagani Abadiano suddenly calls out, holding his classmates back from leaving the room. "I've got an announcement to make."

"Yes, we know. It's your birthday today. You've been speaking of it all week," Ga-Eul is next to speak, rolling his eyes as though even just the thought of being around Isagani displeases him.

"Why then did you not stop over and wish me a happy birthday? So many others did." Isagani scoffs, although his words come across as more taunting than serious. Denying Ga-Eul the chance to form his own sarcastic retort, the birthday boy turns to face the class again. "A party is being held tonight to commemorate. I've already had people send invitations to those I want to invite, so if you're one of them, consider yourself lucky. You'd be making a grave mistake not coming. I am highly regarded for throwing the finest parties in this kingdom."

Apparently, that describes practically every Holder in Arya. Ivy scowls as she slings the strap of her old satchel bag over her shoulder and heads toward the door. She has no interest in staying around and listening to yet another egotistical Holder speak about a jamboree they are hosting.

"You invited me. Why is that?" Athena asks behind her, one leg over the other.

"Because he knows it's a mistake not to invite you," Jade remarks, to which Isagani shrugs with a small smile as though to confirm.

Mr. Abalos' sudden reminder is what brings Ivy to a halt. "Let's also not forget that tomorrow is the fifth year of the Powerless Tournament." She can picture the man's heart swelling with contentment as he speaks, basking in the warmth of the thought of her people fighting and bleeding to death. "Make sure to show up for a chance of winning big prizes. I heard there's excellent goods this year."

Ivy's throat tightens, dread gnawing at her insides. Fighting the urge to slam her hands against the wall and let out a scream, she squeezes them, her fingers curling into tight fists. But they're trembling, her nails digging into her palms, the pain grounding her amidst the tempest of her anger. This is all nothing but a game to them, mocking her people and betting on them while they battle to their deaths for their entertainment.

"Well, I hope this year brings the same thrill as the last did," Jade

"The list of this year's participants will be called out this evening," Mr. Abalos

Of course, none of you find this sick. Ivy scoffs as her eyes trail from the man to Isagani over to Jade. Their eyes are gleaming with utmost delight and they can't stop grinning. When she comes across Athena, the girl is looking back at her, and though she's got her own grin pasted to her face, it's more deriding than anything else. Athena knows how the subject makes her feel. Even without having to look, she knows Ivy is frowning, and that pleases her.

Ivy turns to the rest of the class, then. Some of them have already piled out of the room but the ones that are still yet to leave have expressions that are quite difficult to interpret to Ivy. Are they angry? Excited?

Have the terms of the tournament changed during her absence of three years? Ivy has only been to one tournament, thus far. Other Powerless beings are startlingly permitted to attend and watch but many refuse to come. Why wouldn't they? It is far too unbearable watching their own people fight to their deaths, after all.

Ivy reaches for the door but before she can make contact with it, Isagani calls her back.

"Hold on a second, Eun." The boy reaches into his own bag and pulls out of it a piece of paper. "I wanted to do the honors myself." As he approaches her, his grin broadens.

Realizing what he's planned to do, Ivy chuckles. "You really think I'd come to your party?"

"It'd be fantastic if you could make it, actually," the boy responds, appearing unaware of the bewildered expression Athena is wearing behind him. "I mean, you did something wondrous yesterday. Unearthing a Royal's dirty secret is no easy job yet you managed to pull it off."

"You can't be serious!" Athena blurts out.

"So, what if I am?" Isagani dares. "You really don't still believe that Queen Matilda is an honest woman, do you, Athena? It was proven to us all that she manipulated us and—"

"Shut it!" Athena barks. "I can't believe you would even say such a thing."

Ivy reaches forward and takes the invitation from the boy. "I'll think about it."

Shortly after stepping out of the smothering room, she feels a finger tap her shoulder. Her eyebrows raise instantly at the sight of who it is behind her. She has to admit even her heart jumps a little. Sour almond-shaped eyes stare back at her. Clover. Clover is the one there when she turns. Like an arrow from a bow, the past comes crashing back into Ivy's head.

"I wouldn't go to that party if I were you," Clover whispers.

"Of course, I'm not going. Do you take me for a fool?" Ivy's tone is sharp and harsh. She wants to add something snarkier but she knows better than to stay petty over something that occurred many years ago.

"They planned that act together—Isagani and Athena," Clover continues in a low voice as if she's completely forgotten who she's speaking to. "I overheard them discussing how they were going to fool you into attending. They've apparently got a surprise for you there."

Ivy, dissatisfied but amused with the perception these people hold of her, as if she'll forever be as weak of a target as she was years back, sighs with frustration, accompanied by a subtle mockery. A chuckle leaves her mouth. "Well, they're going to have to do better than that."

An awkward silence follows. It is an unavoidable nothingness—a quiet that is deafening.

At first, Ivy's eyes linger on the two necklaces Clover is wearing, of them being her Mauve Amulet and the other an ordinary dazzling silver swan pendant. She remembers Clover was wearing both that day.

In the middle of the beating, one of the attacking Holders yanked her swan necklace away and Clover wept as though her life depended on it. It was only after Ivy threw herself into the fight that the Holder tossed the necklace aside, allowing the wailing girl to pick it back up.

Ivy deduces that the necklace holds significant sentimental value to Clover, evident by her tight grip on it compared to her Amulet, as though it's worth a lot more than the pendant that grants her powers.

Clutching onto the strap of her bag, Ivy turns.

"You should stay away from him."

This brings her to another stop. "Who?" comes her question, although she has a good guess.

"Mr. Abalos, I mean. I may not know that man well but I keep detecting danger from him."

So now, you choose to help me. Ivy immediately shakes her head at the narrow-minded thought. How pathetic of her to dwell on something so trifling.

"And I know this is six years late but thank you."

Ivy's eyes enlarge slightly, perplexed by Clover's words. What did she just say? She is unable to respond, unable to let Clover know just how worthless she finds that 'thank you', yet is only left to observe Clover's face morph into one of sudden fear. Her eyes have turned to someone else and when Ivy follows her gaze, her breath catches in her throat at the sight of Alvin.

Why has Alvin, of all people, caught Clover's attention, and why is she staring at him in such a way, as though she's just seen a monster?

At a loss for words, Ivy watches Clover hurry away.

She turns just in time to see Athena, Jade, and Isagani finally exiting the classroom. Their brief surprise at Ivy's presence quickly concealed. Athena huffs and scoffs at Isagani before storming off, Jade trailing after her. Isagani nonchalantly shrugs at Ivy as a way of telling her that Athena is only exaggerating. The acting is a little pathetic but Ivy doesn't mind the entertainment. Her attention shifts to the man standing by the door.

They exchange glances, the expression on Ivy's indifferent face indecipherable to the man at first. When Mr. Abalos runs his index finger across his neck with a menacing look out of nowhere, Ivy can't help but shudder a little on the inside. He steps back inside the classroom and hastily shuts the door.

You should stay away from him.

Clover does not need to tell her twice.

When Ivy catches sight of a figure she's been longing to converse with, her peculiar teacher is instantly shoved to the back of her head.

It's the same boy who assisted her yesterday, the same boy who sits next to her in Mr. Abalos' class. . . The same boy who asserted that she was no different from Holders. He's staring back at her when she looks at him. Ivy hates to admit it but a part of her still wonders what he meant with those scathing words. Why was he so brutal? A part of her claims not to care—it continues to dismiss the boy's remarks as mere provocation. But a smaller part of her—the part Ivy wishes would go away already—seeks clarification.

Before Ivy can settle on a choice, the boy begins to approach her. *This could also be a manipulative scheme to throw me off my game,* she thinks immediately. He's a Holder, after all. A cunning, selfish Holder.

When he finally nears her, the boy examines his surroundings, taking into account the eyes that seem to be watching and judging them. Mainly her, of course, but it doesn't take Ivy long to discern the slight discomfort in his narrow eyes. Maybe he doesn't like the attention either.

What has he come to me to do? Ivy knows that by standing there, arms folded, waiting for the boy to say something, anything, she's also gradually missing her second class. The bell hasn't rung the second time yet but she knows there's no way she'd be able to make it to that class—wherever it is—in time. And right now, Ivy frankly doesn't care.

"I want to ask you something," the boy suddenly utters. "But not here." He looks around again, then back at her. "Mr. Zhang's room should still be empty at this time."

He doesn't wait for Ivy to respond. Instead, the boy grabs her arm and starts dragging her across the long school hallway. Only after a small gasp escapes her lips does Ivy keep silent, allowing the boy to maneuver her body through several other students here and there. Does he really want to talk to her or is she just being led into a trap? She remembers this one time when Benecia was invited by this girl for tea only to step into a trap where she was beaten by other Holders that were waiting for her. Ivy ponders over whether it's best to break free from his grasp and walk off while she still can.

Eventually, the boy stops in front of a door. He hesitates for a moment, the same dreary look still melted to his bonny face, before finally reaching forward, twisting the knob, and pushing the door open. "Mr. Zhang is our academy counselor," he informs, though he knows she doesn't care.

"Why did you bring me here?"

Ivy finds the sound of his chuckle a little disdainful.

"I thought that was fairly obvious. It makes me uncomfortable having that much attention on me."

"Or perhaps, it just makes you uncomfortable being around me," Ivy bites back with a roll of her eyes. When the boy doesn't respond, she knows it's her turn to mock him. "Ah, so you're that type of Holder. So obsessed with what other people think of you, huh? Quite piteous."

"I don't want to be troubled. Is that so wrong?" he says.

Ivy is a bit surprised to see him so calm. She knows of many Holders that would have already lost control and broken down into a fit of rage, throwing out whatever insult that comes to mind.

"On the other hand," he carries on, pacing back and forth, "I couldn't care less what they think of me being around you. You're a Holder, after all. I won't get into trouble. Well. . ." He pauses. "At least, I shouldn't."

You're a Holder, after all.

Ivy's brows furrow. "Please, do not put me in the same category as those animals."

She gave this some thought, especially while burying the man in the village. She knows that as soon as she accepted the Golden Amulet as her own, she would no longer be a Powerless. Adora told her she had no power as a Powerless and that angered her. It angered her and it still does because she knows it's true. In order to stand a fair chance at taking down the enemy, she must don the same object that has been causing this war since the very beginning. But no way will Ivy accept being called a Holder.

"Answer me this. What did you mean back then when you claimed I was no different?"

But the boy only responds with yet another question. "Have you come back for justice or vengeance?"

Ivy's answer is quick. "Both."

"Vengeance on every Holder?"

"On every natural Holder, yes." She thinks about it before adding, "And some unnaturals."

Unnatural Holders may not possess the same fortune as the naturals but they are, at least, relieved of the burden of getting beaten or unjust execution. As soon as a Powerless transforms into a Holder, their past as an ungifted being is immediately forgotten. But Ivy will never forget—the Powerless will never forget.

When they get their Amulet, unnatural Holders take one of two paths. Some of them retain a steadfast connection to their past sufferings and covertly aid the Powerless whenever possible. Others, however, succumb to the corrupting influence of the natural Holders, adopting their malevolent ways. The latter are the ones Ivy yearns to punish.

"And that right there is exactly what I meant when I said you were no different," the boy says. "It's just as my mother said. While seeking revenge, dig two graves—one for yourself."

"I suppose your mother didn't know any better, then. Sometimes, you have to be louder, create some chaos, in order to be heard. I learned that the hard way."

"First of all, never speak of my mother that way!" His voice is calm and low but forbidding. "All you do is prove me right, Ivy. You don't even try to hide your immorality either."

"Immorality?" Stunned, Ivy freezes in her tracks, smoldering with resentment. How dare this boy state that she's no better than those unsympathetic Holders out there? Is she hearing this right? She's no better than the same beasts that would repeatedly assault her people? "What a wooden-headed boy you must be. Obviously, it seems you have very poor judgment. Or are you only speaking nonsense because you're afraid that your people's end is near?"

"You came back for vengeance, did you not? Well, the best revenge is to not be like your enemies and you're already failing at that."

"I'm not like them!" Ivy insists. The sudden raise of her voice stuns her. Not only did she practically scream back at the boy but the emotion behind her voice could be effortlessly detected. Anger.

Oh, no, no, no. Did she just get provoked?

Did she just falter?

Ivy mentally slaps herself as she watches the boy exit the room after a scoff. Did she not learn a thing from her training with Adora? All those hours the woman invested teaching her the importance of patience, even in the face of triggering circumstances—did she forget her lessons?

But he had no right to insult me like that!

No, your reaction was unwarranted.

But—

Ivy, Adora talked to you about this!

Before she thought the boy to be someone worth listening to but that was a blatant error. The boy is just like the rest. Arrogant, caviling, and undoubtedly not worth her time. He doesn't get to judge her.

Especially when he knows nothing about her.

word count • 4948

12 | Fragility

CHAPTER TWELVE — FRAGILITY

A boy is watching her the moment she steps out of Mr. Zhang's room.

He's in her class as well, a boy about an inch taller than Reuben, with a curly undercut. The moment her eyes land on him, he turns away but it's too late. Ivy has already caught him.

Yet she thinks nothing of it. The boy is only one of many.

In an instant, he leaves her mind as she concentrates on the new task at hand. Finding her next class. Yesterday's trip to the Royal Palace may have been worthwhile but Ivy also lost out on a great opportunity. While she wanders about like a lost hound, students bustle about her as though they have been attending this academy for years. As if she isn't already late enough. Perhaps, she should have followed that wooden-headed boy since they share the same teachers but Ivy was in a bit of a daze for a while after the unexpected little argument with him. When she stepped out of Mr. Zhang's room, he was, by that time, gone.

After another minute of walking down the hallway in search of a familiar face, she exhales with relief when her eyes catch Poppy's friend, Ga-Eul, leaving a room. But from the smug look on Ga-Eul's face, Ivy instantly realizes that something is going on. Only when she nears the room the boy ran out of and picks up the strange sounds of another whimpering does she finally understand what that something is.

It's another pupil from her class, round black-rimmed spectacles over his glistening teary deep-set eyes, a line between his perfect thick eyebrows, and a hand pressed against his plum lips, struggling to suppress his sniffles and whimpers. What Ivy walks into is a boy sobbing on the dirty floor of a janitorial closet.

Ga-Eul... What did he do to him?

"Hey, Are... Are you alright?"

But as soon as the spectacled boy realizes he's been seen in such a state, he swiftly swipes his sleeve over his eyes, stands up, and dashes past Ivy without a word. Ivy's grip on her paper tightens as she watches the boy hastily make his way across the hall, bumping into one student after another.

Only after she catches sight of Poppy herself does Ivy relax. Millions of Holders may despise her but the petite doe-eyed girl seems friendly enough. Ivy has been keeping an eye on her in class—not that she means to, but she can't help it either. It's not like the girl is going to be of much help yet there's something about her that piques Ivy's interest.

"I don't suppose you know what that was about, huh?" Poppy says. When Ivy stays silent, Poppy sighs and her shoulders drop. "I honestly have no idea what Ga-Eul has against that poor boy. Then again, we've only been friends for a few days and his private affairs are not my problem."

Poppy's eyes shift down to the schedule in Ivy's hand and chuckles. "You're searching for Mrs. Singh's class, aren't you?" She waves a hand back and forth as she begins to walk, motioning for the older to follow. "Well, hurry, then. We're already late."

By now, the hallways are bare with the exception of monitoring guards. Ivy wonders why Poppy isn't already in class. She also can't help but notice how much Poppy seems to be in her own little world as they walk. Something could be bothering her but Ivy doesn't care enough to ask.

By the time they eventually reach the correct class, every other student that has already arrived is exiting the room with an older woman walking along behind them. She casts a look of displeasure toward Poppy and Ivy for their tardiness, regardless, with her concentration settled on someone else, Ivy doesn't bat an eye.

Reuben Kang.

So, that is the disreputable boy's name. Ivy overheard another boy calling for him.

Such a wicked heart that boy possesses.

Tempted to figure out why he said such harsh words earlier, Ivy observes him from time to time. It appears pathetic and it is. At least, she thinks so. In fact, another girl called her out on it, making a sudden bold claim that she is interested in him.

"I mean, look at him!" the girl even added.

Her classmate is absolutely wrong. Everything about that boy screams repulsive.

At the same time, Ivy can't help but find herself a bit intrigued. Is the boy truly out of his mind or does he have a good reason for comparing her to those reprehensible Holders out there? If so, what could that reason be? He claimed she was just as bad because of her plans for vengeance but Ivy still doesn't see how.

Despite the dirty looks she keeps sending Ivy's way, this next teacher is a lot more. . . bearable than Mr. Abalos. The woman is able to capture Ivy's full attention with just a couple of words: "We're going outside." And once they are out there in a vast field not too far from the academy, the woman makes the class sit in a circle before clarifying that she prefers to teach outside where there is more space and nature encircling them.

"My name is Mrs. Singh," she says, standing tall in a snow-white chemise with the strap of a black purse over her shoulder. "I teach my students how to attack and defend using their powers."

"You can't attack with every ability, Mrs. Singh," Athena chips in. Unnecessarily, in Ivy's opinion. "For instance, Poppy's Healing."

"Maybe not." The woman nods. "However, you can undoubtedly protect yourself with every ability." She sends Poppy a small knowing smile. "Even Healing. You just have to get creative sometimes."

The response piques Poppy's interest instantly. "How so?"

"All will be answered when the time comes," says Mrs. Singh, sitting herself down in the middle of the circle. "Everyone understands why this academy opened, correct?"

"Yes, to train us," Isagani answers. "This way, if Outsiders come back, at least, we're well prepared to fight back."

There is that term again. Ivy wonders if Adora knew anything about the Outsiders. If she did, she would have informed her, right?

"Fight back and defend," their teacher adds immediately. "There are those that can't fight, such as children, so it's our duty to protect them."

Ivy's breath hitches when Reuben opens his mouth to speak. Back then, he looked almost smug as he insulted her. Now, his expression has altered back to distress, almost as if that is his everyday look.

"But the academy is still giving out positions, right?"

"Yes, of course," Mrs. Singh nods. "This academy is the same as every other. If you do well during your time here, you'll be rewarded with a gainful job, and if you don't, well, you either don't get a job at all or you get stuck with a very poor one. Nonetheless, the main purpose of it is to train you for the Outsiders."

These Outsiders, it seems, are a group of individuals, not well-regarded and likely originating from another kingdom, that will not leave Arya alone. A war may be coming. Now, Ivy's concern lies in determining whether this impending war will hinder or advance her scheme.

Perhaps, the involvement of the Outsiders could expedite the downfall of Arya.

"So, what are we doing out here?" Jade questions.

"Good question. Before I come to that, however, everyone, stand and form a bigger circle." As she gives out her instructions, the woman rises from the ground and pulls out a whistle from her black purse. "Make sure the circle is big enough for a fight in the middle."

While everyone obeys and takes several steps back, Mrs. Singh scans the class before pointing to a pupil at random. It's the same spectacled boy caught sobbing minutes ago. "Come out in the middle," she orders in her gruff voice. The boy gives a small nod, awkwardly adjusts his spectacles, and walks out of his spot.

"I will now call upon another student," the woman announces. "Both selected Holders will battle until there's one winner. The loser will go back to their spot and I will call upon a third to come fight the winner. This will carry on until everyone has fought. . . Or until we run out of time."

Almost like the Powerless Tournament. Ivy's breath trembles as she exhales. The remembrance of that perilous competition persists, refusing to vacate her thoughts.

"In order to assess your abilities and evaluate your performance in combat, it is imperative that I observe your approach to both attacking and defending against opponents. By doing so, I can ascertain your strengths and weaknesses, with the ultimate goal of assisting you in eliminating the latter," their teacher adds. "You only get called upon once. The duration of your participation in the combat circle will be determined by the number of victories you achieve, a metric that I will diligently monitor."

Like a glowing ember in her soul, excitement begins to dance in Ivy's core, a river bubbling through her veins, unlike the feelings that would wash over her when in Mr. Abalos' classroom, and not just because the man gives her the impression of a night slayer. Sitting at her desk, listening to Mr. Abalos talk non-stop about things that do not concern nor interest her half the time gives her too much time to ponder. On one hand, she doesn't mind it as it presents her with the chance to think more about her scheme, yet on the other hand, her nightmarish daydreams often love to take over.

"Mrs. Singh, I would love to go against him!" Ga-Eul shouts out of nowhere, swinging his arms urgently and aggressively.

Concluding that his idea is sound, their teacher nods. Ivy isn't certain but she swears she sees a tinge of menace in Ga-Eul's elated eyes. There's something about fighting the timid spectacled boy that seems to elevate his mood. Ga-Eul is already cracking his knuckles as he steps inside the circle, his eye contact with his opponent strong. Ivy is, at once, thrown back to the little fight she chanced upon and ponders over what the reasoning behind it could be.

Perhaps, the both of them have known each other from a young age and have had a feud since then. Or perhaps, Ga-Eul is just another scourge who loves to prey on the weak.

Seconds later, Ivy shakes her head. Whatever issues these two boys have with each other is none of her business. She can't afford to get distracted, especially over such a trifling matter. Instead, she drags her focus back to Mrs. Singh, and watches as the woman raises the whistle to her thin lips.

It's not only Mrs. Singh who keeps track of everyone's strengths and weaknesses. While the rest of the class observes the fight for mere entertainment, Ivy's face remains serious.

The fight between the boys does not last long at all. In fact, it ends quicker than it started and whether that may be because the spectacled boy is too weak or Ga-Eul is simply stronger than she thought, Ivy has yet to figure out. It starts with Ga-Eul flashing his opponent a colder stare and perhaps, the spectacled boy made a mistake returning his gaze because in a matter of seconds, he's down on his knees, coughing violently.

What ability did Ga-Eul just employ?

Ga-Eul's towering, muscular frame gives off a formidable appearance. Even now, his opponent struggles to get himself off the ground, his hands grasping onto the grass of the field as desperation gleams in his dark shattered eyes. In a way, the spectacled boy reminds Ivy of the Powerless that would fall to their knees and continually beseech Holders for mercy.

Mrs. Sing blows the whistle as soon as she sees no point in furthering the fight.

"I fear for whoever is going up against Ga-Eul next," Poppy comments with a toothy smile. "His Dehydration is both astounding and terrifying."

Ga-Eul folds his arms, displaying and silently boasting his slight muscles with a proud grin. From the corner of her eyes, Ivy catches Isagani rolling his.

As if just remembering that his opponent is still down on his knees, his body weakened and his face pallid, Ga-Eul raises a palm and on top of it, a glass of water formulates in a blink of an eye out of thin air. With the glass in hand, the boy approaches his opponent.

He toys with the spectacled boy at first, shifting the glass away anytime his opponent makes a reach for it and moving it toward him when the boy looks like he's on the brink of giving up. Only when Mrs. Singh calls him out on it does Ga-Eul end the childish game and eventually hands the drink over.

Dehydration and Water Generation? Ivy should have known. Ga-Eul owns a White Amulet, after all. The powers he possesses are not only marvelous but beneficial as well.

As Ga-Eul makes his way back to the middle of the circle, his opponent watches him fiercely. Perhaps, he's angry that he lost the match, Ivy guesses. But as she proceeds to study the spectacled boy further, she finds it difficult to look over the possibility that it could be so much more than that. There isn't anger in the boy's eyes. The look he has is almost. . .disquietude. Wounded, maybe.

"Hmm. . . How about you next?" Mrs. Singh has just finished praising Ga-Eul's performance and lamenting the fight's early conclusion without the spectacled boy displaying any of his abilities. Now, her eyes are on another student, one that Ivy assumes is just as timid as the spectacled boy due to how quiet she's been.

"M-Me?" the girl splutters.

"Yes, you." Mrs. Singh shifts her gaze from the newly chosen pupil to Ga-Eul before returning to the girl. Her squared face cracks a mischievous smile. "What's your name?"

"G-Gisella."

"I do love to pick on the quiet ones first," their teacher admits smugly. "From what I've learned as a teacher, it's always the withdrawn students that have a lot to show. Gisella, you've caught my attention. I want to see what you're made of."

Although the second fight is yet to begin, Gisella's forehead is already perspiring. Ivy can imagine her heart threatening to burst forth from her ribcage. Her eyes dart around, pupils dilated, clearly searching for an escape route. Behind their trainer, Ga-Eul clasps a hand over his mouth, stifling a mocking laugh. It's one thing giving a presentation in front of a class but fighting another student, especially one that seems so imposing and self-assured in their abilities? Ivy can understand her panic. Seconds pass and just when most of them believe she's going to refuse, Gisella sucks in a breath and takes a trembling step forward.

Once again, Mrs. Singh brings the whistle to her lips and blows.

WHOOSH!

Not a second goes by before the entirety of Gisella's figure vanishes into thin air, almost as if she was never there, to begin with. Several eyes search the area but the girl is nowhere to be seen. Even Ga-Eul is puzzled and speechless, his knees bent and face turning from left to right, awaiting his opponent's appearance. He can't use Dehydration on his rival if he can't see them, Ivy notes.

Has Gisella vacated? Ivy assumes it to be the case. Perhaps, she couldn't handle the strain and teleported out of the field. That could be one of her skills. The color of Gisella's Amulet has already escaped Ivy's memory.

Just before Mrs. Singh can blow the whistle again to end the fight that never began, Ga-Eul's body falls to the ground out of the blue. Something—or someone—is on top of him. From his irrepressible gagging and the way his body is flattened into the grass, it's clear to tell Gisella has her arms securely around his neck.

How intelligent, Ivy gasps lightly in awe, to attack while unseen.

Or maybe, she thought too soon. Straight away, Ga-Eul proves to be quick on his feet and reaches a hand over his shoulder, yanking onto something imperceptible. To every other individual, it's as though he's fighting air but they are all further reminded of his opponent's presence once she lets out a startled screech. Ga-Eul must have gripped onto a delicate area of her body, perhaps her ear or her hair. The boy could have even accidentally poked her in the eye. There is really no way of telling, for sure.

When Ga-Eul understands he isn't as tightly bound as he once was, a flicker of hope gleams in his desperate eyes and he tugs whatever he is gripping onto harder, earning a louder yelp from Gisella. Although not a single part of her can be seen, the girl's despairing attempt at yanking Ga-Eul's hand away is easily apprehended. Before they know it, her overanxious voice comes into earshot.

"O-Okay, okay, I give up. I-I give up!"

Mrs. Singh frowns, as does every other student. "What?"

Gisella's body finally takes shape as Ga-Eul reluctantly lets go, and her nervous eyes stare back at the judgmental ones of her classmates. "I said I give up."

"What an idiot you are!" Mrs. Singh thunders, and Ivy can't help but agree. "You should all know better than to give up. You could have even won."

"It's over, a-alright?" Gisella insists, backing away from Ga-Eul the first opportunity she gets, her steps sluggish. "Besides, this is all practice, isn't it?"

Mrs. Singh stays silent for a moment, having somewhat of a staring battle with the girl before Gisella glances away with flushed cheeks. "May I at least know your reason?"

But Gisella can only swallow hard, fumblingly smoothening her tiered plain green skirt.

Their teacher finally nods. "Alright, you're correct. Training hasn't officially begun, which means I haven't started grading you yet. But do remember that once it does begin, you cannot be pulling this stunt unless you want to fail my class."

"I'll keep that in mind."

Even then, Mrs. Singh refuses to let it slide. "Do you really believe the Outsiders are going to be merciful? That they're going to stop just because you say you give up?" Now, her face has turned crimson and she's screaming at the entire class. "Your goal is to be the protectors of Arya, that is why we're training you. If you had no interest in fighting, why, then, are you even here? Why waste our time?"

Gisella's shoulders slump and her eyes glisten. She dares not look the woman in the eyes.

"Let this be the first and last time!" After shooting the trembling girl one last captious glare, Mrs. Singh turns away and carries on with her process of choosing another student.

This time, Ivy pays no attention to her selection. As she watches Gisella return to her spot around the circle, she contemplates what the girl's reasoning could be. Surely, there must be one, right? But in the end, all Ivy can come up with is that Gisella simply backed down out of a sense of impending defeat. She hopes Gisella realizes that behaving in such a cowardly manner makes her look more like a fool than losing a stupid fight.

When Ivy's attention returns to the middle of the circle, her eyes are quick to enlarge at the sight of the boy their trainor has chosen next. It is none other than Reuben himself.

"Well, the best revenge is to not be like your enemies and you're already failing at that."

Unconsciously clenching her hands as she fixes her vigilant eyes on the boy, Ivy exhales slowly. Reuben's quiet and lethargic demeanor makes it obvious why Mrs. Singh chose him.

Ga-Eul and Reuben are diametrically opposed to one another. While Ga-Eul is prepared to engage in combat with a challenging stare fixed on his face, Reuben, on the other hand, looks like he's silently wishing Mrs. Singh selected another pupil rather than him.

The woman waits for the fighters to face each other before blowing her whistle for the fourth time. She may not know what Reuben's powers are—many of the students here do not, aside from his Invulnerability that was used in a certain presentation—but Ivy is fully aware, and she realizes straight away that unless Ga-Eul has another power other than Dehydration, this fight may not go anywhere. Reuben and Ga-Eul as rivals may only result in a never-ending battle. Ivy is sure of it.

Ga-Eul stares studiously into Reuben's eyes. Reuben stares back. Seconds pass. Nothing. Mrs. Singh and the class wait for the fight to begin but Ivy knows it started the moment the staring commenced.

"W-What kind of power are you using?" Ga-Eul demands, bug-eyed with eyebrows knitted into a deep frown. "How are you not drained yet? You should be feeling dehydrated."

After those words, Ivy confirms two things. Ga-Eul can use his Dehydration several times a day. Reuben's Invulnerability also works for the inside of his body.

"Oh?" Isagani sneers. "Looks like Ga-Eul has finally met his match."

"Shut up!" Ga-Eul snarls, his focus never leaving Reuben. "It'll only be a matter of time."

"I don't think what you're doing is working," Clover comments.

Ga-Eul finally stops and turns to look at their trainor. "Impossible. H-He's—"

"Immune?" A smile dances on Mrs. Singh's lips as she finishes his thought, displaying an air of admiration. "Is it perhaps. . . Invulnerability?" she asks Reuben. "I find that power quite remarka—"

WHACK!

A scream sounds from Ga-Eul.

Gasps sound. Eyes widen. In front of them is Ga-Eul, in a state of pain, no longer standing as his knees give way and collapses to the ground. One of his hands is pressed against his bleeding forehead and a rock, stained with his blood, lies nearby. The same rock Reuben picked up and threw out of nowhere.

"W-What was that for?!" the injured boy hisses through the pain.

Reuben approaches the rock. Ivy is certain she isn't the only one who catches his fingers trembling as he picks the small weapon up.

When Poppy enters the circle to help out her wounded friend, Mrs. Singh is quick to stop her, demanding she returns to her spot and allows the fight to proceed.

Reuben presses a hand against Ga-Eul's neck, just effective enough to prevent him from rising. However, before he can strike Ga-Eul's forehead with the rock again, Mrs. Singh blows her whistle.

"I can see the terror in your eyes, Ga-Eul," the woman states, pointing to an empty spot around the circle. "You already lost the moment you grew afraid."

"I had no idea we could use any tactic against our opponent!" Ga-Eul urges, shoving Reuben away once he releases his grip. "Otherwise, I would have smashed his head first."

But Mrs. Singh disregards the angry boy. "Fantastic quick thinking," she says to Reuben, who, once again, remains silent. "On the other hand, it makes me wonder if Invulnerability is the only power you wield."

Ivy isn't sure if her words are meant to be insulting and telling from the puzzled look on Reuben's face, she sees she's not the only one.

"I already know who I want net inside the circle," Mrs. Singh declares, and with unwavering certainty, she turns to a student standing on the opposite side of where Ivy is. Their teacher must have prior knowledge of this pupil because she addresses the chosen student by her full name. "Calliope Era, please step out."

The girl selected next for combat exhibits a quiet demeanor, yet her eyes scream noxious. Her deadly gaze, devoid of any other expression, fixates upon Mrs. Singh and her opponent. Had she not been trained prior to her return, Ivy knows an unsettling sensation would surely overcome her. She almost fears for Reuben.

Almost.

As both fighters converge upon her, Ivy's line of sight is limited to observing only half of their faces. Before Mrs. Singh can blow her whistle, the staring competition between Reuben and Calliope begins.

But Reuben shouldn't have stared back.

Ivy immediately understands this the moment the look on his face alters all of a sudden. Whatever power Calliope is using must work in a similar way as Ga-Eul's Dehydration. Despite his desire to avert his gaze, Reuben finds himself unable to do so. The slight, repetitive shaking of his head and visible struggle to disengage from his position are telltale signs of Calliope's control over him. If only Ivy could see what power the boy's rival wields. At this point, she despises surprises.

Calliope never moves out of her spot either, indicating that her power is not of a physical nature. That is the only undeniable fact Ivy has gathered thus far. While everyone else struggles to comprehend Calliope's tactics, Reuben finds himself ensnared in her grasp.

Then, out of nowhere, Reuben's hand shoots up to cover his mouth, emitting a faint whimper. Mind Control? Ivy guesses again, tapping the tip of her foot against the ground with intrigue. She's not sure of that speculation but Calliope's Black Amulet is beaming and Mind Control came first in everyone's head. Aside from Mrs. Singh. The woman wears a knowing grin, suggesting she understands exactly what Calliope is doing to Reuben.

When Reuben falls to his knees, overwhelmed by his emotions, the atmosphere within the circle becomes increasingly uncomfortable. But that is also when Ivy eventually unravels it all.

Calliope is making him see something that isn't actually there.

Whether this manipulation is part of Mind Control or not, it is undeniably happening and it does not take the others in the circle to realize it. What could she be making him see? Whatever it is, it must be strong enough, brutal enough, to weaken him so much that he'd break into sobs. From the moment he looked into Calliope's dark, uninviting eyes, Reuben never even stood a chance.

And then, the whistle blows.

word count • 4326

13 | sanctimony

CHAPTER TWELVE — SANCTIMONY

MINUTES after an unavailing search for the boy, Ivy finds herself seated at one of the pristine tables inside the academy's large dining hall. As numerous students form a line for their turn to buy their meals, the young girl leans against her chair, gazing intently at the ceiling while pondering over Reuben Kang's actions, as well as hers. Why did he run?

And why did she search for him?

Did Reuben go home? If he couldn't handle the stares he got from his fellow classmates, then he must have. How contemptuous these people can be. But what did he see? What image that frightening girl put before his eyes could have been so troubling that it caused him to dash off? This question can't leave Ivy's head no matter how much she attempts to place her thoughts on something else. She was so certain that the boy is just another manipulative Holder yet, is there a possibility she could have been wrong?

Is Reuben even a natural Holder?

"Aren't you going to eat something?"

When she picks up the familiar soft voice, Ivy gradually turns her head to face the petite owner. Poppy spares her no second glance as she takes a seat on the opposite side of the long table, gently setting her tray down while she is at it. With every fiber of her being, Ivy refrains from licking her lips at the sight of the delectable dishes. But her stubborn stomach is soon to fail her, rumbling audibly within seconds.

On one side of the girl's tray are bowls of white rice and Filipino-style chicken adobo. A plate with a small slice of cassava cake rests on the other side. Very expensive meal, Ivy figures, and to stop herself from going crazy over the rich and mouth-watering aroma of every single meal that fills her nostril, she repeatedly reminds herself of the plan she's made to head to the market later. Astoria is sure to cook up a delicious bite to eat with the ingredients she purchases, whether it be something as simple as porridge.

"Get the rose pudding," Poppy offers. "It's low-prized. Just one opal." She must think Ivy can't afford the overpriced meals served here.

"I'm not hungry," Ivy mumbles. If it wasn't for the fact every student is required to stay in the dining hall during this certain time, she wouldn't be here at all. She's the only one seated without a tray and Ivy is sure Athena will ridicule her for this sometime later.

She's not wealthy but Ivy isn't poverty-stricken either. Before she passed, Adora gifted her with a number of jewels, knowing the young girl would need as many as she could get her hands on during her elaborate scheme. Ultimately, Ivy came to understand that every little thing her mentor received from the Golden Amulet—whether it be ingredients, tapestries, or jewels—was only handed to her because she wished for them. Adora made sure to use the Ten Wishes the Golden Amulet granted to her advantage.

This is why Ivy has a sack of jewels resting in a hidden room she found inside the dead man's little torn-apart shelter. Yet she loves to play poor—not for pity but so she would be underestimated.

According to what Adora informed her, the power of Ten Wishes will always automatically reset once a new being becomes the owner of the Golden Amulet. But the pendant is selective. Not every wish gets granted. Even now, Ivy is still yet to make her first. Just as she wants to ensure that the wishes she makes benefit not just her but the Powerless as a whole, Ivy refuses to spend any of her jewels unless necessary. And buying a meal in the academy is not necessary. She doesn't have a job and right now, she's not intending on getting one either. Her head is far too concentrated on other plans, therefore, the jewels she currently owns are sure to run low if she's careless with them. Not to mention, Benecia's family already promised her food at least once every week, no matter how many times she declined due to her immense guilt.

"Are you not afraid of starving to death?" Poppy smiles. Yet rather than the mocking grin Ivy anticipates, it appears sweet and a bit of concern seems to linger in the girl's doe eyes.

"The human body can survive up to twenty days without food," Ivy responds with indifference. "I'm not worried at all."

Poppy's gaze lingers on her for a while, her concern now accompanied by pity. Ivy grimaces at the sight. She watches as Poppy shifts her chair back and rises, her fingers reaching for the small pink purse she placed down beside her tray. The younger returns to the lengthy line, leaving Ivy alone once again.

Only then does Ivy become aware of a series of snickers sounding behind her. Swiftly turning around, she comes across a small group of girls that abruptly cease their giggles as soon as her eyes meet theirs. Her lips curve into a threatening sneer.

"If you've got something to say," she taunts, "stop being cowards and say it to my face."

One of the girls pauses mid-bite, rolls her eyes, and retorts, "Oh, we've got plenty to say. But why waste our breaths on a miserable witch like you?"

Ivy's eyebrows raise. "Do any of you not grasp how peculiar that sounds? Waste your breaths on me? I've been the only thing on your mind since yesterday. Your speaking ill of me behind my back proves it. Again, cowards."

"You better watch that filthy mouth, Eun Calinao!" the girl seated in the middle almost rises as she points a finger at their foe. "Don't think you're well protected just because you possess the Golden Amulet. It'll only be a matter of time before your deceased body is dragged to the Pits of Death, and I, for sure, cannot wait."

"Is there a problem here, ladies?"

With her eyes and ears centered on the laughable girls, Ivy failed to notice Poppy approaching them. The delicate girl is holding onto a second tray, topped with cabbage chowder, rose pudding, and napkins, this time. She must have cut to the front of the line.

"I knew you to be sweet, Poppy," one of the girls begins again with a hint of disdain on her arrogant face, "but willingly being around her? I expected better from you. How are your parents going to feel knowing you've become friends with the same girl that challenged the Royals?"

"Keep your nose out of my life," Poppy scorns. Disregarding the girls' captious expressions and continuous insults, she sits down and slowly shifts the tray she is holding toward Ivy.

"What's this?" Ivy folds her arms, her eyebrows knitted into puzzlement.

"You need to eat something." Poppy reaches for her spoon while she speaks, avoiding eye contact as though a bit of her is embarrassed. "The training in this academy isn't going to be easy at all, especially when you're going through them on an empty stomach."

But Ivy pushes the tray back with a scowl. "I don't need your food."

Mortifyingly enough, her stomach chooses to grumble just right after her rancorous response. Poppy chuckles, her slight uneasiness fading as amusement takes over.

"Won't you just have a bite of that, at least?" She points to the small slice of bread resting in the cabbage chowder. "Have a bite of anything, Ivy."

After wavering for what seems like forever, she eventually picks up the spoon on the tray and cautiously pokes at the pudding, as if expecting it to explode in her face at any moment.

"Oh, please!" Poppy rolls her eyes as a small giggle leaves her mouth. "I didn't poison the food if that's what you're so concerned about. Eat. You'll regret it later if you don't."

Ivy would disagree but. . . free food.

She scoops a very small portion of the chowder and brings it to her lips. "Don't think that we're all of a sudden friends because of this, Poppy." She glances away from Poppy's brief flushed cheeks, opens her mouth, and places the portion on her tongue.

When was the last time she tasted such a high-priced delectable meal?

Ivy and her dear friends constantly spoke of earning enough jewels to buy anything they desired one day, but they often found it difficult to even earn enough that would keep them alive until the next week, especially when their hard-earned gems were often stolen by Holders. For Benecia and Delyth, their jobs were not as gainful as they always dreamed of. It was mainly onerous for Benecia since she had a whole family that depended on her jewels as much as she did. Delyth didn't have a family, at least, not anymore, but she worked in such a dishonest area where the Holders would never pay her what she truly earned. Nevertheless, Delyth was not permitted to argue about it. Beggars can't be choosers, after all.

Ivy's employment as a maid was only possible thanks to the Calinaos. Her adoptive parents ensured she worked in a wealthy area where

Holders were always willing to pay big for cleaning something as small as a table, and just at the thought of gaining so many jewels for each household she cleaned, Ivy couldn't help but rejoice and fill her friends' ears with the tremendous news. While unaware of the fact her parents had a different plan for the jewels she made. For every bag Ivy earned, she was to give her parents ninety-eight percent of it—to "help out" with the family, they said—and two percent was hardly enough to buy the meals or anything else the girls yearned for. Of course, they could save up but with Alvin and his own set of friends consistently forcing her to hand over every gem she owned, Ivy was left indigent.

When Ivy's gaze returns to Poppy, a sudden realization strikes her. In that moment, she is thrown back to the questions she was contemplating prior to Poppy's arrival. With slight discomfort, Ivy clears her throat, drawing the girl's attention back to her before shifting her half-empty plate of cabbage chowder aside.

"Do you. . . Do you know Reuben well?"

"Reuben?" A tad bit surprised that the boy has been brought up all of a sudden, Poppy leans forward. "No, I don't. Yesterday was the first time I met him. Why do you ask, Ivy?"

But Ivy doesn't answer. "What about that girl?"

"Who?"

"That girl Reuben faced."

"Oh." Poppy pauses for a second before lifting a finger and pointing to something.

Ivy turns and a small gasp leaves her mouth the moment she lays eyes on the same girl that caused Reuben to run.

"You mean her?"

"Yes. Her."

"Her name is Calliope," Poppy starts, tearing her gaze away from the girl and returning to her cassava cake. "I don't know a thing about her either but I'm assuming she possesses the power of Fear Inducement."

"That would make sense." Ivy nods. "She's got a Black Amulet, after all."

"And she looked so terrifying during that fight." Poppy shivers. "Holders of Black Amulets are scary, don't you think? What's scarier is that a lot of them tend to abuse their abilities too."

"Oh, so you admit Holders can be careless with their Amulets?"

"Of course, I do." The corners of Poppy's eyes crinkle. "I don't need to be a Powerless to know that my people are screwed in the head."

And by 'screwed in the head', do you mean the torture they subject my people to? Ivy scoffs a second after her question. Of course, she doesn't. She's a Holder. A natural one, too.

Ivy turns to look at Calliope again. Fear Inducement, huh? Had she been the same girl from three years ago, the thought of having Calliope as a classmate would completely horrify her. But now. . . "Reuben is such a coward," she finds herself saying out loud with a chortle. The same boy that insulted her ran away the first chance he got as though his life entirely depended on it.

"We don't know what Calliope made him see," Poppy argues.

"That does not matter. He's a Holder, after all," comes Ivy's spiteful response, digging her spoon into the rose pudding. "Holders hardly have any fears."

"That's quite audacious of you to say."

Ivy half-shrugs. "I'm not wrong."

"Oh, but you are, Ivy," the petite girl bites back. "Not all Holders are the same, you know. Many of us have fears. Everyone does. Perhaps, we're just better at hiding them than your people."

Ivy places her spoon down with a small huff. "I don't think you understand my definition of fear." She scowls as she wipes her bottom lip with one of the napkins on her tray. "Yes, your people have fears but theirs are more like 'am I going to become wealthy one day?' 'If I wear this dress, will I look like a disgrace at the party?' 'Why is so-and-so becoming more well-known than me?' 'What can I do to get Queen Matilda to adore me more?' That is not the type of fear my people face. The only Holders that truly understand are the unnaturals but sometimes, even they start to forget and give in to your people's wicked ways."

Ivy can still recall the face of an unnatural Holder from when she was much younger. This unnatural, upon receiving an Amulet from a dying woman, made the conscious decision to sever ties with his own family. The man would watch the same people he claimed to love get beaten, listen to their desperate pleas, and not do a thing. Perhaps, Ivy guesses, this sudden behavior stemmed from a profound fear of the potential consequences that would befall him if he was to help his family. The relentless cycle of abuse must have taken its toll on him, of course, and from the moment that pendant became his, he swore he would do anything never to have a hand lay on his body again. It was logical but Ivy still found it inherently cruel.

"Wow." Poppy pauses, a clear look of disbelief drawn on her smooth slim face. "You're wrong about that, Ivy. You're absolutely wrong." Her shoulders drop, wounded eyes staring daggers at the other. "I can't believe you would say such a thing. Holders do face fears. Real fears."

Ivy scoffs. "Do you stand for it, Poppy? The ill-treatment?"

The unexpected query momentarily halts Poppy's train of thoughts. It's as if her head is struggling to process the words. After seconds of stuttering an incoherent answer, her hands involuntarily clench and, making sure to lower the volume of her voice due to the open ears that still surround them, she leans in closer to Ivy and discreetly points to someone new.

"I want you to take a look at that girl over there."

It's Clover. She's pointing at Clover.

"What about her?"

"Do you not see how Clover is sitting all by herself?" Poppy's finger shifts directions, pointing to yet another group of giggling girls, this time. "And do you not see the way they are looking at her with such repulsive eyes, whispering, and cackling amongst themselves? They're not the only ones."

The last time Ivy properly examined the dining hall was to see if Reuben came back to eat. She's never thought to look in Clover's direction. Now that she finally does, she can see Poppy isn't wrong. Although some students are sitting at the same long table as Clover, there exists a significant physical distance between them and her. They make minimal effort to conceal their contempt, often resorting to gestures of mockery and acts of aggression. They're pointing, laughing, throwing any items they can get their hands on at her.

But remarkably, all Clover does is stay calm, her eyes solely focused on the meal before her as if it's the only thing that matters in this godforsaken world.

Ivy can't believe it. This is the same girl that would burst into tears and run off the first chance she got? Clover's composed demeanor is something she never thought she would ever get to witness.

"Why are they treating her like that?"

Before, it was because they believed she was unappealing in sight, however, right now, Clover looks anything but unappealing.

"Clover helps the Powerless," comes Poppy's response, which immediately leaves Ivy frozen. "Her secret was uncovered just two weeks ago. She was caught providing food to a homeless Powerless."

"Her?"

"Yes, her." Poppy chuckles softly at the mix of disbelief and shock Ivy's face has contorted into. "Can you believe it? She's abominated left and right and yet still has the audacity to show her face."

Ivy's eyes dart around the hall searching for confirmation, seeking reassurance that what she's hearing is not just a figment of her imagination. As though some higher power has heed her thoughts, further evidence comes straight away. One student approaches Clover and, with a mere cackle, slaps the girl's meal out of the table. The dishes hit the floor and shatter in an instant. Laughter erupts.

With this much hatred coming from all of them, Clover aiding the Powerless makes sense.

Ivy turns to look at Poppy again. "What does Clover have to do with my previous question?"

Poppy lowers her head, her eyes fixed on her plate. A line has appeared between her round brows. "Clover's courage is something I admire and aspire to have one day. She hasn't left the academy like I would have if I was in her position. But. . . You don't understand, Ivy." She sinks in her seat, her lips pressed together, dismay overtaking her face. "It's difficult. It's really difficult." Her voice quivers.

For Ivy, the laughter in the background has blurred together and vanished, replaced by a hollow silence. There's this look in Poppy's eyes that seems as though she longs for an escape, a reprieve from the heavy burden of whatever it is that's stopping her. So perhaps, she may have been a little too fast to judge Poppy. Perhaps, Poppy isn't this sheltered little princess she believed her to be.

Or Poppy could be manipulating her with all this talk about wanting to be just like Clover. After all, she finds it strange that such a well-known girl like her, who's got so much to lose, has chosen to take a seat at the same table as the kingdom's most hated. Poppy speaks about herself like she's some coward but doesn't she realize that sitting with Ivy Pearls is already one of the bravest things one can do? Of course, she does.

Because she's faking all of this nonsense.

"People are saying it'll only be a matter of time before Clover is killed and I fear that's true," the younger carries on when Ivy doesn't say a word. "The Hunter is still alive and well."

"The Hunter?"

Poppy gives a solemn laugh. "You've missed quite a lot, Ivy."

Ivy refrains from chuckling. Poppy is a pretty astounding actor. Well, two can play this game.

She sets her palms down flat on the table, brows drawn together. "Alright yes, I've missed quite a lot, so please, explain to me who this hunter is and why you sound so terrified of him."

"Nobody knows who the Hunter is." Poppy half-shrugs. "All I know is that he's this mysterious figure who's gained infamy for his merciless killings of Holders suspected of betraying the kingdom."

She comes to a sudden pause, staring intently at the table. Right then and there, Ivy can see the look in her eyes morph into unexpected terror. Something seems to have struck a chord with her. Poppy's breathing has even grown uneven, her voice trembling, words stumbling out in disjointed fragments.

"B-betrayed. . . Betrayed. . . T-the kingdom. Oh, my goodness."

"What?" Ivy questions, although in her head, she wonders if this is just another tactic at play. She's not the tiniest bit surprised that such a person exists, but rather by the fact that it is Holders who are being targeted instead of her own people. Nevertheless, she cannot help but be captivated by the fear that has taken hold of Poppy. If this is indeed a meticulously planned endeavor, Ivy has to commend the girl for her acting.

"N-nothing," Poppy splutters, shaking her head. "I just realized something, that's all."

Ivy doesn't buy it for a second. If this Hunter truly has Poppy gripped in terror, then Poppy's concerned eyes tell her much more than she's letting on. But Ivy doesn't push the conversation and turns to look at Clover again. So, she helps the Powerless? Poppy couldn't have lied about that, at least, right?

"There she is!"

An unexpected cry from a student draws the girls' attention away from their current thoughts to the other side of the dining hall. A girl seated at Athena's table, whom Ivy immediately acknowledges as

Akira Ito, has risen from her seat and is pointing rather accusingly at another student who Ivy assumes just entered the room. If not for the fact she recognized the second student at once, Ivy would not have taken any interest in whatever drama Athena and her friends are choosing to cook up this time.

It's Gisella, the same girl who gave up in the middle of a fight with Ga-Eul. The girl's pigtails swing slightly from side to side as she hastily makes her way to the hall's little shop. Although Akira carries on with her judgmental pointing and jesting, the girl pays her no attention. But Ivy can still discern the hurt in Gisella's eyes.

"Wait, I don't understand," Athena cries out. "What did she do?"

Akira noisily clears her throat as though getting ready to deliver a great speech. "I was visiting one of my father's good friends the other day," she begins, more as an announcement for every riveted ear while unable to take her impious eyes off of Gisella who's pulled out a number of jewels from her pocket, "and when I entered his bedroom, I caught this slut lying naked in his bed."

Several gasps sound. Noses crinkle. Mumbles arise. Ivy doubts even five percent of the students in here know who Gisella is but the news is enough to get them mocking. Gisella lowers her head in apparent shame as she hurriedly places her jewels down on the counter and utters something to the academy chef. Even the woman behind the counter, who's turned red, can't help the jeering chortles that fly out of her mouth. Occasionally, she would attempt to suppress them or pass them off as coughs while preparing what Gisella ordered. Ivy knows she is sure to go off gossiping about what she just heard once she's off work.

"How come this is the first time I'm hearing of this?" The corner of Athena's mouth quirks up. "How humiliating. Are you that needy, Gisella?"

"She was really sleeping with your father's friend for jewels?" another one of Athena's friends questions, a look of distaste directed to the center of attention.

"What other reason would there be?" Akira remarks, her lips drawing back into a snarl. "Look at the jewels she's got with her. Those most likely came from him. A revolting slut, that one is."

Gisella swiftly seizes the plate of banana rolls she requested from the woman behind the counter and turns to leave. Yet before she can make it to the door, Akira steps up and blocks her path.

With a derisive snicker, the girl continues, a hand on her jutted waist. "Did you really think I'd allow you to exit so easily? How many more men are you secretly sleeping with for jewels, Gisella? The audacity you have to come back here after doing such a thing. How pathetic."

Right then and there, a new voice emerges, interrupting the tense exchange—a voice that Ivy, still acclimating to its boldness, hardly finds familiar.

"But Akira, your actions, or at least your intentions, are equally if not more pathetic than Gisella's alleged misdeeds."

Athena scoffs. "What do you want, Clover? I advise you to refrain from entangling yourself in this mess. . . Although, I don't think that really matters since things aren't looking good for you either."

"Well, if your friend knows what's good for her, if she doesn't want me to finish the rest of what I have to say, she'd stop pestering Gisella."

Akira merely laughs. "Ah, Clover, you never fail to amuse me, you know that? Just when I think you'd finally stop worsening your situation, you prove me wrong." With folded arms, she gradually begins her way towards Clover, her rotten smile widening by the second. "Why pretend you've got something good to say? To save someone who's clearly in the wrong? Clover, darling, if you know what's good for you, you'd better turn around this instant and stop acting so brave."

"Oh, God." Poppy gulps and lowers her head.

"I do have something good to add." Clover grins, just a few feet away from where Akira is standing. "How did you say you caught Gisella again? Oh, right. You walked into the man's room and saw her lying in his bed. So. . . May I ask what you were doing in that man's bedroom, to begin with?"

Akira's jaw tightens. The question seems to catch her off guard for a moment.

"What would a fetching girl like you be doing in an old bum's bedroom?" Clover pokes her chest once she's near. "You don't do charity work, Akira. . . Unless you were helping him some other way?"

Akira swats her finger away. "If you must know, I was bringing him some baked goods." She turns away from Clover and looks to the eyes staring back at her. "My mother had just finished baking and asked me to send him a basket. Of course, I objected. I wouldn't be caught dead around a man like him. But you know how my mother is. She's too sweet of a woman, you see. When I arrived at his place, he was busy so he asked me to drop the basket off in his bedroom." A small proud smile forms on her face, then. "That's when I caught the slut putting her clothes back on. Any more questions, Clover?"

The teasing smile on Clover's face has yet to fade. "No. . . No more questions." She shakes her head and takes a few steps away from

Akira. "I just find it quite strange that you described the same woman who threw a fit about Mrs. Cao being wealthier than her as sweet."

"My mother is a good woman!"

Ivy scoffs under her breath at the words. Even Holders can confirm that the woman is far from sweet. Mrs. Ito would never take time out of her day to do anything for anyone.

If you're going to lie, at least, make it a good one.

"What are you even trying to prove, Clover?" Athena yells.

"Listen." Displeasure clouds Clover's features as she makes her way over to Gisella, who's stood still as if glued to the floor. "I don't care what you do with your life, Akira." She takes Gisella by the arm. "But don't be such a hypocrite about it."

And with that, both girls walk out of the hall.

word count • 4587

14 | Welcome to Angora

CHAPTER FOURTEEN — WELCOME TO ANGORA

DRIED blood.

A lot happened that day but dried blood is what stuck to Ivy's head the most to this very moment. Dried blood and terror. The terror that overtook Benecia's face. She made an effort not to let it paralyze her but terror stole her words. Terror mounted with every stride she made. Terror stabbed at her heart. Ivy remembers standing near Brightfell River that day with weak knees and a hand clasped over her mouth, her body sweating, weak, and confused. The flowing water and the soft, agonized whimpers that escaped her lips were the only sounds she could hear for several minutes.

And Ivy recalls how wrath replaced Benecia's terror. She was screaming with hot tears welling up in her weary eyes, screaming for retribution or justice—anything that could atone for the horrifying state

Delyth was in. Delyth, the helpless child whose body was sprawled over Benecia's back that day, immobile and covered with dark bruises and dried blood. Perforated by unending anguish, it was difficult for either Ivy or Benecia to consider what could have happened if they had not found the battered girl at the time that they did.

Ivy's anger at the recollection springs to life almost immediately. Her snow-white horse's neighing as she comes to a stop in front of the house they live in is what pulls her back to reality.

Ivy takes a good look at the structure. They must depart as soon as possible. She came to that finalized decision after finding the owner lifeless. Not only does this place give her an uneasy sensation, as if something dreadful is bound to happen at any given moment, but it smells and appears to be in danger of collapsing.

If she wants her plan to go off without a hitch, locating a safer area is a must.

The village of Angora is quiet but there's nothing unusual about that. It is so small that the only seven houses built in it sit so near to each other, impaired. One of the doors opens, and a mother and a little boy step out. The woman, dressed in a filthy white gown and brown shoes, is clutching onto two large baskets with a worn-out leather satchel bag hung over her shoulder. From time to time, she would warn her son to stick close to her while hastily searching through the contents of the bag. She appears to be counting something. "Twenty-two pearls. Four jades. Three ambers." And she would repeat the words over and over again.

Too concentrated on the number of jewels she has inside her bag, the woman loses focus of her surroundings. She doesn't spot the rock right in front of her and almost trips over it. She doesn't notice her son leaving her side once again. And she doesn't see Ivy sitting on her horse, watching her intently.

The little boy approaches Ivy, his mouth wide open. "Is. . . Is that a real horse, ma'am?"

Ivy peels her eyes off the woman and stares at the boy, instead. He is no more than eight years old with ruffled black hair, dressed in a shirt that is far too big for his tiny body and sandals he must have already grown out of squeezing his feet. He isn't wearing any pants—at least, Ivy doesn't think he is—but the massive shirt looks more like a dress on him and covers his bottom. Possibly his father's, Ivy guesses.

"Yes, it's a real horse," she responds. "Would you. . . Would you like to pet her?"

The boy instantly nods and waddles toward the animal. As if on cue, Snow lowers herself to his height, allowing his short arm to reach her head. As he continues to stroke the horse's soft fur, unable to conceal his delight, Ivy observes him. His neck is bare.

No Amulet.

"I've never seen a real horse before," the boy carries on, a grin emerging from his lips. "Actually, wait. . ." He suddenly pauses, directing his gaze to the ground, deep in thought. "I have seen a horse before. Just yesterday. Right here in this village. It was so incredible!"

"You saw a horse yesterday?" Ivy asks as soon as a possibility dawns on her. It could have been the guard's horse—the same guard who murdered the man. Of course, if anyone was home at that time, they would have seen the horse or even spotted the guard's face. But Ivy hasn't thought to ask around, primarily because she doesn't know anyone here.

"It was black and big," says the boy, a great deal of distance between his hands to express how big the horse was. "There was a man on top of it too. It was actually a guard, which is so strange. Nobody ever comes here. I thought he was going to bring us some food but Mama said he'd come to capture us so she made us hide."

I don't suppose he saw the man's face.

"Fenghua?!" a voice edged with fear cries out all of a sudden, tearing Ivy's gaze away from the boy and coming back to his mother. The woman, having just realized that her son is not near her, has let go of both baskets and is dashing toward them, her satchel bag swaying from side to side.

"Fenghua, what did I say about sticking with me?" she snaps, grabbing the boy by the arm and yanking him away from Ivy and Snow.

"I just wanted to see the horse!"

Only then does the woman take a good look at Ivy, surprise and confusion crossing her face at the same time. "I-it's you. Eun Calinao, isn't it? What are you doing here?"

"I think she lives here, Mama," the boy answers for Ivy, his eyes still stuck on Snow.

"W-Why?" the woman interrogates, taking a step back. "What have you come here to do?" Her eyes then shift over to Ivy's shelter, and without giving the girl a chance to properly respond, the woman points a shaky finger at the structure. "Where's Haru? Huh, where is he? Did he agree with you staying here with him?"

"Calm down," Ivy says. The woman doesn't know yet. She may not have been here when the guard came to commit the crime. "I haven't come here to hurt anyone. A-And. . ." She slowly slides off her horse and faces the woman entirely. "The old man's gone."

Realization dawns on the woman's face. "The guard yesterday. . ."

"I-I'm sorry. I possibly should have informed you earlier. I didn't know Haru was close with anyone in this village. He never spoke of anyone else other than his family."

The woman shakes her head. "We weren't that close. We just helped each other out here and there, but that's it." Even so, she is on the brink of tears.

"I haven't come to hurt anyone," Ivy repeats.

"I know. Not us, at least." The woman exhales heavily while fiddling with the strap of her bag. "I suppose... It's just better to steer clear of you." She takes her son's hand again, more gently this time. "I don't want what happened to Haru to happen to me or my son."

Those are her final words to Ivy before she turns and hurries away, dragging the little boy along.

——..∘ ☽ ▫ ☾ ∘..——

Mommy, can I come along?

I want to go outside! Why can't I come? I want to go outside with Big Brother, Daddy, and Uncle.

I want to go outside!

I want to go—!

Ivy's eyes flutter open and for a brief moment, she is unaware of her whereabouts. Her shoulders loosen as soon as her ears pick up Snow's calm neighs coming from outside. In the center of what Haru referred to as the living room, she is perched on a grubby gray ottoman. In front of her is a small table, which is what her head was resting on before she awoke. This is where the man ate his meals, as well as did his vital work. Haru was a writer—or at least, he aspired to become one. Prior to his passing, he enjoyed telling stories to young children in his spare time but hoped to advance in his craft with effort and time.

Ivy sighs, scratching her head. What was that about? This isn't the first time she's had a dream like this one—each more perplexing and overwhelming than the last. In fact, she's already come to a conclusion that perhaps, these aren't just dreams but memories, instead. There is never really anything to view in these sights. All that can be made out is a little girl's plaintive voice, whose identity Ivy is all but certain is her given how close the voice is to one she had years ago. Of course, not that she completely recalls what she sounded like before the age of eight.

Ivy did her utmost to understand these dreams back when she was still fifteen. She never did end up comprehending a single bit of them since every notion she proposed seemed far too absurd. And when she commenced her plan of justice with Adora, her concentration slipped from the memories every day. Even when she awoke breathing heavily from a new vision, Ivy never cared enough to figure it out. Adora and the plan were the only things that truly mattered to her.

Until now.

It is a particular name that leaves her frozen on the ottoman for a few seconds. Big Brother.

She has a brother? Not Alvin, of course. At least, she hopes the little girl in her dream isn't referring to someone as treacherous as Alvin. And who in the world is Uncle? Another vexed sigh falls out of Ivy's mouth.

Is the woman in her dreams her mother? Her. . . biological mother?

It was at thirteen that Ivy learned she could not remember a single thing from when she was younger than eight. One rainy day, she, Benecia, and Delyth were seated in Benecia's tiny bedroom, discussing their favorite childhood memories. When it got to her turn, Ivy had absolutely nothing to share and not because all her memories from a young age were terrible but simply because she couldn't recall any one of them—not even the faces of her biological parents or siblings she may have.

Ivy knows she was adopted when she was eight years old. She finds it a little strange that while she can clearly recall waking up in Liezel Calinao's arms, everything before is vague, as if she hadn't lived until that point. Ever since her adoptive family realized she never received her Amulet, they never stopped reminding her how much regret they had for picking her up by the riverbank. According to what they said, Ivy had been wrapped in a blanket and sleeping in a large oval basket.

It was clear as spring water that someone had deliberately left her there.

Someone abandoned her.

Ivy rises from the ottoman and, in an effort to divert her thoughts from her perplexingly unknown childhood and upsetting adoptive family, her mind travels back to what was troubling her before she stepped inside the structure. If anyone is to ever ask her about a particular moment in her life that she recalls in its entirety despite having occurred so long ago, Brightfell River springs to mind first. Delyth's beaten body haunted her day and night after Brightfell River. It still does.

She often muses over what would have occurred if Delyth didn't go investigating Gozar Agulto. Would her dear friends still be alive? Maybe not, given that at the time Gozar was angry and afraid at the mere thought of someone figuring out and spreading the news of the cruel business he covertly ran. But she would have, at the very least, had more time with them. If only Delyth didn't go farther than what was safe for her. Yes, Ivy adored her friend for her courage when it came to unearthing the truth yet it was also that same courage that got both her and Benecia killed.

"I found her like this."

Benecia wept more than her that day. Her friend was panting like a hound. She clutched at her chest, fingers trembling as if trying to keep her racing heart from jumping out of her body.

"I was on my way here when I found her body hidden behind a rock. That's not it, Ivy. The rock wasn't just anywhere. It was near Gozar's cave. I heard the sound of men laughing."

Delyth did not die that day. She was killed the next, along with Benecia who supposedly assisted her with the 'crimes' the guards claimed the girls committed.

Ivy walked inside Delyth's house early that morning after a rushed breakfast on the eleventh of March only to be greeted with two deceased bodies—one lying on a bedroom floor upstairs and the second downstairs near the kitchen entrance. There was blood everywhere. At first, Ivy was not even sure if the remains belonged to the same girls she'd seen just the other day since their faces were mangled to bits.

It wasn't just the horrid sight that almost made her pass out but the foul smell as well. Flies had already gathered around the two bodies. Yesterday night. That had to have been when this happened. Benecia had offered to stay with Delyth and keep her company. She let her family know that she would return the next morning, and because her adoptive parents never allowed her anywhere aside from work, Ivy couldn't join them.

Before, Ivy was too much in shock and agony to make complete sense of what happened. Gozar massacred them—he had to have. She knows it was him. The smug look on his revolting face as he watched the bodies get pulled out of the house said it all. The girls managed to find out his secret but before they could share it with the kingdom, the merciless man silenced them. Guards only found the bodies because she screamed for help. In fact, each one of the men seemed startled at the sight. They hardly knew Benecia and Delyth. So, how then could they claim that it was because of some broken rules that left them in that state?

They would have told Ivy not to worry, that they were going to figure out who did such a thing if the girls were Holders. No, instead, they stood down because Gozar ordered them to. They fabricated that entire story because Gozar ordered them to. Everything was done under Gozar's orders as if he was the King of Arya himself. Being close friends with the Royals sure has its perks.

On the day Benecia discovered Delyth's body near Gozar Agulto's concealed cavern, she told Ivy of her decision to gather her entire family and flee the kingdom, and despite Ivy's attempt to caution her about the dangers of the wild, Benecia adamantly refused to be dissuaded. In fact, that particular day marked the very first time Ivy saw her friend at her angriest. The intensity in Benecia's dark, fiery eyes conveyed her unwavering determination to protect her loved ones at any cost, even if it entailed resorting to violence.

"I've already made up my mind," Benecia firmly stated, "and once my family learns what Delyth just went through, I'm confident they'll leave with me without a second thought. Come along with us, Eun."

Ivy wasn't too certain. She had her doubts. While the wild offered the promise of liberation from the overwork and torment they endured in the kingdom, she wondered what would happen if they ever ran out of food or any other supplies. That was bound to happen if they left.

"You think Delyth would come too?"

"Delyth would be foolish not to agree with this plan," Benecia responded with a small scoff. "Powerless beings have no life here. Why must we endure all this nonsense? It's best we leave while we still can. Sure, it may not be simple surviving the wild but anything is better than this." And Ivy remembers watching as her friend's shoulders dropped, a mixture of defeat and agitation flashing in her eyes, then. "Eun, I'm tired."

Such a shame Gozar got to them first before the plan could be carried out.

Should I clean up this place? Ivy finds herself asking as she glances around. Perhaps, cleaning would work in taking her mind off of these distressing thoughts. It always has.

Yet there isn't really anything to clean. Sure, she could go over the irritating dust that often builds up in some parts of the shelter, but Haru did his best maintaining the cleanliness of this place. The lack of furniture and decorations contributes to its neat appearance. If Ivy has to guess, it's the tottering floor and cracked wall that are in dire need of replacement. And the frayed carpet only makes the floor look worse.

Ivy heads outside, instead. Going for a ride on Snow would help too, that is, if she can manage to avoid people that are sure to swarm around her once they see her.

Before she can untie the horse, someone catches her eye. It's Fenghua, skipping joyously toward her while sporting one of the greatest grins on his loveable face. When he approaches Ivy, he waves enthusiastically while spewing out a few lines about how he and his mother have just come from the market.

"It felt so strange." His eyes expand. "I've never been around so many people. And there was so much food there. Mama was able to fill up both baskets."

Ivy laughs. "Good to see you too."

Immediately, the little boy goes to pet Snow's lowered back. "I can't wait to eat the delicious meal Mama's making," he carries on, merriment dancing in his wide eyes. "It was our birthday yesterday so a friend of hers from work gave her extra jewels. We bought so much food—a whole lot more than we normally buy."

"It was your birthday?" Ivy raises her eyebrows, taking Fenghua's word choice into account.

"She gave birth to me on her birthday." His grin broadens. "So we have our birthday on the same day. Isn't that amazing?"

Ivy is about to respond when she suddenly recalls what the woman told her earlier. Her lips tug into a small sad smile. "You should go back to your mother, Fenghua."

"I wanted to see your horse again. . . Maybe, even ride it," the boy pleads hopefully. "Mama doesn't even know I'm here. I snuck out while she was in the kitchen."

"All the more reason to go back to her," Ivy says. She kneels in front of the boy. "Fenghua, you should stop sneaking out. This is a dangerous world we live in. Your mother's only trying to protect you."

Fenghua pauses with a pout. "Is. . . Is that why she makes us hide sometimes? Who are we hiding from? Are there people out there trying to hurt us?"

Ivy sighs and gets back on her feet. How can she explain the laws of the world to an eight-year-old? She had no understanding of them at that age either. Rather, she was thrown into the face of danger, forced to find ways to fend for herself. She'd hate to see the same thing happen to an innocent little boy who has no clue just how many Holders out there are willing to execute a child. At least, Fenghua has his mother.

"Go home. Run along now."

It takes a while but eventually, Ivy is able to shoo the boy away. She hates the disappointed look his face morphs into before he turns around and runs off.

───..∘ ☽ ▢ ☾ ∘..───

"They're here! Everyone, hide!"

Ivy is in the middle of silently going through her plot in the living room when a cacophony of aghast voices suddenly disrupts her concentration. Although, it isn't just those voices she can hear. The thundering hooves of several horses racing through the village and an army of what sounds like guards shouting angrily come into earshot as well. She tries to make sense of the situation unfolding outside but not even the words that fly out of the guards' mouths give her much of an understanding.

"Guard the exit!" they cry out. "Search the houses!"

A sense of dread coils in Ivy's gut as she rises from her seat. Could it be that the guards have come to finish what they started? So after eliminating Haru, they come back for round two? The thought of the guards barging into Fenghua's house and dragging both him and his mother out causes Ivy mental anguish. They are Powerless beings. These guards are sure to separate them and beat the woman for hiding. Any Powerless being above the age of ten is burdened with arduous tasks and those caught evading their responsibilities are tortured.

Ivy isn't sure how the woman earns her jewels. Fenghua mentioned a friend of hers from work but there is no way his mother actually has a proper job. Powerless beings in hiding never do. They often acquire their jewels through unlawful means. Either his mother is stealing jewels or engaging in relationships with influential men in exchange for them. Those are the only ways, at least, for a woman in her circumstances. It is heart-wrenching to even think about but those are the only ways.

Without a second thought, Ivy throws her door open and runs outside. "I'm the person you're looking for!" she declares, hands in the air. "There's no need to disturb the other villagers."

The guards appear stunned to see her. Why are they? Ivy wonders. Don't they already know she is living here? Haru was killed for that reason. . . Wasn't he?

"It's not about you, this time," a guard says. And each of them returns to what they were tasked to do as though she doesn't exist in their eyes.

It isn't about her? Then, who could it be? Who are they searching for?

"Bring the villagers out and get them on their knees!" another guard barks, unnecessarily kicking open a door. "The traitor might be hiding here!"

Before the raid on Fenghua's house, the door opens from the inside, and the same Chinese woman Ivy fears for hastily steps out with both hands raised in surrender. Her fingers can be seen trembling but despite her terror, she makes her way to the center and kneels.

"You live alone?" a guard questions her.

The woman nods but that doesn't stop the man from entering her shelter regardless. These guards are, of course, trained to never believe a word from those they suspect. That instills a deep sense of fear in Ivy in a way she hasn't felt in quite some time. Her heart pounds relentlessly in her chest. The woman obviously knew the guards would still search. It makes Ivy wonder where she's hidden her son.

Yet in a wink of an eye, her concerns about Fenghua's whereabouts are abruptly pushed aside when she notices something so perplexing that it renders her motionless. Adorning the woman's neck is a Green Amulet.

She is a Holder?

How can she be a Holder?

It takes two minutes before the guard exits the house, empty-handed. He didn't find Fenghua. Despite her success in keeping her son away from their cruel hands, Fenghua's mother refrains from displaying any hint of delight.

Eventually, all the villagers are gathered. They kneel beside each other, trembling. Among them, a villager carries a baby, no more than a year old. The loud guards have awoken him and he's on the brink of tears. In a desperate attempt to calm him, the man holding the baby sways his body from side to side, but to no avail. Within seconds, the baby's cries fill the air.

The guard who starts to speak ignores the wailing. "I'm uncertain if you know this," he says, "but just twenty minutes ago, a traitor was caught. An Outsider."

Ivy's eyes widen. An Outsider?

"We believe that this man is not alone, however, so guards from every area of the kingdom have been tasked with searching for his partner. . . Or partners. Let's not drag this, alright?" the guard says. "If you are working with this Outsider, we will eventually find out. But I'm giving you the chance to reveal yourself and make this much simpler for everyone, including yourself."

The villagers glance at each other, sweat forming on their foreheads.

"Sir," one of them finally speaks, "I assure you that nobody in this village is an Outsider. We've been living here for a long time now."

"We don't know when these traitors infiltrated our kingdom," the same guard continues. "This spying could have been going on for years and we're only finding out now."

"It's not us!" the same villager insists.

A different guard takes over but he speaks to his squad members rather than the villagers. "There's an opening in this village that allows anyone to enter or leave the kingdom at any time. Why has it been left open knowing that Outsiders could come in?"

"We haven't heard from those bastards in years now," the first responds with a half-shrug and a sneer. "Besides, we don't care if those animals leave the kingdom. They always come back since the wild is far too uninhabitable. I mean, take her for instance." He points a mocking finger at Ivy.

Ivy fights the urge to roll her eyes.

Another guard begins counting the villagers. Sixteen, including Ivy. Seventeen if Fanghua is here.

When he's done with his counting, he declares, "We'll be back. If we see that the number of villagers here has reduced, or even increased, we're taking everyone. Do you hear that? So if you're the traitor, you better stand up now. Think of the lives you've got on your hands."

Nobody stands up. The guards give it another minute, just standing there staring at everyone while waiting for one to stand.

Again, nobody does.

The guards give up. And they leave.

Ivy balls her hands into fists. Marvelous! Now, moving out is no longer an option.

word count • 4422

15 | TIBBLes

Chapter Fifteen — Tibbles

Ivy thoroughly examined Haru's house the other day and she is confident beyond a shadow of a doubt that there never was a stuffed rabbit lying on the floor in the center of the man's bedroom. Why is she staring at one now?

The rabbit doesn't appear like it was intended to be hidden either. Whoever placed it here wanted someone to find it, and telling from the note that's being addressed to her attached to the toy, Ivy has to guess that someone is her.

Eun, remember Mr. Tibbles? the note reads. Ivy sets the piece of paper aside and stares at the animal. Its dark color is accented by a white ribbon around its neck, buttons for eyes, and a small shape of a heart drawn for its nose. Yes, Ivy remembers Mr. Tibbles. The toy was frequently mentioned by the little girl from her dreams—or rather, memories—who referred to it as the only companion she had aside from her family. Ivy, however, has never actually seen what it looks like until now, and despite her best efforts, she is unable to recall a time when she's ever touched the animal, much less held it.

The greater question is who brought it in here.

Ivy grabs the rabbit and exits the room with a small new mission in mind. If she can locate this unidentified person, perhaps, all her questions about her past will be answered. She doesn't have high expectations—Ivy knows better than to anticipate too much. But this can't possibly be a ruse, can it? Yes, she's aware of numerous Holders who deceive the Powerless for entertainment. In actuality, she was one of the unfortunate ones when she was younger. A group of her classmates bribed a homeless Powerless woman to pose as her biological mother. However, this can't be a ruse. No, not this time.

She dreamt about this rabbit.

When she leaves the house, Ivy is instantly brought back to her previous concern. Fenghua.

It is after three sets of knocking—which felt like an eternity—that the door to Fenghua's house finally opens, his mother on the other side. The Chinese woman has shed her white gown in favor of a light gray loose blouse made with fabric not a lot of Powerless beings can afford, together with a skirt long enough to cover the entirety of her long legs. She briefly holds her breath at the sight of Ivy, and muses on why the girl bothered to approach them even after she warned her to stay away. Before the woman has a chance to speak, the head of a young child emerges from behind her.

Ivy plasters a smile on her face from relief. She resists the impulse to reach out to the boy and pull him into a hug, careful not to get attached. Such intense feelings can prevent her from completing what she's come back for. Instead, the girl turns to the boy's mother. "I was worried," she explains. "I just wanted to check to see if Fenghua was alright."

"He's fine." The woman lifts her shoulder in a half-shrug. "I knew what I was doing."

"I figured." His mother most likely hid Fenghua in a place one has to look hard to find. The guard would have to turn the house upside down and he must have not done that. Ivy tilts her head to face the little boy again and raises a hand in greeting. "I'm glad he's got you. Not that many Powerless children are that lucky."

When she realizes the term 'Powerless' slipped past her lips, Ivy bites her lower lip. Her mind reels back to the Green Amulet she spotted around the woman's neck. If Fenghua's mother possesses an Amulet, then the eight-year-old could also be a Holder. But if that is the case, why choose to hide pendants that are of such great value? Why choose to hide, in general? With those special necklaces, they can move out of this Godforsaken village—that is, back when moving out was still an option.

Ivy wants to question the woman about this strange behavior but she knows not to meddle in other people's affairs. "I... I was also wondering if you happened to see someone go inside Haru's house."

"Why, did something happen?"

"I found something that wasn't there before," Ivy answers. "Did you?"

"I did."

It's not Fenghua's mother that replies this time. Ivy turns to see another villager behind her. The woman is old with jaded eyes, a crooked long nose, and soft powder-white hair and can hardly stand even with the aid of her cane. As soon as she takes notice of the rabbit in Ivy's hand, her eyes expand. "Is it a bomb?"

"I... N-No, it's not." Ivy gives the toy another look-over. "At least, I don't think so." In the past, bombs were often disguised as many things, such as furniture, toys, and even jewels. This was so Holders could easily entice their enemies into coming out, knowing that the Powerless would pick up anything they found out of desperation. Although this act has been prohibited for years now, many of her people are still wary. "You claimed to have seen the individual who left this?"

The elderly woman nods. "Well. . . I didn't really see his face but yes, when I peered out my window this morning, I saw him stepping inside Haru's house. At first, I-I believed him to be a Holder but. . ." A pause. "He wasn't wearing any Amulet. I figured it was a friend."

Ivy's hold on the rabbit grows tighter as her gaze falls to the ground. *Whoever this boy is knows me. He has to! But. . . How did he even come to learn that I dwelled in this village? Is it possible I'm being watched?*

She only intends to stay at Haru's house until she finds another more suitable place to stay. Ivy has even moved aside a number of jewels for her second sanctuary. Wherever that may be, she's unsure, but it must be one that is affordable and isolated from every other house. If the guards—and this unknown boy—know where she currently resides, then, so does the Hunter. In fact, this boy could be the Hunter himself with a plan already made to get rid of her. According to what Poppy said before, the Hunter targets any Holder they believe has or still is aiding the Powerless. Ivy falls under that category more than anyone else. Yes, she may not consider herself a Holder but the Hunter undoubtedly would, and she's sure to be next on his list.

Ivy looks back at the elderly woman. "Could you please. . . describe him to me?"

"Well, he was. . ." The elder steps closer to Ivy and puts a hand over her head. "A bit taller than you, I suppose. The sides of his head were shaved with the hair on top tied back."

"What about his face?"

"Hmm. . ." She takes an unsteady step back. "H-he had half of it covered. Again, I-I couldn't exactly see much from where I was."

"Alright, thank you." The younger sighs. The description is not at all helpful—many boys have hair like that. Regardless, she nods gratefully at the woman.

"Are you sure it's not a bomb?"

Ivy smiles. "If it was a bomb, I'm certain it would have gone off by now."

The woman grunts something under her breath. Ivy watches as she gradually makes her way back to where she lives before whirling around to face Fenghua's mother, who's still standing by her slightly opened door.

"He hasn't come to cause trouble, has he?"

"I don't know what to tell you," Ivy says. "This boy, whoever he is, left this rabbit for a reason." And unless the Hunter is smart enough to lure me in this way, I don't believe it's him. Not yet, at least. "I. . . I'll get going then." She gives a brief bow and turns to leave. This is it. With this unknown boy knowing where she lives and half of Arya demanding her head, Fenghua's mother most likely doesn't want to take any chances. This is the last time Ivy would be speaking to either her or her son, she can feel it. And perhaps, that's for the best. At least then, there won't be any more distractions. She can concentrate on advancing her strategy and moving further into her plan.

"Ivy!" Fenghua's mother suddenly calls out after Ivy has begun her walk away from the house.

"Yes?"

The woman seems to waver for a moment, her mouth opening and closing while her eyes scan Ivy's face as though she's in search of something in particular—perhaps, something that'd let her know if the girl is a danger or not. Eventually, she heaves a sigh, threading a hand through her unruly dark hair as her gaze drops to the ground.

"W-Would you like to come in?"

Ivy's brows draw together. "But—"

"I just suddenly remembered something significant a good friend of my mother's often quoted," the woman continues. "Solitude and isolation are painful things and beyond human endurance. She told us that the only reason our people still existed even today was because we had each other. With each other, we found strength. And I think she's somewhat right."

"T-that's very strange." Ivy scratches the back of her head with a small chuckle. "I know someone who says the exact same thing too. I. . . Why are you telling me this?"

"You see, I always want the best for my son. Sometimes, I think that I'm doing the right thing keeping him away from everyone else so he doesn't face the same fate as. . . well, Haru," the woman says. "But then, I see how sad and lonely he frequently gets and it makes my heart ache. I'm troubled by this. Yes, it's hard for a child born so unfortunate to live a fortunate life, but if I can help it when it comes to Fenghua's case, then why not try? He seems to really like you."

Quiet contentment spreads through Ivy, swelling within her. "I think he likes Snow more," she quips, earning a lighthearted laugh from the woman. Behind her, Ivy can see Fenghua grinning from ear to ear. He must feel warm on the inside knowing he doesn't have to sneak around to see Ivy and Snow anymore.

The inside of their house is just as Ivy expected. Tottered floor. Cracked walls. Lack of furniture and decorations. Torn-apart roof. Similar to Haru's house. Similar to every other house in this village. Ivy wonders if any of the villagers have ever attempted to repair the damaged structures. What would happen if it begins to pour brutally? The roof is of no help. Then again, tools aren't low-cost.

An oil lantern resting in the corner of the living room is the sole object in sight. Fenghua's mother carefully settles a large tray down on the floor and calls for the two youngsters to sit. The little boy's mouth drops open and squeals almost immediately, clapping his hands as he eagerly plops himself down in front of the tray. At the sight of the dishes the woman has prepared, Ivy can understand why.

On one side of the tray is a sizable bowl of Chinese sautéed cabbage with vinegar sauce. Red bayberries and jujubes, some the size of a cherry and others as big as a plum, can be found in another bowl right beside a platter of white rice and Gong Bao, a delicacy prepared with cubes of chicken, peanuts, vegetables, and chili peppers. A bowl of pan-fried pork dumplings with cabbage comes next, followed by a tiny plate of spring rolls in the middle.

In a split second, Ivy feels a twinge of pity. Although it isn't her business, she considered the woman's occupation, and seeing these dishes brings her back to her speculations. The ingredients needed to make this tremendous meal most definitely cost more than twenty-two pearls, four jades, and three ambers.

The twenty-two pearls alone can only get her things of poor quality, such as the cheaper fruits that are on the verge of rotting or merely two candlesticks. Add the four jades and three ambers and she can purchase ingredients enough to create a small meal that would still leave both her and her son starving. There is no way the woman can afford all these dishes she prepared. Certainly not as a hidden Powerless.

But Ivy says nothing. It isn't her place to bring it up. And surely not in front of her son.

The woman takes out a jug of milk and pours some into two paper cups before passing them over to Fenghua and Ivy. A small glass of ale is already set in front of her. "I told myself we'd have a good birthday this year," she says with a sigh, bringing the glass to her lips. After a small sip of the drink, her eyes rush over to Ivy. "Well, why are you still standing there? Sit and dig in."

"I-I couldn't possibly—"

"Sit and eat!" Fenghua's mother says again, this time, more in a demanding tone. She picks up the extra spoon she took out and extends her arm toward Ivy so the girl can take it. "Fenghua and I couldn't possibly finish this. We need an additional mouth."

Ivy wavers, but when she understands Fenghua's mother intentionally prepared extra, she gratefully accepts the spoon and sits beside Fenghua. Maybe, two spoons of rice and Gong Bao chicken and she'd be on her way. This is meant to be their meal, after all. She still can't make sense of why the woman cooked so much for only three mouths. Normally, a Powerless would cook as little as possible in order to have enough for the next day. Yet once again, the girl brushes the inquiries off.

"J-Just so you know, I've already eaten," Ivy explains. "I had lunch at the academy, plus my friend's family insisted I ate with them."

"Well then, consider this as a thank you for your bravery," the woman says as she watches her son intently, a warm smile dancing on her lips. Fenghua has already dug in, shoving a sizable portion of a mixture of rice and Gong Bao into his mouth and chewing loudly. From time to time, he'd squeal again while clapping his hands with delight and then lean forward to grab another portion before even swallowing.

"You don't need to thank me."

"Of course, I do. This goal of yours. . . I-I don't mean to put you down, Ivy, but it's next to impossible. But I admire your courage and strong will." The woman sighs as a corner of her heavy-upper lips lifts. "Mrs. Patel spoke very highly of you, Ivy."

Ivy freezes at the sudden words. "M-Mrs. Patel?" She pieces two and two together in two seconds. "W-when you mentioned your mother's friend earlier. . . You were referring to Mrs. Patel, weren't you?"

Fenghua's mother nods. "Mrs. Patel and my mother worked together for a while. The woman was there when my mother fell sick and she was there when my mother passed away." She pauses, taking a bite of a spring roll and swallowing. "Mrs. Patel was practically my second mother. She taught me almost everything that my mother couldn't due to her health, starting from how to cook to how to raise a child." Her eyes crinkle at the corners. "I had Fenghua at seventeen."

How come she's never mentioned you?

Ivy examines the Chinese woman's somewhat rounded face carefully. Her skin is delicate and flawless, at least from what she can tell from just her face, with the exception of a little scar that is still yet to heal on her right cheek and a mole under her lips. The remainder of the woman's flesh is hidden by her long fit, making it impossible for the girl to catch sight of any other bruises or scars that may be there.

"I've been hidden all my life," Fenghua's mother carries on in a low voice. "If it weren't for Mrs. Patel and her family, I would be working as a slave right now. Aside from my mother, only they know of my existence. Not even my father knows—whoever that man is."

Ivy frowns. "So, you are a Powerless."

"Why would you think otherwise?"

"I—" Ivy searches the woman's neck next. It is bare, just as it was ever since she opened the door and told her Fenghua was fine. "I noticed you were wearing a Green Amulet earlier."

"Oh, that?" Fenghua's mother lowers her fork and bursts into laughter. "It's fake."

"But i-it looked so real."

"That's what I said too when I saw it for the first time!" Fenghua cries out. Because of his stuffed mouth, his words come out gibberish.

"Let's not eat with our mouths full," his mother warns with the same small smile. She turns back to Ivy and realizing the younger is still waiting for an explanation, she sighs and twirls the fork in her hand. "Mrs. Patel bought it for me fifteen years ago. There was this sweet couple that excelled in making Amulets back then. They had a secret business and Powerless beings that could afford the pendants often came to them. But we were warned not to wear the Amulets unless necessary." She swallows hard again as her gaze shifts to the floor, her smile slowly deforming. "I would have bought Fenghua one too when he was born, but by the time I'd earned enough jewels to get one, the business had shut down."

Ivy waits patiently for the woman to proceed while she chews on a piece of jujube. She's, of course, heard of this business. The two individuals that ran it were apprehended and put to death in 1989. Ivy was four years old at the time. She finds it somewhat odd that while she can recall key occasions from her younger years with ease, such as the passing of Queen Aqua, her mind instantly turns blank when it comes to remembering anything about her biological family—their names, their faces, anything.

"I could have asked Mrs. Patel to buy one for Fenghua when there was still time but I felt terrible relying on the woman. So I decided to work for the jewels. It was better that way."

Work for the jewels?

Fenghua's mother provides no further clarification regarding how she worked for those jewels as Ivy hoped. Instead, she proceeds to impale a piece of chicken with her fork and redirects the conversation towards the Green Amulet. "I'm afraid if I wear mine too many times, someone will eventually ask me to show off a power, which is something I obviously cannot do," she says. "The secret to surviving this cruel game we call life is to keep a low profile. It's why we live in Angora. Fenghua and I need to continue being nonexistent. I only put on my Amulet when I'm at the market or at work."

"You work?" Ivy questions with a raise of her eyebrows. Perhaps, she shouldn't have. Telling from the look on the woman's face and how she comes to yet another pause, it seems she didn't mean to bring up the fact she even had a job.

"Ever since she started working, she's been earning a lot of jewels," Fenghua chips in, chewing on two dumplings, which, once again, makes his words come out gibberish. "That is why I can't wait to get older so I can get a job of my own and help her out more."

"What do you work as, Miss. . .?"

That is when Ivy realizes she doesn't even know the woman's name yet.

But Fenghua's mother doesn't answer her question and as she speaks, she avoids Ivy's gaze. "I had my Amulet on earlier because I was afraid the guards had come to take away any Powerless beings that were hiding here." Another sip of the ale is taken. "But I was wrong. I spotted four Powerless villagers when they made us kneel, yet none of the guards seemed to care. Or maybe they didn't see."

"They weren't paying attention to your necks. I noticed that too. Goes to show just how vital it is to catch this traitorous Outsider really is." Ivy shrugs. She doesn't want to talk about her job? That is fine with her.

The third part of the Amulet Assessment is coming soon, though.

"Of course, finding this traitor is important to Holders." The woman chuckles. "Yes, Holders believe they'll prevail in this ongoing battle but they also understand just how dangerous Outsiders are."

"Who are these Outsiders anyway?"

"You don't know?" Fenghua's mother looks surprised. "The Outsiders are a collective of Powerless beings that managed to successfully evade capture and escape their kingdoms. None of them are from this kingdom, however, since survival beyond the borders of Arya is impossible. United by a shared desire for retribution, they coalesced into a tightly knit group. At least, that's what everyone keeps saying."

"It sounds true," Ivy mumbles. Indeed, Arya's reputation for effectively imprisoning the Powerless is well-known since no other kingdom has as much forest and water surrounding it as it does. "These Outsiders must be exceptionally skilled and stocked with supplies if some of them managed their way inside Arya."

"Millions of Powerless beings have chosen to believe that the Outsiders are their escape from this torture," the woman says with a despondent sigh, staring at the last pork dumpling perched upon her fork.

Consequently, the Outsiders must possess exceptional skills and ample provisions to have successfully infiltrated this kingdom. It is worth noting that millions of Powerless beings have embraced the belief that the Outsiders offer a means of liberation from their torment. This sentiment is expressed by the woman, who, with a despondent sigh, contemplates the solitary remaining pork dumpling perched upon her fork.

"You don't believe it?"

"It just sounds too good to be true."

For the following minutes, the three of them eat in silence. From time to time, the woman would caution Fenghua not to swallow such large portions to avoid choking. Ivy laughs pitifully. She understands the little boy's behavior all too well. It is the fear of having their food taken from them that often causes the Powerless to eat quicker than necessary—the fear of guards barging into their homes before they even get to finish their meals. It's happened too many times. Who knows when a meal would be their last? Fenghua's mother, on the other hand, eats slowly. Something seems to be on her mind but Ivy resists the impulse to ask her what is wrong. Instead, her head drives back to something that's been bothering her since a little while ago.

"What do you plan on doing for the upcoming Amulet Assessment?"

Due to Arya's tremendous population, the Amulet Assessment, which is only supposed to occur once every year, has been broken down into three parts—one at the beginning of the year, January 9th, the second in the middle, June 21st, and finally, the last near the end, September 16th. The previous Royals pushed on this adjustment to ensure that every single part of the kingdom is searched, including the smallest settlements.

"In exactly eight days, you're going to have to prove to the guards that your Amulet is real."

Passing the assessment is impossible for her people. The only guaranteed way a Powerless can stay hidden is if they. . . well, hide. But avoiding capture is so rare that many people choose not to attempt it.

"You must have a plan," Ivy insists, terrified for the two more than she cares to admit. "I mean, how else have you survived in this village for this long without getting caught? What do you do?"

"It's easy to stay hidden when you know all the best hiding places in Arya." The woman's lips arc into a sly smile.

Know all the best hiding places? Ivy's curiosity sparks. It can't be the wild. Many years ago, the Powerless would flee the kingdom for the day, returning only when they were certain the Amulet Assessment had come to an end. The Royals caught on quickly, unfortunately, and made a new order. On the day of each assessment and seven days after, a multitude of fearsome proficient dogs were to be sent out to scan as much of the forest as they could. Ever since this commenced, anyone who dares to evacuate the kingdom never makes it back.

"You don't have to worry about us," is all Fenghua's mother says to clarify as she stands up from the floor after setting her fork down.

And yet, Ivy can't help but worry.

"By the way. . . my name is Hui-Qing."

word count • 4165

16 | renegade

CHAPTER SIXTEEN — RENEGADE

"ARJUN passed away last year."

The folded piece of paper in Ivy's right hand crumples as she squeezes her fists. She fails to conceal the puzzlement that crosses her face. This response isn't what she expected—it's not what she wanted. As she was putting Arjun Laghari's name on her list, she thought of every possibility—perhaps, the man got into gambling, lost all his jewels, and is struggling to provide for his family, or he would be among the wealthy in possession of more jewels than he knows what to do with, or even be behind bars—but death?

Death never crossed Ivy's mind.

"Arjun came down with an illness last year," the woman in front of her carries on. Although she's complying, her eyes are burning with hatred. Ivy is left to assume that the woman is tolerating her presence solely out of fear of the Golden Amulet.

"But Arjun is a Healer," the younger reminds. "A marvelous one, at that. How could he die from an illness he could easily get rid of?" Arjun is gifted. His exceptional ability makes him a valuable asset, thus warranting his inclusion on the list that Ivy meticulously constructed back when she was still with Adora. The list serves as a tool to facilitate the next step of her scheme. Ivy speculates that the woman in question may be disingenuous, leading to the possibility that Arjun is present within the confines of her abode. Such a scenario would not be surprising to her.

Mrs. Laghari, reminiscent of Ivy's adoptive mother and former friend, shares a similar affinity for the Royals, particularly Queen Matilda. It's no shock that Mrs. Laghari dismisses Ivy's allegations against the queen. Why is it that someone as benevolent as Arjun would develop affection for an individual as duplicitous as her?

"Oh, he would have lived if some bastard hadn't stolen his Amulet." Mrs. Laghari grinds her teeth as she glances away. "And even if he was still alive, what makes you think I'd hand him over to you willingly?"

"Arjun is his own person."

Mrs. Laghari scoffs. "Not anymore, he's not." And she walks back inside, shutting the door in Ivy's face. Although she loathes the woman, Ivy can't deny the love she has for Arjun.

Someone seized his Amulet, huh? The young girl doesn't dwell much on that information. It is plausible a desperate Powerless snatched his pendant when the opportunity presented itself. This incident is not isolated, as numerous Holders have come forward with similar complaints within a single near. Ivy ponders how long it will take for her people to realize that confiscating Amulets will not provide a solution to their predicament.

Stepping away from the door, Ivy examines the crumpled paper. Arjun Laghari is the first unnatural Holder on her list—and the first to be crossed out. Under every possible helper Ivy printed down, there are alternatives. Alas, Arjun only has one. It;s not easy at all finding Holders willing to provide assistance, especially when her plan involves dismantling the Royals.

Aside from those high in power, Healers are the most affluent individuals on this continent. Their wealth stems from the fact that they are the primary source of medical assistance for those in desperate need. However, their prices can be ridiculously great. It's almost as though they derive satisfaction from manipulating people's lives, fully aware that they are the sole options.

Ivy stares hard at Arjun's alternative. She made sure that every name she put down was people whose integrity she could vouch for in the past. But she cannot guarantee that they have remained unchanged over the years.

Let's hope Yufei Rén is still good enough.

He's not. Not in the way Ivy expected, however.

When she walks into his home, her attention is immediately drawn to his arms, or rather, the absence thereof. The sight is both shocking and distressing, leaving her momentarily frozen in place. Ivy's throat feels constricted as if she's just ingested a lump of coal. What happened is simple.

The Holders got to him.

"He was caught feeding some Powerless women near the market," Yufei's mother, who's just a couple of feet away from Ivy, speaks. Ivy tears her gaze away from her son and glances at the woman. There is a tinge of sadness in her voice that feels like a stone in quicksand. Tears trickle down her cheeks like rivers of sorrow. "So, they took away what he used to feed them."

Ivy takes a step forward. Yufei is seated on a sofa, head thrown back and eyes closed, snoring so softly that she can hardly hear him. Her face is as straight as she can get it to be but her chest is beating with an unceasing cadence of despair. How can a being take another man's limbs as a consequence of helping another in need? How can someone be that cruel?

"It was our food!" Yufei's mother suddenly shrieks. "It's not as though he was stealing or anything like that. He was taking our fair share and feeding it to other people." Her heart must feel like it's been torn into two and ripped out of her chest. "What we do with our share should be none of their business."

"When did this happen?" It's a foolish question but Ivy isn't sure what else to say. Perhaps, she should have come back sooner, commenced her ploy quicker. . . No. No, that doesn't matter at all. That wouldn't have stopped this from happening.

"Three days ago," his mother responds. "Ivy, I don't know what you're here for but it can't involve my son. Even if he wasn't in this state, I wouldn't allow him. I don't want my son playing hero any longer. Risking his life. . . and for what? The best we can do is follow orders and steer clear of troubles. The Royals are merciless. Nothing on this earth will ever get them to change."

"No, I disagree." Ivy shakes her head. "Failure to follow the rules, we get executed. Follow the rules, we kill ourselves slower. Don't you see? We die either way."

"Well. . ." The woman exhales sharply. "I'm sorry if I sound like a coward to you but I'd rather live longer than die trying."

Ivy pauses. It is moments like this that make her wonder if, at the end of it all, this will all be for nothing. That, even after everything, nothing is going to change. It is moments like this that make her long for Adora's comforting embrace, yearning for reassurance that she is not mistaken.

"Ivy, darling, when will you stop?" The woman steps forward to place a hand on her shoulder. "It's over! How can we fight against people with literal magic? It was over for us long ago."

But Ivy continues to shake her head. Adora's words come to her again.

"It's not over until my final breath is taken."

———..○ ☽ ☐ ☾ ○..———

She should have immediately gone running the moment she entered one of Findara's biggest fields. Adora often warned her to refrain from indulging her curiosity, yet here she is, standing amidst a sizable crowd that has assembled around Queen Matilda. The queen is seated on her horse right beside a man on his knees. He's clearly a prisoner, as seen by his chained hands, torn clothing, and bloodied body. Holding the end of the shackles to prevent him from escaping is Gozar Agulto himself.

He's still taking orders from her? Is he that loyal or just that stupid?

Although Queen Matilda is speaking, the prisoner captures Ivy's full attention straight away. Not only does she feel empathetic towards the man, especially whenever Gozar strikes him for any sudden movement, but this situation aligns with the second step of her scheme. Ivy remains at a distance but that doesn't stop several people from turning to her once Snow begins to neigh.

"I understand your terror in what I've just informed you," the queen is saying. "But do not concern yourself with this matter. We will eventually find the other Outsiders, regardless of how many there are of them. The Royals never fail to keep this kingdom at peace."

So, the prisoner is an Outsider? Ivy can't see much of the man from where she is yet she can't help but feel even more drawn to him and his people, especially after what Hui-Qing told her about them. Are the Powerless really onto something about the Outsiders being their only hope out of this tortuous kingdom? If so, then some changes to her plan might have to be made. And fast.

"However, this isn't the only reason I have you all gathered here," Queen Matilda carries on. She pauses for a second to gulp at every eye burning with abhorrence glaring daggers back at her. This level of repulsion isn't something she's used to—it isn't something she ever thought she'd have to face. "Ever since we captured one of them"—the woman's left index finger extends to point at the prisoner—"we've been focused on getting answers in whichever way we can and I'm happy to announce that we've finally managed to get something out of this Outsider, something I believe is worth sharing."

Why did they have Queen Matilda, someone whose reputation is undergoing a gradual negative shift, deliver this announcement? Ivy ponders over the potential motives behind such a bold choice for a moment. One possible rationale is that it is an attempt to restore the trust of the people. By having the queen declare wondrous news, it is plausible that a greater portion of the kingdom would be inclined to place more faith in her words. The mechanism by which this would occur remains unclear to Ivy but given the nature of these people and their tendencies for descending to depths of desperation, the theory holds considerable merit.

"Because of this. . . scandal that's been going on," the woman says as she graciously slides off her horse and saunters over to where the prisoner is kneeling, "I suppose it's better you hear it from him rather than me." She grabs ahold of the man's jaw and firmly lifts his head, forcing him to make eye contact with hundreds of enraged but puzzled Holders. "Go on, then. Tell them exactly what you told me. . . from beginning to the end."

The man swallows hard, his terrified eyes scrambling from one Holder to another. How can he be so afraid? He knew what he was getting himself into as one of the Outsiders. He knew what would happen if he got caught. Now, he's here, about to tattle on his own people? These Outsiders don't sound very brave to Ivy. They don't sound like people that are capable of freeing the Powerless from slavery.

"On the fourth of September, we got a-a. . ." The prisoner pauses and gulps again. Ivy can actually make out the sweat gliding down his triangular bony face. "On the fourth, w-we got a surprise visit from Ivy Pearls."

Ivy freezes.

"Y-You may know her by Eun Calinao." The man's chest is still rising and falling with rapid breaths but he looks somewhat relieved. Needless to say, the crowd has begun their murmuring. He eventually looks away and turns his eyes back to the ground. "We live in a very secluded area, a small town outside of Arya, so we don't know how she was able to find us. But she came to us on this day, pleading that we assist her with some revenge scheme she'd cooked up. W-we agreed. Well, of course, we agreed. Her scheme was against the Holders, our greatest enemies. It was the perfect partnership, plus Ivy seemed to already have everything planned out."

"And what was her plan?" Queen Matilda asks.

"To bomb Arya, along with everyone in it."

What—?!

The unforeseen flabbergasting utterance immediately compels Ivy to flee the scene. Either they coerced that man into uttering such a falsehood or he's no Outsider, at all. Yet before she can signal Snow to make a hasty retreat, her attention is caught by Queen Matilda, who, while scanning the crowd during the prisoner's speech, locks eyes with Ivy and promptly gestures for her guards to apprehend her. Understanding the queen's command, all the guards, except for Gozar, hastily depart. So does Ivy.

"I was just going to have my guards pay a visit to Angora and take her away there," Ivy can hear the queen still speaking behind her. "But it seems that's not goi. . ." And her voice gradually leaves the girl's earshot the farther she gets away from the roaring crowd.

Snow is not as trained as the guards' horses. I won't win this chase. Despite that fact, Ivy remains unperturbed. Unless these Holders have all the time in the world to wait for her to stop defending herself, there's no reason to be. Either she will find herself at a disadvantage or she will acquire additional allies. Regardless of the outcome, her plan will proceed as intended, and Queen Matilda will always find herself perilously close to relinquishing her title. Ivy can ask her Golden Amulet to teleport her to somewhere safer as her first wish, but Adora taught her not to overly rely on the pendant. No matter what trouble she's in, she is to first attempt resolving it on her own. The Golden Amulet is and always will be her backup plan.

It is reserved for a more significant purpose in the future, after all.

"No use running from us, Ivy!" a guard thunders behind her. Following after the soldiers is an uncountable number of people, aching to punish Ivy themselves.

Ivy tightens her grip around the reins. The man is right. There really is no use running. As each of the guards near her, she continues to see that. Eventually, one of the men who's caught up to her tugs on his reins harder, bringing his horse to make a sudden swivel and block Snow from moving any further.

"It's over for you, Eun!"

The formulated dust from the horses' running legs clouds Ivy's sight for a moment. Several coughs leave her mouth as the chanting a guard commenced grows louder and louder.

"IT'S OVER FOR YOU, EUN!"

Ivy is encircled. Not just by the self-satisfied guards and their loud horses but by enraged Holders, as well. Most of them used their powers to get nearer to the girl as quickly as they could. Others just ran. It isn't long before Ivy catches sight of a great number of them bending down to pick up the rocks scattered all over. So, that is their plan? Stone her to death? And then what? Have any of them thought about what would be of the Golden Amulet if she was to die?

Ivy scrunches her face when she locks eyes with a boy she was least expecting. It's a boy from her class, the same one she caught staring at her when she exited Mr. Zhang's room after confronting Reuben. Ivy studies him for a moment. Although he's far from her, she can still make out his curly undercut.

"...The sides of his head were shaved with the hair on top tied back."

Ivy shakes her head. No, it can't be. Many boys in Arya have that same hair.

Tired of using her voice, the young girl reaches for the pendant around her neck, resisting the urge to roll her eyes at the foolishness of her foes. Yet before she can even open her mouth, she's met with a sudden bright light that could have blinded her had she not looked away. In a fraction of a second, the light fades and forms into the one thing she was just wishing for moments ago: a barrier. Since guards are far too near to where her horse is standing, the thin bluish-purple force field around her is small and it takes Ivy no more than a second to realize she and Snow aren't the only ones inside it. A third being stands in front of her in a fighting stance, dressed in a dark brown short-sleeved tunic over black pants with ink painted all over his arms. A long sword is attached to his back but what Ivy mainly pays attention to is the glowing bluish-purple Amulet in his hand.

A Holder defending her?

Ivy swallows hard. She does not need saving, definitely not by the same people she considers enemies. Or, perhaps, this man is an unnatural Holder. Why so much ink? No one in this kingdom has ever dared to paint on their bodies in such a way. It's forbidden.

By now, Queen Matilda has arrived on the scene. Behind her is Gozar on his own steed, still clutching onto the shackles and brutally dragging the prisoner along. The man continues to stumble and fall to his knees but Gozar does not stop. In fact, the guard only speeds up, grinning mischievously as the Outsider's body follows along on top of harsh sand while bumping into anything on the way. The grin is soon to fall off Gozar's face as soon as he realizes what's going on.

"Ivy, you will stop this nonsense right here, right now if you know what's good for you!" Queen Matilda barks as her rosy brown horse comes to a halt. "Do you really believe you can win this? Just because you've got the Golden Amulet with you does not make you invulnerable."

"So you admit the Golden Amulet is mine?" Ivy calls out. Although she tries to sound brave, the uneasiness from being around the man in front of her comes in the way.

Queen Matilda scoffs. "This is not about the Golden Amulet anymore, Ivy. You're being arrested for treason."

"All because you forced a man to spit out lies?" Ivy purses her lips, a slight furrow between her brows. She ponders over whether or not the barrier will follow if she starts running. Will the man follow?

"You think everything said against you is a lie." The woman's lips curl and she lets out a derisive laugh, amusement swaying in her wicked eyes. "As to how you managed to form an army of your own, I do not know. All I know is that it's over. This ends here." She points at the unknown man. "Don't allow this child to drag you down with her. You'd think twice about protecting her if you were any intelligent."

The only thing the man does is answer Ivy's question. "Move."

"What?"

"Start moving. As long as I'm with you, you're well protected."

Who are you? Ivy exhales. "I-it doesn't matter. The guards will chase after me." She can't see the man's face. Perhaps, if she can get even a glimpse of it, she'd be able to tell where she's seen him before and why he's helping her. Is he on her list? No, he can't be. The man's voice doesn't sound familiar at all.

Queen Matilda turns to the guards. "Where's Vihaan? He can easily phase through that barrier."

"Today is Vihaan's day off, Your Majesty." one of her men responds.

"Day off?!" the woman shrieks. "For as long as that wretched little thing is free, there is no such thing as a day off. Get him here. Now!"

"You will do no such thing."

When the voice of the king pierces through their ears all of a sudden, heads are quick to turn. The man does not hesitate to start his way toward his wife on his own horse. Ivy watches him carefully. There's something about the look in his dark hooded eyes that stirs up puzzlement within her—a look of anger not for her but for the queen instead, almost as though he's not on the woman's side anymore.

Has he figured out the truth? The sigh that leaves Ivy's mouth is out of slight relief. If the king himself doesn't trust Queen Matilda, others are sure to follow.

"Titus, what are you doing?" Queen Matilda hisses.

"No, what are you doing? What happened to the deal we made?"

The woman scoffs. "Deal? What deal?"

"Ivy is not to be touched until you prove the Golden Amulet belongs to you."

"Titus!" Horror flashes through the queen's eyes for a moment. She glances around warily as she clears her throat. "I-I'm working on that but this isn't about the Golden Amulet anymore. Ivy has been proven to be a criminal. We just got word that she was in cahoots with the Outsiders themselves. She's to be arrested for treason!"

King Titus draws back from the woman and takes in Ivy's situation: the guards surrounding her, the Holders still clutching onto rocks, eyes scrunched together, nostrils flaring, and the barrier stopping them all from pouncing. Raising his hand and signaling for the guards to turn back leaves everyone else rooted to their spots, mouths either agape or mumbling to each other.

"Titus, what are you doing?!" Queen Matilda questions again, this time angrier.

But the man does not pay her any more attention. "From now on, you are only to take orders from me," he informs the guards. "The girl is not to be touched."

"Titus, you can't do that!"

Once again, her cries are ignored. King Titus points to the prisoner. "Take him back to his cell."

"Ivy has made plans to bomb this kingdom!" a Holder screeches. "Isn't that more than enough to put her behind bars?" A series of agreements comes next.

"Listen, a proper investigation will commence soon regarding this issue," King Titus tries to reason. "As of now, we have no evidence tying her to this crime."

"Evidence?" another Holder exclaims. "An Outsider just confessed to Ivy coming to see them days ago. I'm not certain about you, Your Majesty, but that sounds like enough evidence to put her away. Letting her go is utterly ridiculous!"

For a second, the king's hands seem to quiver with fury. He turns to look at Ivy again, as though expecting her to find a way to calm the thundering crowd. Ivy only snickers. She tugs on Snow's reins and the horse listens, moving away from the Holders. Although the barrier follows, Ivy knows there's no point of having it now. Whether or not everyone agrees with his decisions, King Titus is still in charge. No doubt the Holders will allow their rage to get the better of them and strike back, however.

The man in front of Ivy picks this up too. As soon as he hears Snow slowly shifting away, he dashes towards her and hops on. "Head back to Angora," he orders.

"Not until I know who you are."

"Head back to Angora and you'll get your answers."

And so, that's what she does.

There's a girl in Haru's shelter when Ivy stumbles inside.

No doubt another Outsider considering she's got a rose inked on her left arm.

At first, she's oblivious to the presence of Ivy and her Outsider companion, far too engrossed in the papers Ivy left scattered on the living room floor before she left. These papers bear the imprints of stories authored by Haru prior to his unfortunate demise. During the past several hours, Ivy has surprisingly found solace within the pages of these delightful tales. Perusing them started as a means to alleviate her boredom. Now, she finds herself repeatedly returning to these pages, perhaps in the hope of discovering new content.

The smile on the girl's rosebud lips fades the moment Ivy's voice sounds.

"Who are you? What do you want with me?!"

The girl turns away from the pages and locks eyes with Ivy. Much like the first Outsider, she has an Amulet adorning her neck. This sight presents a perplexing conundrum for Ivy. Aren't Outsiders perceived as Powerless beings that miraculously discovered an escape from their kingdoms?

Perhaps, Hui-Qing got it all wrong.

"Did you write all this, Ivy?" the girl suddenly asks, her coal eyes going round as she holds up one of the papers. "Wow, I didn't think you were a writer. A good one at that, too."

But Ivy entirely disregards her words and demands again, "What do you want with me?"

The girl sighs and allows the paper to leave her grasp. "Not here for small talk, I see." She takes short strides towards Ivy until their faces are only inches apart, her head slightly over Ivy's shoulders. "We're here because our Head insisted we could trust you."

"Your Head?"

"Yes." She gives a half shrug. "Everyone's got a leader. Even us."

"And why does your Head insist on such a thing?"

The girl turns away then and begins pacing back and forth with her arms behind her back. "You were previously a Powerless, were you not, Ivy? I suppose he thought you'd understand."

"Understand why you're going to war with the biggest kingdom on this continent?" Ivy raises a brow.

"We're not going to war. We don't want to go to war!"

"Well, Arya sure seems to think so." Ivy gestures to the door with her thumb. "They're all preparing. They've even got an academy training children from the ages of sixteen how to fight. They've got more teaching young, young children how to hide or what to do if they ever find themselves in danger." She snorts as she lowers her hand. "Arya isn't going to back down from a battle they're training for."

"Yes, we know!" the girl shrieks, her breaths quickening. "We know, Ivy. That's why we're here."

Ivy frowns and tilts her head to the side. "Wait... You're here because you think I can help you stop this war? Is that it?"

"We do not have as many people as Arya does. Not even close. While we're merely in the hundreds, they're in the hundreds of millions." The girl gets close again. This time, her eyes are glistening, pleading. "We're going to lose this war. Even worse, we're going to lose all of our people because there's no way any of us are making it out alive. Ivy, we don't just have soldiers. We have children. So many little children who are unaware of what's about to happen. There's a whole town full of them and they're all about to die."

Ivy's brows snap together. "And you think I can protect them?"

Both at once, the girl and her Outsider friend glance down at the pendant around her neck.

"Is that what this is?" Ivy shifts away with a glare. "Because I have this Amulet, I'm all of a sudden capable of shielding an entire town?"

"Did you not come back to Arya to get your people out of slavery?"

"And how would you know that?" Ivy challenges.

The girl lets out a small, teasing laugh as though the question is one of the stupidest she's ever heard. "My people always know what's going on in Arya—the biggest dramas. We relish in them, really. Some of us walk amongst you and you don't even realize it. It didn't take long for us to learn who the true possessor of the pendant was and neither did it take us long to understand why you'd even bothered coming back."

"And so what if that is why I'm back?"

"Don't you understand, Ivy? We're your people. The Outsiders are a group of Powerless that, yes, found a way out of their torturous kingdoms but are still suffering."

Now it's Ivy's turn to glance down at the girl's pendant. "You don't look very Powerless to me."

"I—" The girl takes hold of the crystal on her chest. "I'm an unnatural." She nods over to her friend. "So is he. We're two of the only four Outsiders with Amulets."

Ivy turns to look at the man behind her. "Which kingdoms are you both from?"

"Arya."

"Thegn."

Ivy gasps as she switches her gaze back to the girl. "You're from here? But. . ." She thinks back to what Hui-Qing told her. The Outsiders are a collective of Powerless beings that managed to successfully evade capture and escape their kingdoms. None of them are from this kingdom, however, since survival beyond the borders of Arya is impossible. . .

"I left Arya when I was seven," the girl explains. "Days after my parents were slaughtered. The Outsiders found me and welcomed me with open arms"

Ivy studies her again. She's about the same age, perhaps a year younger. Which means the Outsiders have been around since I was, at least, six. "How come I've never heard of you people until now?"

"We try our best to stay low," the man behind her answers.

"Royals knew about us from the very beginning, however," the girl adds. "They did their best to keep us a secret. They believed that if people knew of our escape, the Powerless would be motivated to attempt it. We were doing so well hiding until two of our people got caught two years ago and a fight sparked."

"Now, some of them have been caught again." The first Outsider grunts. He looks like he wants to drive a fist through a wall. "We never learn our lesson."

"Hey, hey, hey." The girl steps forward and rises to her tippy toes to place a gentle hand on his shoulder. "How else are we meant to know what's going on in Arya? How else are we meant to know what they're planning? If some of us weren't here, we never would have found out that they're preparing for war."

"But now that we've got Ivy on board, we don't have to do that anymore, do we?" the man asks as a smile plays on his lips and his dark bushy eyebrows raise.

Ivy scoffs lightly. "Has news of me owning the Golden Amulet spread outside of Arya already?"

"Just us." The girl shrugs.

Of course, the news hasn't reached other kingdoms. Ivy expected this. It is already bad enough for Matilda that her kingdom wants her head but having other kingdoms involved? No more waiting for a miracle or for some more evidence. The woman will be executed on the spot.

"Listen," the girl begins again. "What you're doing right now is good. If everyone is far too concentrated on this whole Golden Amulet drama, they'll hardly pay attention to us."

"The trainings are still going o—"

"Yes, but," she cuts Ivy off, "if it weren't for you returning and showing everyone how deceitful Matilda is, this war would already be happening. My—our people would already be dying."

Ivy presses her lips together, her hands slowly unclenching.

As though she needs any more assurance, the girl places her hands on Ivy's shoulders and gives a small, warm smile. "We're not your enemies, Ivy, I promise. You and the Outsiders are on the same side."

Ivy sighs and takes a seat on the floor, as though the weight of everything she's just been told is far too great to keep her body standing. The girl makes a point. It would be strange to regard these people as her foes when they're all fighting the same battle.

"Well," she says, glancing from the girl to the man. "What plan do you have in mind, then?"

word count • 5154

17 | Poppy Winters

CHAPTER SEVENTEEN — POPPY WINTERS

AT the mere age of six, Poppy Winters experienced her first encounter with death.

This particular day remains etched in her memory, a trigger that refuses to fade. In fact, as she's seated there at the large dining table, a spoon in hand, an untouched plate in front of her, and voices rattling off with such exuberance and enthusiasm in the background, it's all that can occupy her mind. The worst part—the part that pricks at her heart the most even today—was that she could have prevented that day. If only she visited Mrs. Duong and forewarned her of the impending execution, perhaps her life could have been prolonged.

She knows what Mrs. Duong would say. "It was not your fault. You were just a child." But age doesn't matter. Not to Poppy. Just because she was six does not mean she did not know every little detail of the plan. She was fully aware of the impending arrest, the prepared rope, and the location of the execution. While her parents unknowingly discussed the plan, Poppy fortuitously eavesdropped from the other side of the living room wall in the middle of filling her favorite pink cup with milk.

It seemed her own father had been the one to report the woman, in the first place. How hard could it have been to scramble out the door and dash to Mrs. Duong's house to warn her to run or hide? How hard could it have been to say no to her mother when Mrs. Winters insisted she stayed inside all day?

Poppy's affection for the woman was unwavering and enduring. Despite her reluctance to admit it to her parents, Mrs. Duong held the position of her dearest friend. In fact, the young girl occasionally found solace in pretending the woman was her mother. Whenever Poppy claimed to be visiting a friend, she would secretly divert her path to Mrs. Duong's residence. There, she would be greeted by the enticing aroma of freshly baked cookies and a refreshing glass of milk, thoughtfully prepared and placed on the knitch counter. The woman would then settle herself down comfortably on the living room floor with her knitting materials ready and wait for the child. This clandestine rendezvous had become a weekly ritual.

So, why didn't she run the first chance she got?

Perhaps, it was due to her mother's insistence on her remaining indoors. Although the door was left unlocked during daylight hours, Poppy's fear of disappointing her parents prevented her from venturing beyond its threshold. They expect her to listen and obey at all times and she has never done the opposite.

The next day, she saw the woman's dangling feet, her closed eyes and sealed lips, the rope around her neck. Death—when someone becomes completely motionless and is unable to open her eyes. That's how much of it six-year-old her understood thanks to her teacher. Poppy remembers walking in on her parents arguing with her teacher that she should never have told a child such a thing.

"Why was Mrs. Duong eshechuted?" She remembers her six-year-old self asking. Poppy thought her visits to the woman were secret but with the way her mother didn't question how she even knew about Mrs. Duong and her execution, it seemed she was already aware of it.

"Poppy, darling, she was a bad woman," her mother told her. "Not only was she a Powerless but she stole and lied."

"Stole what?"

"Oh, Poppy, she stole almost everything. Food, jewels, furniture, medicine. She took something of value from people. She didn't care about anyone's feelings, only what she could get her selfish hands on," her mother said. "Such a horrendous being does not deserve to breathe."

Why did she believe her mother?

Well... Mothers know best, don't they? They are seen as the epitome of wisdom and honesty. It's the idea her mother instilled in her since the moment she could comprehend words. They never deceive their children. At least, her mother would never deceive her, so, of course, she placed unwavering trust in her mother's words, as any child would. Yet even as her perception of Mrs. Duong shifted, Poppy was burdened with a persistent guilt for failing to warn the woman. She struggled to reconcile the image of her trusted best friend—a woman who practically baked and knitted all day—with the reality of her deceitful nature.

Thinking about it now, it stings realizing that her own viewpoints were solely shaped by her parents' teachings. They instilled in her the belief that their opinions were infallible, leaving no room for alternative perspectives. Her parents never told a lie. Such was the narrative they imparted upon her.

When she got older, Poppy understood that her mother didn't entirely lie to her that day. Mrs. Duong did steal and lie. She did take something of value from other people. But Mrs. Duong did not deserve to die... because the things of value she took were not frivolously squandered or hoarded for personal benefit. Instead, she sold them in order to provide basic necessities such as shelters, groceries, and clean water for her people. The individuals from which she took these valuables were Holders who consistently denied the Powerless their right to essential resources. The feelings she turned a blind eye to were the hostility Holders expressed for having these things taken from them.

Her mother didn't lie. But she certainly did not provide the complete story, either.

Mrs. Duong's actions, while unlawful, were driven by a sense of equity and a desire to rectify the injustices faced by the marginalized—something Poppy knows she would not have understood during then.

You cannot lie to yourself anymore. You're trapped.

Trapped.

Poppy can't believe that such a simple word carries a weightier significance. Previously, it evoked images of a helpless mouse manipulated into entering its own prison and law-breakers confined behind bars. That is until her teacher—the same woman who shared the heart-rending news of how she could never see Mrs. Duong again, alive and well, and hug her, or eat her freshly baked cookies or tell her how her day went—sat her down and shed light in great detail a heavier meaning of the word, a meaning she often overlooked because her parents convinced her otherwise.

"If you need help, Poppy, know that I'm always here," her teacher even added.

Her teacher's offer of assistance served as a beacon of hope amidst the bleakness of her circumstance. At least, that was before her parents banned her from seeing the woman again.

"We're just trying to protect you, Poppy. We're only doing what's best for you."

How many times has she heard those words fall out of her parents' unscrupulous mouths? How many times has she been led to believe that everything she's had to do is for a better future, a future that her mother often describes as one that any Holder and Powerless would kill for, only to realize that all her efforts have only served to feed into her parents' greed and hunger for more power?

"Poppy, darling, how are you doing today?"

For Poppy, the insipid conversation has already blared in the background long ago. She is there at the long dining table but not quite there. This detachment, if discovered by her parents, would undoubtedly displease them. It goes against their expectations of her.

Their primary objective is for her to establish a reputation and forge connections within their social circle.

She not only has to be seen but remembered.

Poppy finds herself surrounded by rules, from the Royals and the competitions she often takes part in, to the academy she attends and, most significantly, her parents. She can do nothing but adhere to them all, too afraid of the consequences if she doesn't. But perhaps, it's time for a change.

In a calm and confident manner, she answers the woman seated across from her, "I'm fine today, ma'am," while ensuring to display her one-million-gold smile that her parents have often praised for its ability to evoke envy in commoners, captivate boys, and foster friendships with girls.

All around the dining table, a cacophony of laughter, chewing, and cheering fills the air. Amidst the lively atmosphere, Poppy stands out, seated uncomfortably at the left end of the table beside one of the girls her age, looking like a lost hound. Her discomfort is further accentuated by the strapless golden gown she is wearing, a garment she struggles to bear with composure. In contrast, the other girls are donning similar dresses but exude confidence, a quality her mother has cautioned her she lacks. The worst are the tall heels. Poppy has been wearing them since they left for the dinner, which already feels like forever ago, and they are currently murdering her small reddened feet.

It's something her mother insisted she wore because she believed it would make her stand out and outshine the others. Mrs. Winters wasn't exactly wrong. Poppy couldn't help but notice that her attire garnered a significant amount of attention, with more than half of the group commenting on its dazzling and exorbitant nature, while the other girls received only a fraction of the compliments, possibly around three or four each.

Mrs. Winters hoped that by clothing her daughter in such a way, not only would these powerful people see that they possess a keen sense of fashion but that they were wealthy enough to afford such a thing. And once they return home, Poppy is certain her parents will go on and on boasting about how much better they did than everybody else. Everything always has to be a competition to them.

"Ma'am?"

The woman Poppy greeted looks taken back for a second, a hand flying to her exposed chest as a small offended look takes shape on her face. Poppy freezes. Did she just mess up? Her parents would be displeased knowing she angered someone influential. They would never allow her to hear the end of it. But when the woman suddenly bursts into laughter, Poppy instantly understands she was only teasing.

"Don't make me feel so old. Please, just call me Mrs. Lee," she says. "I'm Sa-rang's mother."

"Ah, well then, it's nice to finally meet you, Mrs. Lee."

It isn't. Nobody wants to meet the mother of the girl who threw a fit like a toddler for losing to Poppy in the beauty pageant that recently occurred.

Mrs. Lee leans forward and places a hand on Poppy's bare shoulder. "Your mother wasn't lying. You really are one of the prettiest girls I've ever laid eyes on." The woman chuckles yet, for whatever reason, it sounds more bitter than friendly. "No wonder you won."

"I—thank you."

Poppy swallows. Despite the mindless ramblings of another woman to Mrs. Winters, she can feel her mother's eyes on her, watching and ensuring her daughter's every move is devoid of any mistake. Her mother isn't exactly content with the idea of being anywhere near Mrs. Lee but she knows of the latter's elevated status in terms of popularity and wealth. Mrs. Winters is keen—and desperate but she's good at not showing it—on forging connections with as many influential individuals as she possibly can. It's part of why she had her family move from Goch to Arya.

It is all part of a bigger plan, she often tells Poppy.

"Mother!" Sa-rang shoots Mrs. Lee a glare from where she's sitting. She's been watching Poppy as well, perhaps even a lot more attentively than her own parents have, eager to seize upon any misstep that can later be used for mockery.

The presence of Sa-rang only adds to the pressure. Having one of her biggest contenders sitting just a few seats away from her does little to foster a sense of comfort for Poppy.

In a lot of different ways, Sa-rang possesses certain qualities that remind Poppy of Athena Takao, a prominent figure in Arya, the girl many commoners envy and boys actually swoon for, and the girl Mrs. Winters regards as Poppy's main competitor. It is not surprising that Sa-rang is one of Athena's great friends, either. Such girls love to either pitch themselves against one another or stick together. Perhaps, the latter explains Mrs. Winters' interest in establishing a relationship with Mrs. Lee. From Sa-rang, Poppy can climb her way to Athena and surpass her. Somehow.

Good thing Athena isn't actually here. Her absence spares Poppy from the challenge of having to deal with two hot-headed girls who openly display their dislike towards her.

"Of course, not that I think my daughter didn't deserve to win first place," Mrs. Lee immediately corrects with a small, awkward chuckle.

"No, it's alright. I understand." This time, instead of a simple smile, her response is accompanied by a light laughter. "In fact, I think she deserved to win first place, too. Sa-rang did astounding."

From the corner of her eyes, she can see her mother smile. This is just as she taught her. Be humble and professional. By downplaying her own achievements, she could aim to demonstrate her lack of egotism and garner praise for her graciousness, even towards her competitors. Her mother emphasized that self-praise held little value, as it was the opinions of others that mattered more than anything else—aside from jewels, of course.

But Sa-rang is not having it. Unlike Mrs. Winters, her face is crimson, her forehead furrowed, and her jaw clenched. Smoldered with rage, she slams a hand against the table.

"Sa-rang!" Mrs. Lee hisses as soon as all eyes fall on the girl.

With trembling hands, Sa-rang rises to her feet.

"Sit. Back. Down!" her mother snaps.

Nostrils flaring, the girl stays standing, fist clenched at her sides, her knuckles white.

Mrs. Lee has to rise from her seat as well and get close to her daughter's face. "Sit. Down!" Her voice booms like thunder, each word a sharp crack of lightning.

Poppy has never seen the woman so red.

Finally, Sa-rang listens, slumping down into her chair with a big hmph like that of a toddler. Poppy can see her own mother attempting to suppress a proud smile. The young girl grips her spoon at the sight, knuckles straining against the pressure. It's all just a big competition for all of them.

"You know what?" Sa-rang suddenly declares. "I may not have won that stupid pageant but at least, I don't go around befriending the kingdom's biggest enemy!"

Silence follows. The air becomes tense and awkward as everyone either stops mid-bite or drops their utensil to direct their gaze at Poppy.

Mr. Winters is the first to speak. "What does she mean by that, Poppy?"

Poppy's mouth drops open but Sa-rang refuses to allow her to get a word in.

"I saw her in the dining hall at the academy," she begins. "Poppy was sitting with Ivy, willingly. She looked quite relaxed around her as well, as though she was Ivy's friend."

The look in Mrs. Winters' eyes scares Poppy the most. Her mother's gaze, with its searing intensity, can scorch the very surface of the earth. The sheer force of her stare demands Poppy deny Sa-rang's words. In its presence, Poppy cannot help but feel a sense of anxiety, suddenly compelled to get up and walk out of the room while she's still breathing. Yet, while it's a look that Poppy dreads the most, she cannot negate the raw anger that shoots through her at the mere sight of it. She shuts her eyes as her teacher's words fill her head.

You cannot lie to yourself anymore. You're trapped.

"Think about it," finally, she speaks in a bitter and critical tone, her fingers slowly letting go of her spoon. "Think about it for just a second. You love Queen Matilda, do you not? In fact, every one of you here adores her. How does it make you feel knowing that you love a Powerless?"

"Poppy!" Now, it's her mother's turn to raise her voice.

"Well, I'm not saying it's a bad thing," Poppy carries on, for once in her life disregarding the judgmental looks that she's been taught to obsess over, disregarding her mother's warning that she's been taught to always obey in a heartbeat. "You all consider Queen Matilda your friend. All I'm saying is that perhaps, you've been wrong about the Powerless all this time."

"Poppy—!" her father tries this time.

"Why don't you give the rest of the Powerless the same chance you gave Queen Matil—"

"Poppy Winters, you will shut it right now!" As he screams, her father hammers his fist against the table, each strike louder than the last, reverberating through the room, causing his daughter to flinch. "Queen Matilda is not a Powerless, you hear me?" he barks at an even louder volume, his face surpassing the look of anger Mrs. Lee wore just a moment ago. "No daughter of mine will heed the words of a traitor and disrespect our queen."

You're just saying that because you refuse to believe that you've been deluded all this time.

But Poppy sits in silence, her head hanging low, shoulders slumped, shame apparent in her downcast eyes. She dares not speak her thoughts now, the last bit of the confidence that sprouted out of nowhere dying out.

All of you are blind.

She hates that her eyes are glistening now, tears tracing a path down her cheeks. For once, can she speak her thoughts without sobbing about it like a baby seconds later?

"I apologize for whatever that was," her mother begins, a hand on her chest. "I promise you all that we'll give Poppy a lecture once we get home. This is not a behavior we condone, I swear it."

At those words, Poppy sinks further into her seat.

She knows exactly what her mother means by a lecture.

word count • 2962

18 | ayako

CHAPTER EIGHTEEN — EIGHTEEN

The woman's desk is the same as it was three years ago. No, not the desk itself, as unlike before where it seemed as though it would fall apart at any second, this desk is made of smooth, repurposed wood and stands on strong iron legs. It's one of the contents on the desk that leaves Ivy recalling the past. A cup of hot tea. Even now, she can still recall the uncomfortable sensation of the burning liquid trailing down her back, leaving a mark.

Her eyes dive a little lower until they come across the metal name tag nailed to the front of the desk.

"Who are you?"

The brittle voice sounds no different than the last time Ivy heard it. When she turns, there the woman is, standing tall and thin in a white sheath dress and silver heels.

"Y-You!" Mrs. Kumar fidgets, fiddling with the ring on her finger.

There were always times when Ivy would grow afraid once those old fears ran through her head, when she heard the taunting laughter of years past, when she had been a skinny child and the point of every jest. And she knew she was afraid when those unpleasant memories broke loose of their chains and wreaked havoc on her self-assurance, eroding the person she had worked so hard to construct since those gloomy times. Laying eyes on this woman again takes her back to those fears, to the past when Mrs. Kumar would welcome her into the classroom with yet another gibe, when she'd turn a blind eye to a classmate pushing her fragile fifteen-year-old body to the floor or unintentionally yanking her hair. When Mrs. Kumar always refused to hear her out during a dispute with another being and took out the special whip she kept on top of her bureau, when the woman would move the chairs and desks aside and force her to the floor, allowing every other child to watch as each hit lashed across her back. Constantly seeking an excuse to write her wrong and punish her.

But Mrs. Kumar is somewhat different now. Unlike before when she'd stand tall and make firm and precise movements with her chest pushed out, she seems to be holding her breath, her posture is hunched, and her eyes are darting in every direction, as though unwilling to keep them on Ivy.

"What are you doing in my room?"

The younger revels defiantly in seeing her former teacher like this. She can imagine the woman's heart pounding hard, just as hers had been before she took each strike. "Are you already beginning to sweat, Mrs. Kumar?" She slaps her forehead with a teasing grin. "Why, but I haven't even done anything yet."

Mrs. Kumar's arms remain at her sides but Ivy can see them slightly trembling. Her forehead creases and her anger spikes, yet at the same time, fear has crept up her spine, holding her in a tightening grip. "I have a daughter," she finally says, exhaling shakily as though it took everything in her to let the words out. "I have a daughter, Eun. She's only two!" And now she's shouting and the first tear has slipped through.

Regardless, Ivy does not break her stance and the smile on her face does not quiver. "Good for you?"

"You wouldn't dare take a mother away from her child!"

"Years ago, you didn't have a problem taking a child away from her mother."

"Neither of your parents even loved you!" Mrs. Kumar thunders, her voice cracking halfway and her cheeks stained. "Not your former parents. They gave you up. They didn't want you. Not your current parents. They won't even look you in the eyes. They're ashamed to call you their daughter. You're nothing but a maid to them. You're a Powerless, Eun. What did you expect? To be pampered like a princess?"

"I want to know, Mrs. Kumar, is this your attempt at begging for forgiveness? Because if it is, you're very poor at it." On the outside, her smile is still there, but if Ivy made a claim that the woman's words did not puncture her heart, that would be a lie. *They gave you up. They didn't want you.* Her face is a mask of resignation, a façade that conceals the raw ache of her woe, her true emotions hidden beneath a carefully crafted veneer. She does not need to hear about how she was thrown away over and over again, how her family put her in the hands of monsters and never once looked back, never once regretted it.

Ivy casts one last dirty look at the teary-eyed woman and heads for the door. Mrs. Kumar is another one of those wants Adora warned her to be careful of, an enemy whose demise would flood her soul with sunshine but not impact her people's well-being. Mrs. Kumar is also the person she needs for the next step of her plot—or rather, the woman's ability. Otherwise, she would no longer be here.

Coming back to the academy with rumors about conceivably working with the Outsiders is not how Ivy intended to start her day. Outside of the classroom, troubled voices fill her ears, some of which mumble about how crude she is to want to bomb the entirety of Arya, others questioning why King Titus prevented his wife from seizing her, and the remainder making threats on her life.

"If I were the Royals, I would not hesitate to slay her right here, right now."

"So, why don't you?"

Yet once again, their opinions are of little importance to Ivy.

"What were you doing in Mrs. Kumar's room?"

Clover. She was there during those crude days, three seats away from Ivy as another one of Kumar's students. Although she was never targeted by the woman, Clover saw firsthand what she did to those less than. Ivy gazes at her briefly and continues on her way without a response.

"Hold on a second, Ivy." Clover takes hold of her arm and yanks her back. There's this sudden look in her eyes that brings Ivy to an immediate stop. Clover's jaw sets and her pitch goes lower, steady. She moves closer to the other, almost in her personal space, though it seems she doesn't realize it. "I want to join you."

"Join me in what?" But Ivy already knows.

"You're planning something, I'm certain of it," Clover insists. "I don't know what this something is but I know that all those years you spent out of Arya, you were plotting a scheme. And I ask that I be a part of it."

The worst thing one can be is a coward, not just towards themselves but towards others, as well. Cowards will do anything to defend their physicality even at the expense of their emotional survival because they are willing to become monsters and enable their dark selves to replace their genuine selves. That's what Ivy formerly thought Clover to be. A coward. But after she learned from Poppy about how she aided the Powerless, people opposite of her kind, people deemed undeserving of love and respect, and hearing her now, Ivy knows she misjudged the girl. Yet, there's still something about Clover that makes it difficult to trust her.

"Absolutely not. You serve no use to me, Clover."

"My end is near, Ivy. I can feel it. I know of many people that have been slain just for aiding the Powerless and soon, I will be one of them. Ever since it was revealed that I secretly helped them, nobody has stopped telling me how the Hunter is coming for me. And yet, I keep going. Don't you get it, Ivy? You really believe I'm afraid? The Hunter does not terrify me. The Royals do not terrify me."

Ivy continues to stare at her, a bit wide-eyed. Clover's face has contorted into a mask of intension, brows furrowed, lips curved into a scowl, her very presence radiating a menacing aura that hints at an impending eruption. The Royals do not terrify me. And that's when Ivy gets it.

"Who did they take from you?"

At that question, Clover's eyes instantly soften and her lips slightly quiver. "My mother."

Though she's unwilling to further explain, Ivy understands her hatred even more then, and what causes her to hesitate is not knowing whether Clover wants to join her simply to free the Powerless from their assailants or to get vengeance on those that have wronged her. Either way, they're more alike than she believed.

"I'll think about it."

It's not a yes but Clover understands it's not a no either. A small smile forms on her face. Just when Ivy has turned to walk off, she calls her back again once a reminder snaps inside her head. "Two days from now, you should be far away from that village you live in. The Hunter has planned to set a trap and will be waiting for you then. My Amulet warned me of this."

"Your Amulet?" Ivy doesn't doubt the information but now that she thinks about it, this is the very first time she's hearing of Clover's abilities.

"Danger Intuition." Clover's grin grows wider. "How else do you think I'm still alive? My power's helped me avoid danger. Without it, I would have already met my end a long time ago."

"Why did you not use this power better when you were younger?" Ivy looks at Clover head to toe before she begins to walk away again. "Would have saved you some scars."

——..∘☽▫☾∘..——

Ivy's next class is puzzling to her.

The walls are white, and aside from the small wooden bureau up front and what she assumes is their trainer standing next to it, the floor is bare. Their voices and feet are the only sounds that buzz through their ears. Ivy pauses at the entrance while the rest shuffle inside. If there's one thing she's learned since the passing of her friends, it's that empty rooms are her enemies.

Empty rooms echo her thoughts. They make it easy to relive what happened and they make it easy to imagine the parts she never saw. The piercing shrill of their screams coming to a sudden halt. The smell of dried blood leaving behind a hint of hatred and fury, and satisfaction from their slayer. Empty rooms remind her all over again that she will never see their mesmerizing eyes again. Never to see their smiles that always brightened her day. Empty rooms make her think that some part of it was her fault. Make her believe that she could have saved, at least, one of them. Perhaps, she could have further insisted that they stayed with the Patels rather than sleep in Delyth's house alone. Empty rooms remind her that it could have been her. She was that close to leaving with them and she would have if not for Alvin who ratted her out to Angelo and Liezel. In a way, Alvin saved her but she can't help but despise him even more for that.

Her trail of thoughts are interrupted by the call of her name. When she snaps out of it, Clover is standing in front of her, concern in her eyes. Everyone else has already placed their bags on the bureau and found a spot on the floor to sit. Aside from Reuben, the spectacled boy, Hiroshi Sol, and even the strange undercut boy who can't seem to keep his eyes off of her, the boys have engaged in a conversation, eagerly pointing to something at the back of the room, something Ivy can't see from where she's standing. Athena and Jade are once again sneaking glances at her and whispering among themselves. Poppy has the same look as Clover, and their teacher is tapping her foot impatiently, glaring daggers straight at her.

"Are we going to have a problem?" she calls out in a strong Japanese accent.

Ivy enters and drops her satchel bag on top of the rest without a word, ignoring the menacing look the woman has fixed on her. Now that she's inside, she can see the room isn't entirely as empty as she thought. At the back of it against a wall is a row of swords and daggers of different types and lengths. The sight of them causes her heart to swell with just as much exhilaration as the boys, maybe more.

She sits at an area that distances her from everyone else but not a second goes by before Clover scoots closer. Their trainer pulls open the bureau's first drawer and takes out of it a small box.

"My name is Ayako," she begins, standing tall, her spine rigid with arrogance. Her voice cuts through the air like a sharpened blade, commanding attention and respect. "In this class, I have only one rule." She holds out the box and begins to walk towards them. "No Amulets."

The class erupts in horrified and puzzled shouts. Ayako silences them with a question. "What would you do if you were attacked and you didn't have your Amulet with you?"

"Defend myself without my Amulet. Simple." Ga-Eul shrugs.

The look on the woman's face is formidable. "I assume you know how, then."

"Well. . ." The boy's eyes dart around the room, maybe to avoid eye contact. "I-It's not going to happen anyway because I'll always have my Amulet with me."

Ayako scoffs. "That's what I thought." She shakes the box violently. "In. Now."

Ivy takes off the golden pendant and drops it in the box but she makes sure it's out of sight before the woman can move on to the next student.

As Ayako begins her way back to her wooden bureau, a girl leans closer to a grunting Ga-Eul and tells him, "Well, I heard she's one of the best combat fighters in this kingdom."

"So what?!" Ga-Eul snaps. "There's hardly any need to learn how to fight when your Amulet practically does it all for you." He scoffs, frowning with irritation. "This is a waste of time." Perhaps, it's because, for once, his Amulet is out of his hand and he feels powerless without it, Ivy guesses.

"This is a waste of time, you say?" Ayako's eyes crinkle at the corner, her thin mouth curved into a lopsided grin, one so condescending and enigmatic. "What's your name, young man?"

"Ga-Eul."

"Ga-Eul," the woman repeats. "Why don't you come up front."

"What for?" As he asks his question, the boy rises from the floor and makes his way over.

"You claimed you can still effectively defend yourself even without the aid of your Amulet. I want to see what that looks like." Ayako's narrow eyes scan the rest of the class, her gaze moving from one individual to another. In comparison to the formidable boy standing near her, she appears noticeably smaller, her round face only reaching up to his arms, and her porcelain skin a much lighter tone than Ga-Eul's tan complexion. "Who would like to step forward and face off against Ga-Eul?"

The class goes silent as their eyes shift from one classmate to another, as though waiting for someone else to volunteer. Before another boy, just about an inch shorter than Ga-Eul, can raise his hand, Ivy stands.

At the sight of this, Ga-Eul immediately sneers, staring at the girl as though she is nothing more than a mere insect. Ayako waves Ivy over and asks the class to shift back to give them more space. Ivy exchanges a glance with her opponent and it's instantly clear that this is not a friendly encounter.

I have always wondered what it'd be like fighting the strongest student in my class.

Fighting Adora was challenging. The woman may have looked old but she still had a lot of fight in her. In the end, before she came back to Arya, she won against her mentor. Ivy remembers how proud she was during that moment until she realized it wasn't a win at all, not when Adora was not in her strongest state. Her mentor became weak, became incapable of even dodging a simple attack.

Will all of Adora's training be enough?

She never did get a chance to fight in Mrs. Singh's class. Following Calliope's victory over Reuben, another boy who goes by the name of Ravana was brought to the center of the circle. He lost to Calliope, as well. The bell rang shortly after Calliope's third win against Jade. Now, all Ivy yearns for is the opportunity to face her and Ga-Eul. They are almost as good as what Ivy believes Adora would have been had it not been for her state, and winning against them both would serve as a good enough evidence that she would have beaten her mentor even if she hadn't been suffering.

The moment Ayako gives a slight nod to commence the fight, Ga-Eul charges forward, his fists coming at Ivy with incredible speed and force, yet she manages to evade his attacks through nimble footwork and quick reflexes. Despite her successful dodges, Ivy is struck by the raw power behind each punch, and the adrenaline surges through her veins as she concentrates on finding an opening to strike back.

Seconds after carefully observing her opponent's movements, she finally sees her chance and launches a swift counterattack, targeting the boy's vulnerable spots with accurate blows. The force of her punches against his flesh brings a gratifying sensation, yet it's not enough to take him down. Ga-Eul retaliates with a fierce uppercut that connects with her jaw, instantly inflicting a piercing agony that sends Ivy stumbling back.

She catches herself before she falls but the strike stupefies her. Ga-Eul just landed a blow that's got her mouth tasting bitter with blood yet there's not a hint of hesitation or regret in his eyes. Whether that may be because she's Arya's greatest enemy or simply because he's eager to win this fight, Ivy can't deny the satisfaction that arises within her afterward. Ga-Eul isn't afraid to go far and beyond, which means she doesn't have to be either.

Ivy shakes off the pain and quickly regains her focus, determined not to let this setback defeat her. She moves back in with renewed vigor, exchanging blow for blow with the Aryan boy in a flurry of punches and kicks. The resounding impact of her kicks hitting her mark echoes through the room, eliciting gasps of astonishment from the crowd of students watching the escalating intensity of the fight unfold before them. Ivy can tell she's surprising them with her speed, agility, and the way she's evading Ga-Eul's heavy punches while delivering powerful blows of her own, leaving the boy reeling and gasping for air.

As she deftly dodges a particularly wild swing from the stronger fighter, Ivy quickly darts forward and lands a devastating punch square on his nose, causing blood to spurt forth, staining the floor. Ga-Eul stumbles back, visibly shaken by the force of her blow but Ivy does not take a single moment to recuperate. In his eyes now, dark and irate, she can see that he's underestimated her from the start, and now, he's paying for it.

Ivy adeptly maneuvers her smaller stature to her advantage as she darts around her opponent, never allowing him to get a solid hit on her. Her movements are so fluid and graceful as though she's captivatingly dancing around him, her swift punches and kicks landing with lethal precisions each time. That is, until he regains the strength enough to grab her foot and yank her forward.

Then's the first time she meets the floor. Ivy's breathing grows ragged while beads of sweat form on her forehead. The situation deteriorates further when she feels the force of the boy's fist striking her chest. She can feel the blood ascend her throat and out her mouth. Ga-Eul grips her hair and drags her across the floor. It takes everything in the girl not to scream when her head collides with Ayako's bureau.

For a brief moment, all Ivy can hear is the sound of her labored breathing intermingled with the derisive laughter emanating from some of her classmates. The previously immaculate surface of the floor, once devoid of any blemish, now bears the stain of blood, most of which is hers. In a state of vulnerability, she remains prone, her visage pressed against the ground, her eyes tightly shut, and her hands clenched in a display of anguish, until Ayako's voice pierces her ears.

"Do you yield, Ivy?"

Yield?

Ivy coughs out a forceful expulsion of blood as she places both hands down flat against the floor and lifts herself up.

"Remember this, Ivy."

With every bit of strength she can muster, she stumbles up and stabilizes herself with the help of the bureau before turning to face Ga-Eul.

"Yielding is only for the weak."

Milton Keynes UK
Ingram Content Group UK Ltd.
UKHW050738021224
451755UK00018B/624